A LESSON IN DECEIT

ALLIE SHANTE

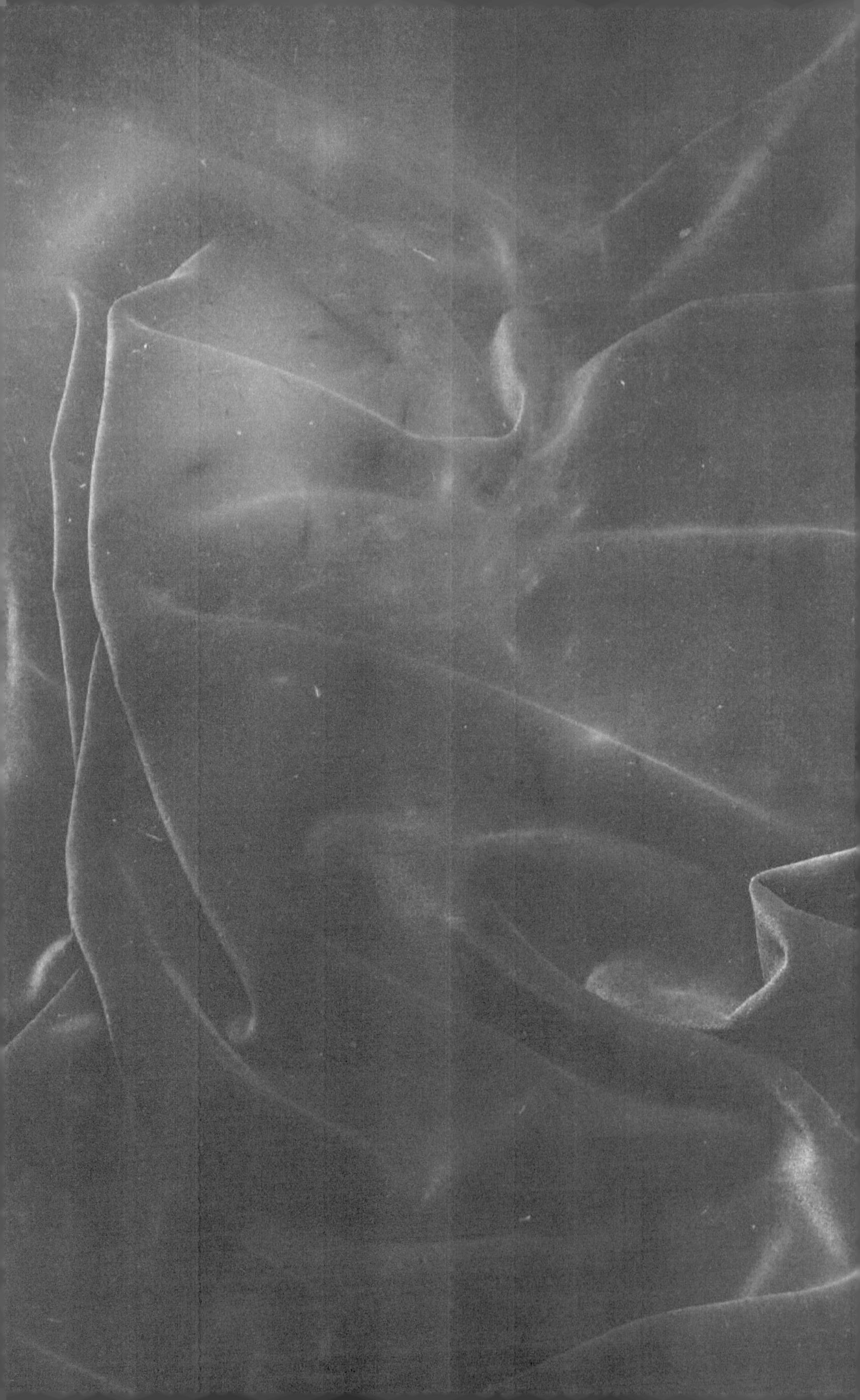

CONTENT WARNING

Parental death (talked about, mild visuals), suspected suicide (briefly spoken), explicit sexual content, underage drinking, very light degradation, shadow play, explicit language

List can also be found at: www.authorallieshante.com

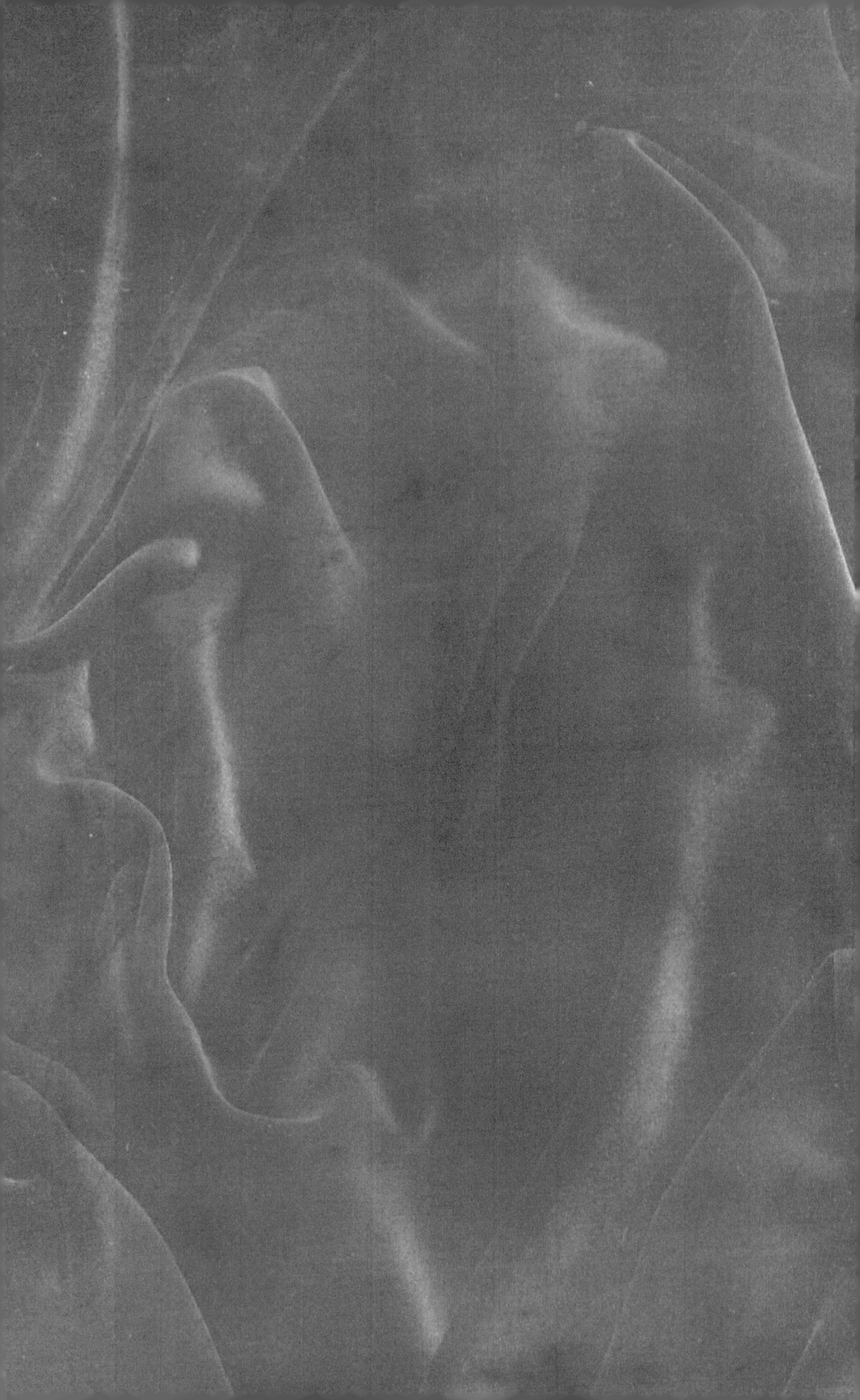

If you like slutty glasses, your boyfriends to have boyfriends and your books spicy, then welcome...

This is a safe space.

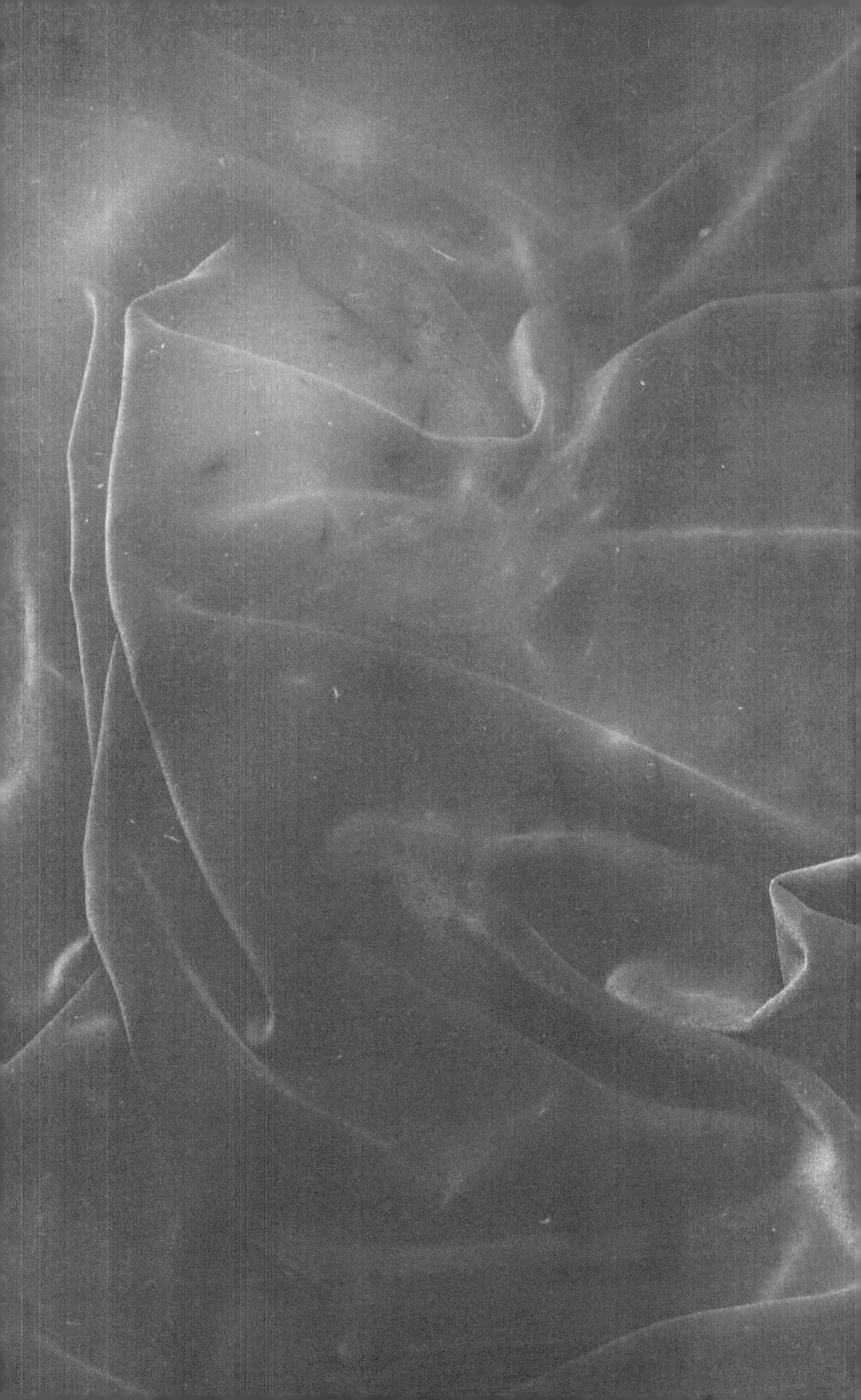

PLAYLIST

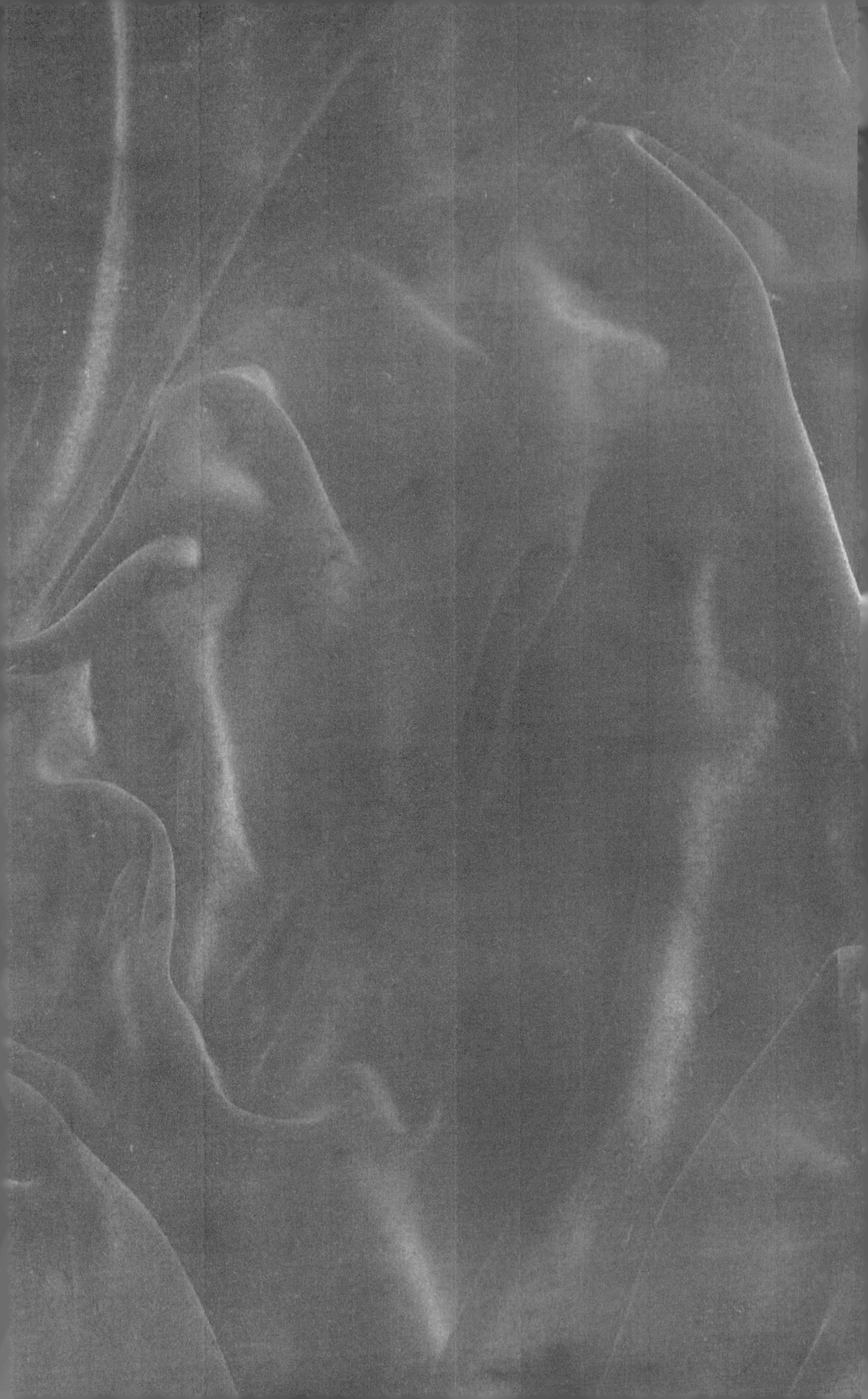

AUTHOR'S NOTE

If you aren't in the mood for spice, I would recommend sitting this one down for a later time. The plot is very much there but so is a whole lot of sexy flirtation and explicit scenes.

If lgbtqia+ or bipoc representation is not for you, then neither is this book.

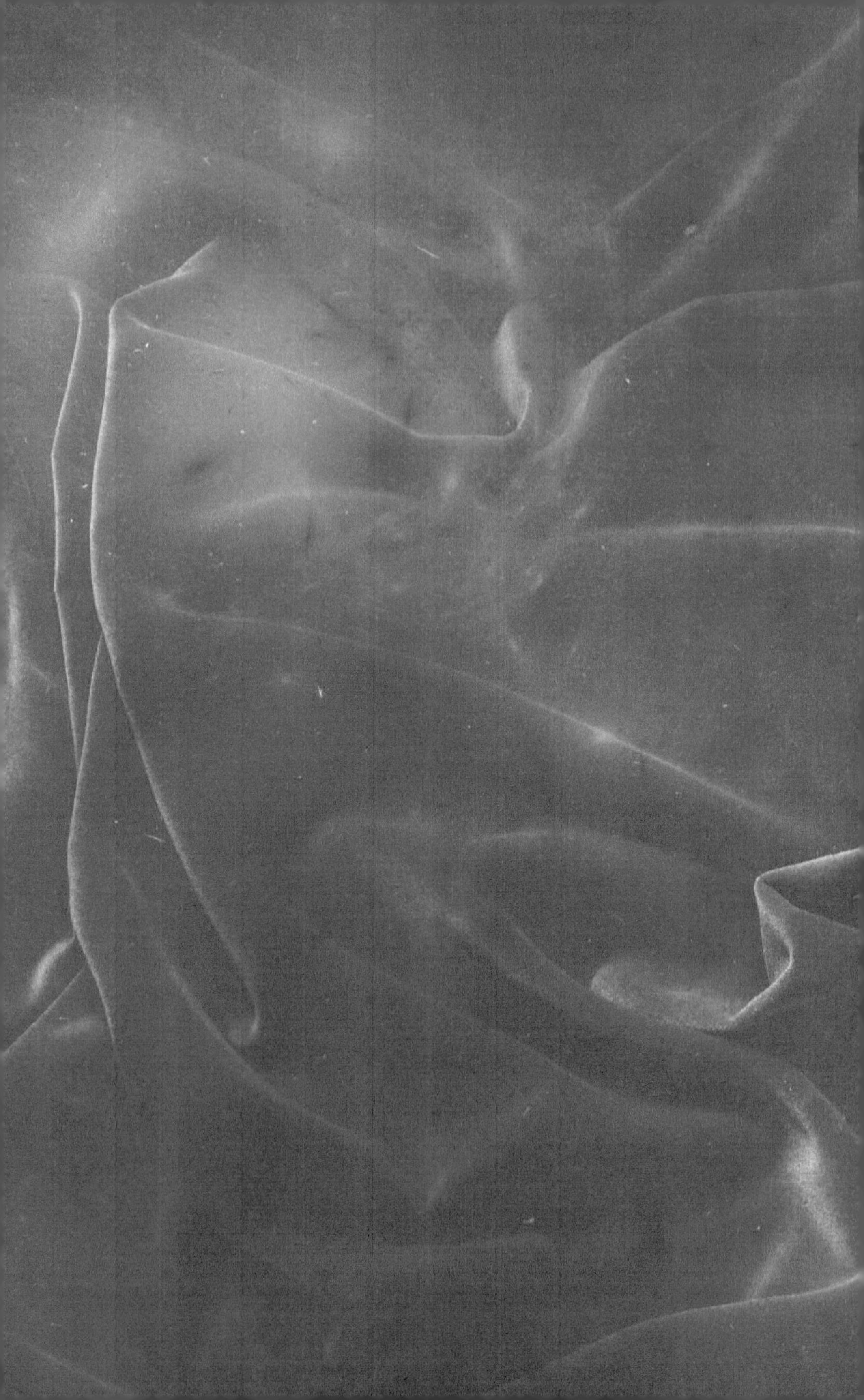

PRONUNCIATION GUIDE

Grayson Ypulong (EE-PULONG)

Corrin (CORE-IN): not CA-REN

Beau (BOW)

Shamir (SHA-MEER)

Sothis (SO-TH-S)

Leif (LEAF)

Lucina (LU-SEE-NUH)

Mystic Riegan (REE-GAN)

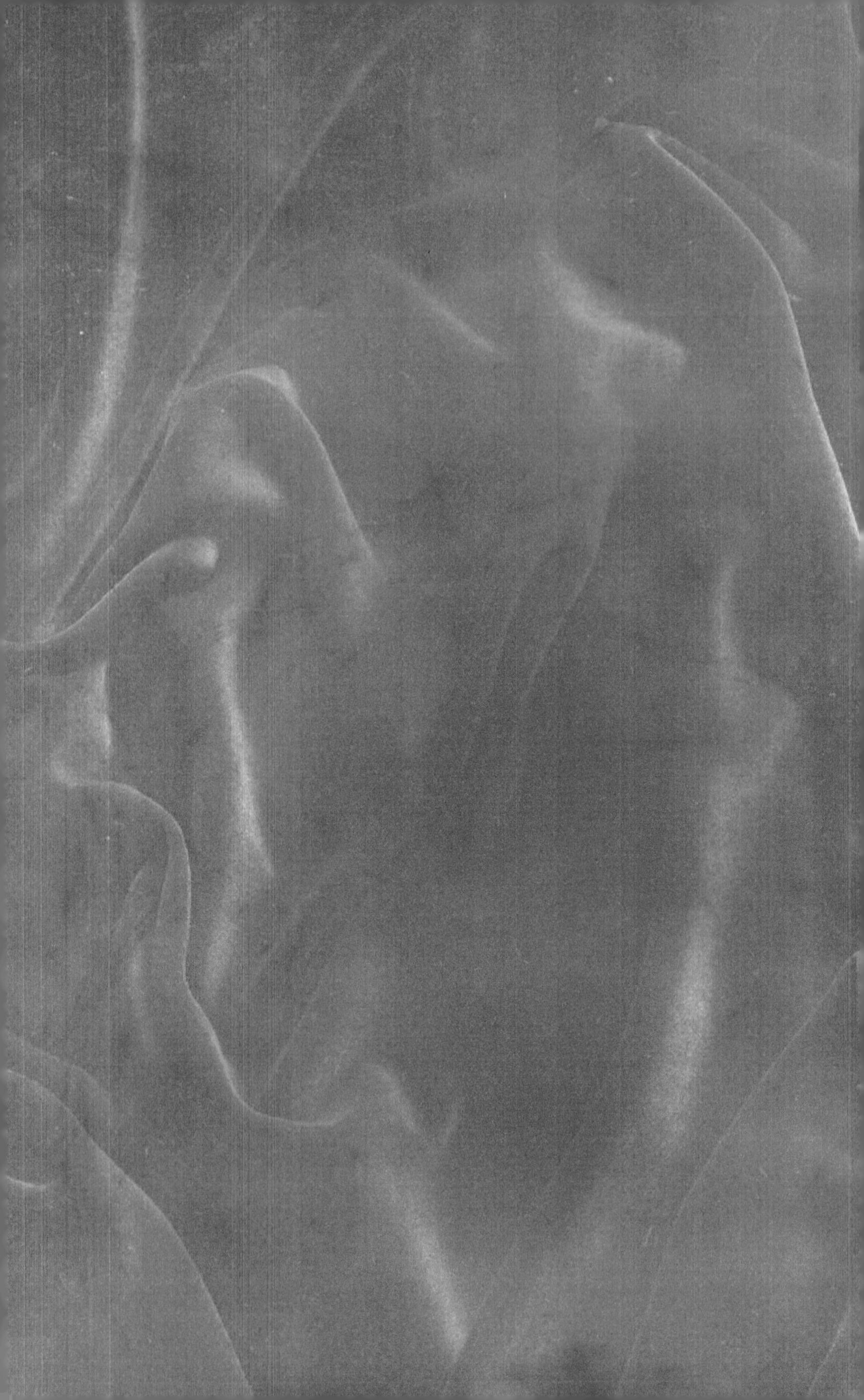

TRANSLATION GUIDE

A Lesson in Deceit has both Spanish and Tagalog phrases throughout, so here is a quick translation guide.

TAGALOG

- *Pare*: buddy
- *Nakakainis ka naman. Napaka killjoy mo talaga. Bakit mo naman kami iniwang dalawa lang ni River?*: you're annoying, and you're also a killjoy. Why did you just leave me and River on our own?
- "No. Okay *lang po ako,* Mom: No. I'm okay, Mom
- *Plano ko pong umuwi ngayong linggo*: I plan to go home this Sunday/weekend
- *Ingat ka*: Take care
- *Aking sinta*: My love/darling
- *Kaya pa kitang dalhin sa langit gamit ang dila ko. Yun ba ang gusto mo?*: I can take you to heaven with my tongue. Is that what you want?

SPANISH

- *Tengo que ir a lidiar con unos idiotas. Te amo. Hablaremos al rato.*: I have to go deal with some idiots. I love you. We'll talk later.
- *Te amo*: I love you
- *Mi amor*: My love
- *Deja de traumatizar a la gente, pinche idiota!*: Stop traumitzing people, you fucking idiot.
- *No todo el mundo habla lobo:* Not everyone speaks wolf
- *¡Que increíble!*: How incredible!

Chocolate PSD
Bar Mock-Up
Read Photoshop Collection
157

PROLOGUE
RILEY

I sure as shit didn't look like the picture on my fake ID.

I would very likely be turned away with a stern look, while I trudged back home with my head down. The big, bulky guy in front of me was clearly going to see that I should not be here. Arcane was one of the smaller bars in downtown San Francisco, but apparently this Saturday everyone wanted a night out, so it was packed. The dress I decided to wear was one that I'd bought spontaneously on a shopping trip with my best friend, Marianne, who confirmed that I might need the black mini dress—that showed way too much of my umber skin—one day. I was starting to rethink our decision when the wind began to pick up causing me to pull my slouchy jean jacket tighter around my chest.

Marianne lightly touched my elbow as she stood next to me. That was her subtle way of telling me to get my shit together and stop fidgeting. I casually turned my head so I could look at her, my braids swinging over my shoulder. Her long blonde hair was tied up in a high ponytail that moved like a pendulum when she walked. She made sure that both of our faces were decorated to her level of perfection before we left my room, while I actively gave my mother very vague answers through my closed door about where we were going.

Well-manicured fingers entered my vision as my best friend grabbed my ID. I looked up at the buff man and he nodded towards the entrance. I blinked, and then blinked again, because if I was being honest, that ID was fucking awful. The worst hundred bucks I'd ever spent. Marianne grabbed my hand and dragged me inside the dimly lit bar, my low heels clicking against the floor. She moved us far enough away from the door and to an empty spot near the wall. Looking over the throngs of people talking at the bar and dry humping on the small dance floor, it only made me even sleepier than I already was. I liked going out, but with it being already April and high school ending in a few weeks, finals, and the dread of college... I wasn't in the mood.

But when your friend calls you crying, spewing an entire story about how her ex-girlfriend is scum and she needs girls' night, you do what you have to do.

Marianne leaned in, speaking into my ear. "Let's go to the bar."

I nodded, starting to head over there but she reached out and stopped me. I turned around confused. If I took any sort of elongated pause, I would probably beg her on my knees for us to go home and turn our girls' night into eating frozen pizza on my couch back in San Jose. She gently tucked one of my braids behind my ear. "Thanks for doing this. I know you've been a little freaked out about graduation. Ainsley is just..." she rubbed her pink painted lips together, trying to find the words to describe her on again, off again, but currently off again ex-girlfriend. "She makes me so fucking mad."

I let out a laugh. "How about you buy me a drink to thank me and then we can scope out someone new that won't have you calling me crying at two in the morning?" I grabbed her wrist, yanking her over to the bar.

We had to weave through a few people before I quickly claimed two empty seats, nearly throwing her onto the leather stool. Purple lights streamed against the brick walls and mist traveled along the ground from some machines in the corners of the building. Arcane had one large bar that had seating wrapped all the way around in an oval shape, while the dance floor situated itself near the left side and a bunch of lounge seating was on the other. My dress rode up my thighs more than I would have liked, but I did my best to stay comfortable.

I noticed Marianne jump off her stool, walking around me. "I'm going to the bathroom. Get what you want and keep the tab open. Please and thank you." I gave her one solid nod, damn well knowing that the words 'keep the tab open' were not something my eighteen-year-old self should be considering. I looked down the long granite bar top, hoping to spot the bartender. He was near the end, speaking to a large group of people, each of them shouting their orders, which told me I wouldn't be served any time soon. There was another bartender near the left side that I attempted to make eye contact with, but I wasn't good at this so that didn't work either.

I just wanted a stupid Sex on the Beach, nothing overly compli-cated. I was patient—at least that's what I told myself when I quite literally *had* to be.

I closed my eyes for a moment, pretending that I was back home with cheap sugar filled snacks and an even cheaper wine cooler. I popped my eyes open when I heard a small clang, catching sight of the cocktail in front of me.

"Sex on the Beach," the bartender offered, giving me a nod before he went to check on someone else. I blinked at the drink, reaching out to tentatively touch it. *How the hell...?*

"You look disappointed," a deep voice inquired to my right. I felt my shoulders stiffen a bit in alarm, but more so because I've never had a simple voice melt my insides. I moved a chunk of my dark braids off my shoulder and let them hit my back before I turned to face who this was.

He settled himself onto Marianne's stool, running a hand through his messy waves of dark hair. Small pieces of it curled and hit his forehead. I noticed two silver studs in his ears. One of his elbows was propped up onto the bar, and his dark green eyes were so intensely set on me that I had a hard time maintaining eye contact. I didn't back down from his staring; he was hot, but he didn't intimidate me.

"I'm not. I just...um..."

"You just what?" he pressed, leaning back a bit, regarding me. I noticed the way his eyes quickly scanned my body, a look of appreciation appearing on his face. He slid his index finger over his chin, giving me a glimpse at some of the tattoos that adorned his knuckles. I let my eyes travel up his hands to his exposed arms that were covered in tattoos as well. There was a skull, various vibrantly colorful roses, and even a chain in grayscale.

"Not a Sex on the Beach fan?" There was a slight mischievousness in the way he asked.

"No, it's my favorite, but I just didn't order it." I looked over at him, but his face never morphed into confusion like it should have at my answer.

"Well, I guess whoever ordered it for you got really lucky then." He raised one of his dark brows, shrugging one of his shoulders. He casually raised two of his fingers, calling the bartender over. The young guy hustled over and leaned forward to hear my dark-haired stranger's order. "Whiskey, whatever is your best one."

He let his eyes fall on me again, angling his body more so that it felt like we were in our own little bubble. The grey shirt that he wore tugged against his arms and clung to him like a second skin. I could almost see more tattoos peeking out the top of the shirt; I was way too interested in knowing what the design was.

"I hardly think you should be drinking it anyway since you're underage."

My eyes nearly bulged out of my head as I whipped my head around, hoping no one heard him. "Excuse me, why would you say that?"

"Because it's true."

My mouth gaped open at his utter audacity. He was correct, but I didn't want to give him any sort of satisfaction with that fact. "I hardly think you should be speaking to an underage girl, so I think this conversation is over." I shook my head and confidently grabbed my free cocktail, taking a long, much needed drink.

I heard a rumble of laughter next to me which caused me to put my glass down and zero in on the dimple that appeared in his cheek. The bartender returned with his drink, setting it lightly on the bar. The presumptuous stranger wrapped his long fingers around the glass and brought it to his lips. I couldn't help but watch him swallow the whiskey, the way his throat moved or the way his lips wrapped around the edge of the glass. I shouldn't have been thinking about my mouth on his neck or what his lips would feel like on certain parts of my body, but here I was being a fucking weirdo.

Another fit of choked laughter came from his throat as he set his drink down, tapping his fingers against the glass. Both his eyebrows were raised as if he was surprised. I needed to find a way out of this, or for fucking Marianne to come back. I eyed the area where the bathroom was located, noticing the long line of women. *Damnit.*

"I'm only twenty-one, so I'm pretty sure I'm free to speak to an eighteen-year-old."

I had started to reach into my bag for my phone when I froze. "How do you know how old I am?" My eyes turned into slits as I stared at him. I wasn't interesting enough to have a stalker, but this guy was treading dangerous territory,

He placed a hand on his chest, his finger tattoos on display. "I'm not a stalker, I assure you. Give a guy a chance, Riley."

I immediately shifted off my stool, putting a small amount of distance between us. *He said my fucking name.* "What the fuck!?"

He slowly got up and placed his hands on my stool, inclining his head towards me. "Isn't that your name?"

"Yes," I hissed, attempting to back up but a group of what looked like rowdy college kids were in my way. "I don't know you, so it's very stalker-like to just casually know things about someone. I really think you should...." I let my words fall away when I flicked my eyes to my drink. The fucked-up puzzle pieces of this situation started to come together. I pointed at my half empty glass. "This was *you.*"

He remained firmly in my line of sight. "I assumed a pretty girl would like a guy to buy her a drink. Her *favorite* if I'm not mistaken." There was that glint of mischief in his eyes again. "You are quite a loud thinker; I would advise you to work on that."

I opened and closed my mouth like a damn fish, trying to find my next comeback. My mind halted. *You are quite a loud thinker.*

I moved my body around my stool and shoved him, but not so aggressively that we caused a scene. My palm was flat against his stomach as I pushed him against the bar. His abs were easily felt through the comfortable fabric of his shirt. He looked down at me as my hands lingered.

His tongue poked out, licking at his bottom lip. "Fuck, your thoughts are going to kill me."

He was taller than me to the point where I needed to get on the tips of my toes, but now was not the time to realize how much his height turned me on. "Are you reading my mind?"

He gave me a small smile, that dimple shining. It made his face light up in a way that shouldn't have been cute. "Perhaps."

"You want to get a girl to talk to you, try not to invade her fucking privacy, *asshole,*" I reprimanded, turning on my heels to get far away from the mental magic wielder.

This had to be my first negative interaction with a magic user, and I'd known about magic my entire fucking life. Magic users were an essential part of our society. They were key factors in hospitals, science labs, and even security. Learning about them was in our curriculum.

I was very aware that I'd gone to schools that integrated magic wielders, especially in middle school when a girl in my history class accidentally shifted in the middle of her oral presentation because of her anxiety. They weren't hidden from the world, but after a few instances like the one I'd had, they started implementing dampeners, only to be worn while in school or in government facilities—unless you were an employee of some kind. Puberty tended to be a time when those that held magic may be a bit unstable—especially shifters and the ones that wielded elemental magic.

Magic only and human only schools were always a choice, giving individuals the option to separate themselves, which sometimes was better depending on the person. My parents had asked me once if I'd wanted to transfer to a human only high school and I'd given them a confused look and said, "Why the hell would I do that?" Marianne was staying at the integrated high school, so I would too. That was the end of the discussion.

There were a vast majority of magic only and human only colleges as well, but there weren't many unified ones. There was at least one in every big city in the country, which included the one closest to me right here in San Francisco: Mystic Riegan University. I'd been there a few times, since my dad worked as their liaison for human-magic relations.

He made sure that everything was fair and that all students were taken care of and treated with the respect they deserved, regardless of their upbringing. He made sure all mediations went straight to one of the school counselors and even set up weekly meetings with students that transferred from schools that didn't intermingle, just to make sure they were alright. I was more than proud to tell people where my dad worked and what he did. It also had everyone, especially my teachers, assuming I would attend in the fall. As beautiful as Mystic Riegan's campus was, it wasn't somewhere I saw myself.

Just like I didn't see myself *here*, with a telepath that thought he could use his powers to win me over.

I felt a large hand grab my arm and suddenly I was maneuvered to a small, secluded hallway that led to the back entrance. A few employees, cigarettes in hand, were already moving towards the big steel doors. My back was pressed against the wall and my mental invader loomed over me. I didn't feel unsafe, but that didn't mean I was thrilled to be in this position either.

This area of the bar didn't continue the purple strobe lights, but just maintained a purple hue of color around the ceiling and the overall lighting was still dim. I could make out that his skin wasn't pale like Marianne's, but he had a slight tan. He placed both hands on either side of my head, giving me a much better view of his tattoos, but any desire to admire them was gone now.

"I could hear your thoughts from outside the bar. That's what I meant by being a loud thinker. They were coming off like nervous chatter in your head. When I heard you mention wanting a drink, I thought that might help and be my way to talk to you. A selfish endeavor, but it worked."

"Still an invasion."

"Hmm and practically daydreaming about me having my mouth on you makes you such a saint?" He tilted his head to the side, smirking.

I opened my mouth but quickly closed it. I attempted to settle my mind, not wanting him to find more incriminating things to hold against me. I took a deep breath, rubbing my lips together. "I'm sorry for thinking those things, okay? You shouldn't have used your powers to try to hit on me, and I shouldn't have been thinking about you inappropriately."

He squinted at me as if he was trying to understand my words, as if what I said was in some foreign language he didn't understand. "I'm flattered you think I'm attractive, Riley. The feeling is mutual." His eyes moved over my face. "Very much so."

His face was inches from mine, but he didn't make a move to get any closer. It was like he knew how to build the right amount of tension by just his presence alone. "How about we go back to the bar and talk? It just so happens to be my birthday, so it would mean a lot if you kept me company." He smirked at me. "And then maybe I'll consider doing all those things you want me to do to you."

I rolled my eyes. "Presumptuous. I'm sure you have friends coming to celebrate with you, besides there are a ton of women here that would love for you to read their minds and do all the right things. Please don't waste your time thinking I'm some kind of prize to be won."

He dropped his head, shaking it. "I've heard the thoughts of nearly every woman and man in here, but the only thoughts I even remotely want to consider are yours, gorgeous." He moved his face back into my view, pulling one of his hands off the wall and cupping my chin. His thumb moved over my jaw in a gentle motion that sent an unwanted tingle down my spine. "The dirty *and* the tame ones."

I narrowed my eyes, wanting to tell him to stop touching me, but the part of my brain that was seeming to malfunction didn't want him to stop. I almost felt my body melt against the wall behind me—*almost.*

"Do you even have a name? Seems only fair since you know so much about me," I asked, choosing to be polite, even though he didn't deserve it. "Happy birthday by the way."

He let out a small laugh, continuing to delicately caress my skin. "It's..."

I felt a hand grab me and yank me from my stranger's overwhelming presence. Marianne's stunned face had me sighing and wanting to explain a situation I didn't even know how to comprehend. "Riley, what the hell?"

I turned my head to the man now leaning against the wall, one of my braids practically slapping me in the face. "It wasn't me, okay. It was him."

He raised his hands up, laughing. "I'm sorry for invading your thoughts, gorgeous. I'm not sorry about why I did it."

I scoffed and so did Marianne. I watched her as she eyed him. "You're River St. James?" I saw her tongue pressing into her cheek, a telltale sign that she was collecting every piece of information she knew about someone.

He winked at her, nodding. "Guilty."

I shook my head. "Is that supposed to mean something?"

Marianne gave him a raised eyebrow but focused on me. "Nope, not to you." She grabbed my forearm, dragging me away from him. Her ponytail swung as she looked over her shoulder. "Use your powers on someone else, River. Your reputation precedes you, believe me. Leave her alone."

The lack of information I was getting about this man just intrigued me more. Marianne moved in a determined fashion, but I found myself sneaking a look over my shoulder.

He had that mischievous smile again. His voice rang out through the music. "If I promise to not use my powers on you ever again, do I get a date?" There was a joking nature in his voice, but also a hint of sincerity, and I didn't know why I liked that so much.

I didn't even fucking *know* him.

Marianne huffed, wrapping her arm around my shoulders. "How about we just go to your house and eat popcorn drizzled in chocolate and those tiny pretzels you like? I can drown my Ainsley sorrows in empty calories."

I blew out a breath, nodding in response. Once we were outside of the bar, I waited while Marianne tapped her phone to bring up the rideshare app. It would be a long hour ride home. I wrapped my arms around myself, looking up at the dark sky. I scanned the people waiting to get into Arcane, wondering how many of them had powers and how many of them were just simple humans like me.

I chewed on my bottom lip, fiddling with the ruby gemstone my mom gave me for my twelfth birthday, needing to find something to do with my hands. I looked towards the entrance of the club, wondering what River was doing. River St. James must be quite popular if Marianne is revoking her stamp of approval already. He had annoyed the hell out of me, yet he had this alluring way about him that in a matter of two minutes I already wanted to dry hump him. I didn't feel like diving into what that said about me.

"Riley, come on." Marianne called when a black car rolled up in front of her.

I started to make my way over to her, while at the same time I was mentally giving my number to the telepath who had my pulse racing. I could do *one* date. It didn't have to mean anything.

1
RILEY

"**M**y birthday is like three months away, why are you asking me this now?" I laughed, sliding off my bed. The soft carpet hit the bottom of my bare feet as I padded over to my desk. A scoff came from behind me. "Besides, we *just* celebrated your birthday." That was last week, which also happened to be the last week before spring break for the unified community college I got accepted to at the last minute.

"You had class on my birthday, but we got to spend the entire night in bed together, so I'll forgive you," River teased. "But aren't you happy I was well prepared and had everything fucking perfect for your last birthday?" he asked, with a tone that came off like he knew the answer, but he just liked hearing me say it out loud.

He *had* been well prepared, but that didn't mean he was well liked. Scratch that...he was well liked by everyone but Marianne. The minute I had told her we had been talking, she nearly popped a blood vessel in her head. When I'd told her I'd agreed to a date, I thought she would combust right then and there.

"RIVER ST. JAMES! YOU'RE ACTUALLY GOING ON A DATE WITH HIM?" *Marianne screeched as she pushed open my bedroom door.*

I stumbled out of my closet, the dress I had decided to wear not fully pulled down my legs. "Well hello to you too."

She pointed her finger at me. "When you told me that you guys were just talking, I thought it was just some mindless flirting. He's hot, I get it. I just don't want you to get into some hot guy mess that you can't get out of."

"He's been nothing but polite since we started talking."

"Oh right, cause having you pinned against a wall was just the politest meet cute."

I stared at her, not really interested in having the same conversation in person that we'd had over text. She only knew about River due to her college tour of Mystic Riegan during the summer of our junior year and apparently, she had overheard some things she didn't like. "You've really yet to explain to me how he's so bad. Is he a womanizer? Does he do drugs? Does he have a violent history?"

Marianne sat on the edge of my bed. "No, it's that power of his. It gives total invasion of privacy and lazy behavior when it comes to dating. You were pissed at him for doing it in the first place, or have you forgotten?"

I walked over to my floor-length mirror, examining my outfit. She narrowed her dark brown eyes at me as if she was waiting for a response. "He apologized for that. If he does it again, he's out. Hot or not, he knows where I stand." I raised one of my eyebrows, turning to look at her. "Lazy dating?"

"Come on, Riley. The guy doesn't have to try. He knows everything. He has no need to work for it if all he has to do is get into your head and boom! Every single detail right there. It's like taking a test you already have all

the answers to and being fake surprised when you pass. Studying isn't required for people like him."

I huffed. "You are a little insufferable, you know that?"

"I care about you. And until he proves himself, he's less than worthy." Her face softened as she pushed off my bed, walking over to me. Her eyes glanced over my outfit. She scrunched her mouth to one side, tilting her head sideways.

"I wouldn't have it any other way." I stuck my tongue out at her.

She went over to my closet, grabbing a jacket off a hanger and quickly ripping the one I was preparing to put on out of my grasp. "Wear this one. One thing though, keep your legs closed, and don't sleep with him tonigh-...."

"How's my babygirl doing?" Marianne jumped at the sound of my dad's voice. I gave her a warning look before giving him my full attention. He'd asked me way too many questions about my date, but backed off when my mom told him that I would be home before eleven and would text them when I got to the restaurant. I'd been on plenty of dates before, but this was the first time I was going out with someone who attended the university my dad worked at. It practically stunned me when my dad knew exactly who River was; it probably shouldn't have surprised me, given that River's dad was the Dean of Mental Magic and his older brother, Asher, was a professor for the same department.

"All good here." I awkwardly twirled in a circle as if showing my dad that the fact that I'd gotten dressed meant my stomach wasn't flipping from nerves.

He looked as if he was holding back a laugh. "Well, you look beautiful. That boy better recognize that." Marianne nodded, agreeing with him.

I pinched the bridge of my nose. "He is going to be here soon, so can I finish getting ready?" I moved past Marianne, but my dad caught my arm before I could get past him as well.

"You have a good time tonight. And I promise I'll be nice." He smoothed his hand down my braids, giving me a warm smile that always put me at ease. "Well, nice enough." I gave him a small smile, looking into his brown eyes that had tiny lines forming at the corners. I favored my

mom more when it came to looks, but I had a special kind of relationship with my dad that was something I could never put into words. He did almost run over my last boyfriend for breaking up with me through a social media app, so for that he was the best dad in the world.

"Thanks Dad." I kissed him gently on the cheek.

LITTLE DID I KNOW THAT RIVER WOULD SHOW UP ON A MOTORCYCLE AND I would have to awkwardly situate myself on the back of his bike in my dress. I shook my head as I looked over my unusually messy desk. Normally, it would be clean enough to eat off of, but the amount of time River had spent at my house and then how much time I'd spent at his house he shared with his brother had cleaning falling to the low end of my priorities. I smiled to myself when I found what I was searching for, hiding it behind my back when I turned to face him.

He was stretched out on my bed, looking right at home. He had both his hands behind his head and the most charming grin on his face, showcasing that dimple that made my stomach flip. The sunlight from my window made the colors of the tattoos that covered his arms more vibrant than usual.

I sauntered over to him, propping myself up on my bed with my knees. "Fine, we can talk all about my birthday, but..." I handed him what I was keeping hidden, earning me scrunched eyebrows as he looked at it.

"A book?"

"You promised me that you would start reading more books that I like. Actually, you promised me that you would start reading generally." I shoved the book at him. He pushed himself up so that his back was parallel to my headboard. River grabbed the book from my hands, examining the cover.

"Alright, gorgeous. What's it about?"

I bent over so I could collect my braids together, pulling the hair tie off my wrist and securing them at the top of my head. "It's the first in a series. A witch has a human boyfriend, who is awful to her, so she ends up seducing and sleeping with his dad."

River pressed his lips together, but his green eyes glittered with just a hint of intrigue. He flipped over the book, reading the back. "I mean a girls got to do, what a girls got to do. I might know some witches that would use this as a self-help book."

I waggled my eyebrows as I sat down next to him, watching as he flipped through the first few pages. "Also, his dad's like a super hot demon."

My boyfriend tapped my gold hoop nose ring with his finger. "You don't have to sell me on it, I'll read it."

I leaned over and kissed his cheek. He turned his head and captured my lips, leaving the book on the bed so he could cup my face with his large hands. He angled his body closer to me, kicking his leg over mine so that he was straddling me. I looked up at him, settling into my pillow.

He kissed my lips again, softly, the kisses descending to my neck and collarbone, while his hands found their way to the hem of my shirt. "Can we talk about birthday things now?"

I giggled. "I'm turning twenty, not twenty-one. It's not something to really be all that eager to celebrate."

He licked a line up my neck and brought his lips to my ear. "Not true. You'll be officially out of the ages that end with 'teen'. It's a moment to remember, gorgeous."

"I think you just like spoiling me." My words came out breathy when he dragged his hand up and grabbed my breast. I felt his chuckle against my throat, his warm breath dusting over my skin. Over the year that we'd been together, he'd only slipped up once when it came to reading my mind, and he'd had to grovel his way back so that I could trust him again. His power was a part of him and a learned behavior, but for some reason, I was worth keeping it in check over.

I looked over the restaurant, my eyebrows raising at how nice it was. It was over the top fancy and in a part of town that I knew I couldn't afford with my tutoring money. The interior was cherry wood, large mirrors adorned the walls, while elegant sconces created light that gave the space an intimate atmosphere. River had given the hostess his name and she'd walked us to a table near the back of the restaurant.

She placed our menus down, letting us know that bread would be coming out soon. River had quickly pulled my chair out, waiting until I was comfortably seated on the plush velvet cushion, before pushing it back in.

"I would have been fine with that diner that's near my house." I pointed out, lightly grazing my fingers over the white tablecloth. I looked to my left, noticing a man focusing on a fork he had floating in midair with a piece of steak on it. He let the fork move over to his date, who had her mouth slightly open so he could feed her.

I had secondhand embarrassment from how corny it was.

River gave me a confused look. "Why would I do that?"

I shrugged. "I don't know. Seems like a place you take someone if you are trying to impress them."

"So, what if I am?"

"I prefer to be impressed by conversation, not sophisticated restaurants."

He leaned back in his chair, his crisp button down pulling against his defined chest. "I'll have you know I happen to really like the food here, and they make a really good Sex on the Beach, which I know is your favorite." I opened my mouth to remind him of my age, but he waved his hand. "Don't worry, put your fake ID away, gorgeous. It's fine. My conversation is pretty on par, so I'd like to learn about you authentically. No mind reading." He leveled his gaze at me. The way he refused to look anywhere else had me wanting to rub my thighs together from the heat that rushed between my legs.

I crossed my legs, getting more settled in my chair. I picked up the menu, flipping it open and holding it up to my face, only letting my eyes peek over the top. "Impress me."

Two hours and too much pasta later, I was laughing so hard I had to hold my stomach. I had learned so much about this man, and he had eagerly asked so many questions about me. Every topic from my family to my friends, all the way to what I wanted to do after high school was discussed. He just nodded when I told him about community college, letting me know that that's exactly what his best friend, Grayson, did before he got a scholarship and transferred to Mystic Riegan.

He talked about growing up in Berkley and eventually moving to San Francisco at a young age with his brother. River told me the whole story about how immensely freaked out he was the first time his power emerged. I had giggled, considering that hearing people in your head was probably something no one is prepared for. He admitted that he hadn't always used it with the best intentions, and I appreciated his honesty. He spoke vaguely about his brother and even less about his own parents. It felt like a delicate subject so I wasn't going to push.

The waitress set our dessert down, smiling at each of us before leaving us alone again. I grabbed one of the forks, digging into the chocolate cake, when I realized that River was staring at me.

"What?"

He licked his lips and smiled. "Nothing. I'm just having a really good time."

"You don't miss being able to read my mind?"

"Not in the slightest. I kind of like not being able to know how you'll respond. It's kind of a rush. Bit of a turn on."

My cheeks started to fill with heat and I suddenly became very interested in the cake in front of us, picking some of it up and placing it in my mouth.

He picked up his own fork, sliding it around the chocolate sauce underneath. "There is something I do need to tell you."

"Is this where everything goes downhill?" I asked, swallowing down my piece of cake.

He shook his head laughing. "No, gorgeous. Well, I hope not."

I nodded, absentmindedly, not really knowing what else to do.

"I'm pansexual. Is that a problem?"

I blinked and blinked again. I wasn't upset. If this was who he was, I was more than fine with that. I did want to clarify something, so I could fully understand. "Okay. Remind me what that is again?"

He stuck a piece of cake in his mouth, swallowing it before answering me. "Sex and gender aren't something I consider when it comes to my attraction. I just like you for you."

I tapped my fork against the plate, considering his statement. "People have a problem with that?"

River let out a hmph as he ate another piece of cake, letting me know that it had likely been a problem for others in the past.

"You'll have to do better than that to make me dislike you." I smirked at him as I pointed my fork in his direction.

"Are you trying to turn me on even more with that fucking smirk of yours?" He tilted his head, the studs in his ears glittering from the light on the wall near us.

I took in a breath, nearly choking on nothing but fucking air. "Can I ask a personal question?"

"I'm an open book."

I pressed my lips together, pulling my napkin from my lap and placing it on the table. "I'm just curious. Have you been with both men and women or...? Totally fine if you have, but I'm going to have that one on my mind for the rest of the night if I don't ask it now." I heard myself rambling and willed my tongue to stop working. "Or you can tell me to fuck off."

River's deep laugh eased the tension in my shoulders. He placed his hand under his chin as if he was utterly enthralled by me. "Yes Riley, I have."

I mirrored his hand placement. "Cool. Well, I haven't. Man or woman. Is that a problem?"

A stunned look clouded his facial features for only a moment before he rallied. "No, not at all."

I felt River tuck his fingers into my athletic shorts and start to shimmy them down. I placed my hands over his, stopping him.

"My door is wide open."

He looked over his shoulder, then let his face fall into my neck. "I'm sure your mom won't hear a thing."

I batted him away, sliding out from underneath him and standing on the side of my bed. We'd had sex exactly one time in my bedroom, and I was paranoid the whole time that finishing—at least on my end—was more work than I would have liked. I'd been less nervous when I'd lost my virginity to him. It was also probably my subconscious remembering when my mom found my birth control pills and the conversation it led to. The minute we'd started having sex I'd tried both elixirs and the pill. While elixirs lasted longer, they tasted like absolute shit, so I'd stuck to the pill ever since.

"Neither one of my parents love the fact that you hang out in my room constantly."

"We can always just close the door."

"Yeah, we both know my mom would come in here and lecture me on how while I *am* in college that I still live under her roof and don't pay rent so I can do this *one* thing for her. Cue 'the mom glare' to both of us as she leaves the door open and walks away."

My boyfriend laughed. "See I thought all those times we had dinner and all those outings we did together to get to know me better basically gave me the okay to spend alone time with their daughter." He stuck his tongue behind his front teeth.

"They probably think you'll corrupt me."

River moved off my bed, causing me to step back so he could stand in front of me. He was tall, about six-foot, but he always strained himself to get down to my five-foot five level. "Pretty sure we are way past that." He leaned down to kiss me and I felt his erection through his pants.

A knock at the front door made us both jump. I pulled away from him, walking over so I could lean against my door frame. We had two windows on either side of our front door, and I could make out blue and red lights flashing outside. I heard my mom open the door, muffled voices and then I figured she had stepped outside when all I heard was silence.

I felt a presence at my back. I looked up to see River looking down the steps towards the windows. His eyes were a little narrowed and looked as if he was lost in thought. I knew he was using his powers, and I had no desire to tell him to stop. A sharp cry pierced my ears, causing me to look over at my front door and then I heard a thud as if something had landed against it.

River stepped away from me and when I peeked over at him, his mouth was slightly open, his eyes darting from left to right. He looked like he was in shock. I looked from my front door to my boyfriend, not really understanding what just transpired. I took a step closer to him, reaching out to grab his forearm.

"River, what's going on?"

His usually excited green eyes didn't have their shine I recognized. "Riley, I don't know how to..."

The front door opened and the sound of sniffling and choked sobs filled my ears. I watched my mom slowly close the door behind her, her hunched shoulders shaking with every single cry she let out.

"You should talk to your mom." River nodded towards the stairs, leaning back against my door frame.

I didn't think twice before I took the stairs two at a time and grabbed my mom's shoulders. It took her a moment to focus on me when she looked up as if she was seeing me for the first time. I looked over at the windows as the blue and red lights disappeared.

"Mom, what's wrong? What's happening?"

I tried to steady her when I noticed her whole body was shaking. She sucked in breath after breath, her tears streaming down her face.

"Mom, talk to me. You're scaring me," I pleaded, using my fingers to tuck her dark curls behind her ears and hold her face up so that she was forced to look at me for longer than a minute. We looked so much alike, from our dark eyes and umber skin to the way our bottom lip was just a tad bit fuller than the top. They were simple things, but right now I noticed it all.

"R-Riley," she stuttered my name, as if it took so much out of her just to say it.

"Mom, why don't we sit down?" I tried to pull her towards the kitchen, but she wouldn't budge.

"Riley, I- I don't.... they said..." She looked down at her hands as if they had the answers.

My voice started to shake. "They said what?"

Fresh tears formed in her eyes again. "Your dad. They said..." she hiccupped, "they found him at the school."

I shook my head, not understanding.

"They couldn't do anything. He's g-gone. Your dad is gone. He's dead." She fell against my body, wrapping her arms around me for leverage. I instinctively held her back, my body feeling stiff.

There were a million questions I wanted to ask, but words couldn't find their way out of my mouth. I didn't care what I did for my fucking birthday or that I needed to consider whether I was going to continue community college or transfer out. None of that mattered, it all seemed too trivial to even consider.

I just held my mom as tight as I could. And even though it felt like she had no strength to do anything but cry, she squeezed me back.

2
RILEY

I zipped up my last suitcase and lugged it down the stairs. River had insisted he could help me with everything, but he'd done enough these last few months. I rolled the bag next to the other two I'd previously brought down, scrubbing a hand down my face. I looked over at the entryway table, focusing far too hard on a framed photo of me and my parents.

I remembered the day we'd taken that. My dad had to take the phone from me because my arm wasn't long enough to capture us in the frame. I was thirteen, and we had gone to a baseball game. The school had given discounted tickets to faculty and even though my mom absolutely despised sporting events, she went simply because my dad loved baseball and because he'd promised her that a date night full of adult conversation and lots of wine would be in their future. We were all smiles in that photo and I felt tears start to form, but I blinked them away.

I didn't understand how I had any tears left at this point.

"Riley," I heard my mom call from the kitchen. I let out a slow breath, knowing exactly how this conversation was going to go. I placed my hands in the pockets of my shorts and walked towards the kitchen.

My mom had the dishwasher open, meticulously putting things away like her life depended on it. I wrapped my fingers around the edge of the kitchen island. When she finally noticed me, she set the plates she had down and looked over my shoulder. I knew she was seeing my bags and backpack filled with last minute shit I didn't know where to put.

I snuck a glance over my shoulder as well, shaking my head. "You act like this is a surprise."

She brought her hand to her forehead, rubbing it with her fingertips. "I know, honey. I just really don't think you've thought this through."

My eyes widened. "We've had this conversation multiple times. I've run you through the pros and cons. I told you I would call you every week. What more do you want from me?"

My mom closed the dishwasher harder than I assumed she'd intended. "Riley, no matter what you tell me, I will still think this is irrational. You could stay at the community college another year and *then* transfer. What's the rush?" She held her hands up as if her understanding my decisions was a lost cause.

And to *her*, it was.

We'd come back from my dad's funeral and after a week of crying non-stop, I'd sat up in my bed and focused on the facts. The only thing the police and the school had told us was that he had fallen out of his fifth-floor office window. I heard accusations that he jumped, or that alcohol was involved and that he slipped due to inebriation. It was all so fucking ridiculous. My dad drank, but it was an occasional beer or maybe a glass or two of wine with my mom. The school didn't want a scandal and there was no sign of foul play, so it was deemed an accidental fall.

Mystic Riegan slowly but surely went back to normal, and River came around nearly every day, despite the one-to-two-hour distance between us. Or he sent Grayson, who normally just sat in silence, reading with me in my living room. He loved books just as much as I did, so to him, it wasn't a big ask to keep me company. Marianne called or video chatted all the way from Virginia to check on me whenever she didn't have class. I appreciated the sentiments, but nothing felt right and everyone at that fucking school seemed to move on or attempt to.

This man wasn't their dad, so why should they care? Accidents happen, yes. I would have accepted it if it didn't seem so suspicious. I couldn't ask River to ask his dad more questions, especially when he liked to keep his talks with his dad to a minimum. I couldn't just show up on campus crying and screaming that I wanted someone to listen to me.

I just needed to get closer.

It hadn't taken me long to open up the Mystic Riegan transfer application and fill it out. My dad had always wanted me to attend, so now I was. I'd told my mom what I'd done *after* I'd received my acceptance and filled out all the housing paperwork as well.

I lifted myself up on the counter. "Mom, I'm leaving today. Can we just pretend like you support me in all this, so we can have a normal goodbye?"

She let out a sigh. "I support you in whatever you do, but I just feel like you are trying to, I don't know, prove something by going. I just don't think it's healthy to head straight into the place where your father..."

"*Fell?*" I finished for her.

She closed her eyes. Eyes that used to be decorated with red circles due to continuous crying all through the night. "Is that what this is? Are you off to play detective?"

I swallowed hard, toying with my nose ring. "No. Besides, it's not like anyone would believe anything else anyway."

She cocked her head to the side, her dark loose curls following behind her. "Excuse me?"

I waved my hands, hoping to move on to any other topic. "Nothing, absolutely nothing."

"Is this so you can be closer to River?"

I let out a soft laugh. "That's a very mom thing to ask."

"That doesn't answer my question." She narrowed her eyes at me.

I shook my head. "If I wanted to live with River, I could. He offered, but I'll be in a dorm with a roommate. I've done all the legwork, stop worrying." Due to my dad's extended time with the university, they had taken care of my housing and books. My tuition was heavily discounted, and my dad had made sure to keep a separate account in the bank just in case I decided to transfer to a larger university.

I walked up to my mom and wrapped my arms around her waist, snuggling my head against her chest. I heard her heart thud, the beat starting to ease as she placed her hand on the back of my head.

She dipped her head down to kiss the top of my braids, whispering, "Maybe I'm making all this fuss because I'm going to miss you."

I could feel my tears wanting to make an appearance again. Without my dad, she wouldn't have anyone here to calm her down whenever she broke down sporadically throughout the day.

Halfway through my freshman year of high school, she decided to go back to school and get a degree in computer science. She worked as a data engineer which kept her plenty busy, but if I knew anything about my mom, she would find a way to do her work, while still finding time to fret over me. The woman had even offered to pay for an apartment close to home so I could still have what I wanted, but I needed to be as involved in this school as possible. I couldn't tell her that though, so letting her assume I wanted to get the full college experience was how I'd played it. She was pretty good friends with Marianne's mom, so she could get her out of the house more often, but I knew it wouldn't be the same.

I hated lying to her; I hated lying to anyone. She had fallen prey to whatever the police and the school was telling her. I couldn't make myself just accept their words without validating my own theories. I really *was* going to get an education, so that *had* to count for something...right?

Our tender moment was shattered when I heard my mom yelp and pull away from me, looking down at the floor. Paws padded on the kitchen floor and the sound of a thunderous tail hitting the cabinet doors on the kitchen island had me giggling. My mom placed her hand on her chest, shaking her head at Beau, my two-year-old pitbull. His grey coat still shined from the bath I'd wrestled him into yesterday.

"*He* is another reason I wish you would reconsider." She narrowed her eyes at the dog, who simply looked up at her with his big innocent eyes.

"I would if I could, but do not pretend like he hasn't brought a smile to your face on multiple occasions." I raised an eyebrow at her. She huffed, bending down and petting my furry companion on the head.

Beau had ultimately found me. I had decided to take a walk alone after the funeral, continuously assuring River and my mom that I was alright and wound up collecting a walking buddy. He had scared me half to death when he'd come from a bush, seemingly unscathed and pretty well taken care of. He had curled his body around my legs and panted, lifting his big head up for me to pet. I'd called River to come get me, receiving a wide-eyed look when he'd pulled up and saw a dog sitting next to me on the curb.

We'd taken him to a vet, quickly learning that he wasn't chipped. I went home and made a deal with my mom that if no one claimed him in two weeks, then he was mine. Those two weeks were filled with Beau climbing in my bed while I cried, falling asleep in my lap while I read, and greeting both me and mom with the most enthusiastic response whenever we came home.

I bent down next to her, scratching Beau behind his ear. "You gonna take good care of her, buddy?"

He tilted his head as if he was telling me something without words. He did a little hop and licked my face, almost knocking me over. A knock sounded at the door, gaining a sharp bark from the medium-sized dog between us.

I wiped my hand down my shorts, heading towards the front door. I pulled it open, smiling when I saw River and Grayson standing there. My boyfriend gave me a hug, kissing the side of my face before moving to greet my mom. I looked around Grayson's tall frame to see a midsize SUV parked outside.

Grayson followed my eyes, chuckling. "Your boyfriend thought it would be a good idea for me to borrow my parent's car instead of my sedan to take you." He stepped inside, taking a look at the minimal amount of luggage I had. "Hmph, River strikes again."

I shook my head, narrowing my eyes at my boyfriend. "I would have happily taken the train." I'd taken the Caltrain plenty of times, seeing as it had stops at all the places I was familiar with. I had liked using it ever since the first time I'd ridden it with my dad. I'd even gotten lost on it one time, on purpose, which got me grounded for a week for giving my mom a heart attack.

River rolled his eyes from his place on the floor, happily scratching Beau's belly. "That's a joke, right? It would take over an hour, maybe more to just get to the city alone. How about you put all that saved up money to use and put a down payment on a car? Or you know what? Just come live with me."

I heard my mom cluck her tongue causing me to let out a long sigh. "Driving is a nightmare here, at least for me and I don't know... you ever think I might enjoy public transportation?"

In unison they all looked at me and said, "No."

I was about to protest when I felt arms around me, pulling me into a hug. Grayson's voice settled near my ear, whispering, "River continues to borrow Asher's car because he believes that he can do all things with just his motorcycle."

I wanted to shake my head remembering the story River had told me about how a year or so before we met, he had sold his car in favor of the motorcycle he currently owned. River in a motorcycle helmet did things to my insides that I'd never felt before, but that didn't mean I thought the idea was very smart. His brother's car was nice whenever he borrowed it, but Asher was the type that wanted it back in pristine condition, which meant that after he picked me up when I'd found Beau, we'd gotten the car vacuumed and thoroughly cleaned.

"I heard that, dickhead," River scoffed, walking over to us.

I giggled, always feeling this comforting warmth when Grayson Ypulong was around. I pulled away from him, keeping my hands on his forearms that weren't as covered in tattoos as River's, but they were getting there. His skin had gotten some sun over the summer, so his olive complexion looked more tan than usual. Unlike River, Grayson's multitude of tattoos all meant something special to him, especially the ones that had to do with his family, regardless of how and when he got them. From what I'd witnessed he was close with his parents, and they only ever treated River and I like damn near royalty every time Grayson would drag us out for his family dinners. "I didn't know you were coming. River didn't mention it."

Grayson shrugged, running a hand through his dark hair that ended right at his earlobes. The strands looked so soft and shiny; I had to stop myself from reaching up to touch them myself. His eyes were almond shaped, turning up slightly at the corners and were the darkest brown I'd ever seen. "River told me you were moving into the dorms today, and I like to be helpful." He winked at me. "Also, you know you're my favorite if I had to choose between the two of you." He reached for my sides, his fingers finding the spots that tickled.

I batted him away, catching my breath from my laughing fit. My eyes immediately found the one tattoo on his arm that I had been present for. He'd decided on a random Tuesday night to get his *lola's* name tattooed in loopy cursive on his bicep. That was the same night I discovered *lola* means grandma in Tagalog. Every so often, he would throw words I didn't know into sentences, so he could give me a tiny language lesson. It was kind of our thing.

"Can you get the bags?" River delegated, pointing to my luggage.

Grayson winked at me again, pulling out his keys and pressing a button to open up the trunk to the SUV. He pocketed his keys and pointed his fingers at the luggage. Black shadows escaped his fingertips, whipping around and wrapping around my bags. The tendrils lifted and hauled them towards the closed front door. Grayson pointed his other hand at the door, letting more black ropes release themselves so that they could turn the doorknob.

We all watched as his shadows worked, effortlessly placing my bags into the trunk. Beau waited patiently by the door, keeping an eye on the black wisps that slammed the trunk closed and then disappeared as if they were never there.

"Show off," River muttered, playfully slamming his shoulder into Grayson's. I heard my mom chuckle from where she stood off to the side.

"You ready? We leave now and we should be able to make it there to get you settled in and off to the orientation assembly." Grayson explained, hooking his thumb over his shoulder.

"Orientation assembly?" I asked, wrinkling my nose.

Both boys nodded. Grayson waved me off. "You'll see when you get there."

River turned and pulled my mom in for another hug, giving her shoulder a squeeze when he let her go. "She'll be in good hands, Mrs. Monroe." He looked over his shoulder at me and smirked.

"I'm still convinced she's getting out of here just to play house with you." My mom's tone was full of humor. I knew it was a way for her to try to calm herself so that she didn't completely combust after I was gone. I planned to come back to see her, whether it be River driving me, train, or rideshare.

My boyfriend scoffed. The amount of times he'd proposed I live with him was astronomical. He nodded his head towards my mom, the silver studs in his ear glinting in the sunlight that came through the window. "Tell your mom goodbye like a good girl and let's hit the road." He raised his eyebrows and smiled at me while I stared at him with my mouth open. Grayson cackled loudly, following him outside.

I sighed, both me and my mom taking equal steps towards each other until we were fully embraced.

"Call me when you get there, please? And call me when you get settled in your dorm. Also, please call me when you are going to bed, I want to know how your day went." Her voice had a faux calm that was familiar, since I tended to do it as well. She rubbed my back in soothing circles as if she knew there was something else on my mind but refrained from asking.

"I will, Mom. I promise. We can Facetime and you can let Beau in on the call." I heard a bark and the sound of a vivacious tail.

She leaned back, kissing my forehead. Her hands smoothed over my braids, her face scrunching up a bit. She was trying not to cry, and fuck if she didn't make my own eyes well with tears. I whispered, "I'll call you the minute the school comes into view, okay?"

"Okay. I love you, always and always." She kissed my forehead again and lightly pushed me towards the door.

I fingered the gem around my neck, swiping a finger under my eye to remove the tear I could feel wanting to fall further towards my cheek. "I love you too. Always and always."

River and Grayson leaned up against the SUV, patiently waiting. River tilted his head down to catch my eye. "All good?" His voice was soft and understanding.

I sniffed, nodding. "All good."

He gave me a small smile, tilting his head further down so our foreheads were touching. He kissed me quickly, reaching up and rubbing his thumb over my bottom lip and then kissing me again.

"You guys are disgustingly hot. I could stand and watch you for hours, but can we get a move on. Hustle, hustle." Grayson joked, clapping his hands in rapid succession.

River grabbed his friend's head and mussed up his hair, tugging on a few strands to pull his head up. He pressed his lips to Grayson's cheek in a chaste kiss. "Fuck off, but let's go. I'm driving though." They had always had this very touchy, close-knit relationship that I never questioned because River always had a way of making anything and everything seem like the most casual thing in the world. I had always wondered if they'd ever been together at some point, but it wasn't my business, so I kept that thought to myself. I knew River didn't care about the idea of men or women, but Grayson just seemed like his type, although Grayson could be everyone's type if I was honest.

Grayson paused as he was rounding the front of the car to the driver's side. "It's *my* parents' car."

River shrugged, giving me a once over that was dedicated for when we were alone and he was prepared to make me sore for a few days. He looked back at Grayson. "Yeah...unless you want me fingering her in the backseat, I think I better drive so my mind can focus on something else besides wanting to taste her p—"

"River!" I shouted, moving towards the back door.

Grayson casually dropped the keys in his hand. "Solid reasoning. I accept, but I'm not sitting in the back because you drive like you're on a motorcycle and not a four-wheel drive." He jogged over to the other side of the car, stopping when he saw my face. "What?"

"He...I...ugh, I don't understand you guys. Like me, you should be fucking mortified."

He let out a short laugh, shaking his head. "Nah, I mean he makes a valid point. You have seen yourself, right?" He narrowed his eyes at me as if I was insane for not leaning into being desirable to my boyfriend...or to anyone.

I closed the door behind me, securing my seatbelt. River turned the car on, his green eyes finding mine in the rearview mirror. "Sometimes I really wish I hadn't promised not to read your mind."

I gave him a confused look while he put the car in drive, hitting the gas. "Are you planning on elaborating?"

He shrugged, turning right. "Mmm, no. You'll elaborate to me whenever you're ready, gorgeous."

I tried to keep my composure while I'd set myself up to transfer schools. I really thought I'd played it cool. River was never one to assume, but I guess with me, he had to go on assumptions and inferences alone.

Grayson turned to look at me from over his seat. "You ready for Mystic Riegan, *trouble*?"

"Trouble?" I raised an eyebrow at the nickname.

He snickered, eyeing me suspiciously. "My shadows know trouble when they see it. Deny it all you like, but I think trouble is exactly what you're planning.

3
RILEY

River pulled into a parking space and cut off the gas, leaning back in his seat. He never did well with traffic, so this drive had gotten on his nerves more than usual. I looked out my window to see a long row of cars parked next to us, groups of people hauling items out of their trunks. I'd spent the last twenty minutes on the phone with my mom and I couldn't deny that I missed her already. I took a peek out of the front window, taking in as much of the university as I could.

When we were getting closer, you could see the rust-colored tops of the buildings and the beige mass timber that made up the majority of the academic buildings. There were four massive parking lots that aligned perfectly to each section of Mystic Riegan housing. A brick barrier surrounded sections of school, with gates leading inside. Gates that were wide open at the moment. The brick took up most of my view of the lawn, but from the few times I'd been here with my dad, I knew they paid a lot of money for landscaping and used a few green witches to help maintain it. Students got college credit if something they helped with aligned with their major.

I jumped a little when I heard my door open and saw Grayson holding his hand out. "Out you go."

I grabbed his hand, letting him lead me onto the pavement. I squinted up at the sun beaming down on us. It was hot, but not as hot as it was going to get. The short breeze made my braids move, slightly slapping me in the face. I leaned down, letting my hair dangle as I stretched out my hair tie around them, creating a messy bun on top of my head. When I straightened, a single braid sat in front of my face.

"Missed one." Grayson pointed out, holding onto the end and moving it from left to right. "It's cute though. Leave it."

I heard the trunk close, right as River placed my weekender bag on top of my luggage. He had put his sunglasses on, particularly the expensive ones I'd bought him for Christmas. He swatted my hand away when I tried to take one of my bags, rolling one of them to Grayson.

A massive amount of heat drifted past my face and I screeched, seeing River's large hands grab my arms and pull me back. I looked over seeing a ball of flames fly through a few more groups of people, eventually disintegrating. I reached up and touched my cheek, wondering if it had singed my skin.

"Fucking watch it, Jensen!" River yelled, looking past me.

A guy an inch or so taller than me jogged over, waving his hands. "Fuck! I'm sorry. It wasn't meant to go that far out." He had blonde hair that was buzzed on both sides and left long at the top, the ends flopping over his eyebrow.

River stepped in front of me, shoving Jensen back with one of his hands. "Yeah, that's what you said the last time when you forgot to wear your fucking dampener and almost set your dorm on fire!" His voice was getting even louder. He pointed over to me. "You're lucky you didn't burn her, because I would fucking kill..."

Jensen rolled his eyes, backing away from us. "That was one time and I was a freshman, so sue me. I said I was sorry, for fucks sake." He nodded towards me.

River and Grayson both looked at me as if confirming that the apology was enough. I also noticed the eyes that were on us and I had never been more embarrassed. I tucked my stray braid behind my ear. "Yeah, it's fine. Scary, but fine."

A black shadow came out, wrapping around Jensen's chest and turning him around. Another shadow pushed against his back, shoving him in the other direction. "The lady forgives you so off you go, fucking idiot."

Jensen looked back at us as he walked, rolling his shoulders as if Grayson had left him with a small chill. Jensen suddenly stopped, lifting his arm up at a very slow pace as if he was trying to stop it and then his fist connected with his jaw. He stumbled sideways, holding his face. He was seething when he turned around to look at us, mainly River. My boyfriend didn't use the parts of his powers that included influencing someone's actions and thoughts frequently; he primarily used it when he was younger. Nowadays, when he thought that it was necessary...no one was safe. River simply smiled at him and waved. "Throw a fireball at my girlfriend again and I'll make you think you want to suck your dick, got it?"

A few people snickered around us, while others just looked on in varying confusion.

I placed my hands on my face, groaning.

"Something wrong?" River asked, locking the car and throwing the keys at his best friend.

I waved my hands around me, noticing a few students with lingering glares and a few muffled laughs. My goal wasn't to try to impress anyone at this school, but I didn't love the idea of already making a pariah out of myself before I'd started any of my investigating. "Um, let's see...you couldn't have handled that with a little more subtlety?"

River ran a tattooed finger over his bottom lip. "Not really, no."

"You're ridiculous."

He shrugged, pulling the handle of my bag up, rolling it. "The guy almost struck you with a fireball, excuse me for being concerned. I didn't beat his ass or mentally debilitate him, so be grateful, gorgeous."

He was walking in front of me, while I followed behind him, so he didn't see the way my body automatically shivered with the thought of him hurting someone for me. I'd never actually seen him fight, but I knew he could. I always just saw him as the sweet guy who forced me to walk on the side closer to the buildings when we strolled down a sidewalk, so he could be the one near the street. I hadn't seen many guys do that before, but he claimed it was a common gentleman practice. Gentleman went out the window when he then proceeded to lean me against his motorcycle and attempt to finger me, but honestly, I wasn't complaining. And I likely never would.

We stopped at the gates, as did many others, causing me to raise an eyebrow. River reached into his back pocket, pulling out two rings and handing one to Grayson. I looked around seeing students take out bracelets, earrings and even necklaces. River placed the ring on his finger, contorting his hand into a fist before relaxing.

"Dampeners?" I asked curiously. I knew about them, but I had never truly witnessed them in action. Growing up, kids always already had them on when in school, so I didn't know how magic wielders felt putting them on. What it felt like to have your power become nearly dormant.

"It's like a vacuum inside of yourself. All the power just goes poof." Grayson snapped his finger. "Well, okay, you can still feel it, which honestly is kind of worse."

There were plenty of students who didn't have dampeners, letting me know they were human. I knew this wasn't the entire student population, but it seemed as if the ratio of humans to magic wielders were equal enough. That thought had me considering my dad's place in how well the two types of students mixed. He wasn't the reason they got admitted or even decided to integrate at all, but he was sometimes the reason they stayed at the school. He had a way of making you feel like he truly understood you, even though he had likely just met you a few moments ago. My heart constricted and I had to catch my breath before I started sobbing in front of my future classmates.

I felt a tug at my elbow, seeing Grayson pull me along gently. There was a small wave that washed over you when you went through the gates, like you knew you were entering a place with so much power while also trying to maintain normalcy. The lush green lawn came into view and no brochure or word of mouth could have done this campus justice. There had been changes since I was last here. They had built a giant breezeway between two of the buildings, glass taking over each side. Newly planted white alder trees decorated the open space, and freshly cut hedges outlined the brick wall. A large fountain sat in the middle with benches surrounding it. The walkways were sculpted out with red clay, creating the rickety sound of wheels against it as students brought their stuff in.

There was a large sign directing towards different areas of the campus. Mystic Riegan was one of the biggest campuses in California, even including the human only schools. When a sign said left, you didn't know how far left you were actually going. The directory indicated that up ahead would lead us to the academic and administrative buildings. I tilted my chin up to try to look as far out as I could. I knew we were on the east side of the university and my father's building was north. I would have to carve out time to make my way over there, or hopefully my class schedule placed me in its vicinity at some point during the day.

I hadn't realized I'd stopped walking until I heard my name being called. I looked over to see River and Grayson waving their hands, motioning for me to hurry up. My phone buzzed in my shorts pockets. I pulled it out, seeing Marianne's name across the screen. I sent her a quick text that I would call her back and hurried over to the guys.

WE HAD TO SHOVE PAST A FEW PEOPLE TO GET TO THE ELEVATORS AND THEN down the hall to my room, but after a quick tap of my university ID that doubled as a keycard to my dorm room, we finally were at our destination. The room was what I'd expected for a university dorm. Mid-sized, two twin beds on opposite sides, two simple work desks, a decent bathroom and one closet.

Grayson rolled one of my suitcases to the middle of the room and whistled. "Damn, your room is smaller than mine."

River scrunched up his face. "You have a single, of course it's smaller than yours."

Grayson rolled his eyes. "Hey now, my scholarship covers a lot and when the form asked me to check a box on what kind of dorm I wanted, well, I went for the one with privacy."

I giggled. "Right. *Privacy*. This coming from the guy who admitted during our first time meeting each other that he prefers a particular brand of lotion when he masturbates."

River held his stomach as he doubled over in laughter. Grayson wagged his finger at me. "There is nothing wrong with being partic-ular about what I'm rubbing on my dick. I'm happy I could make such an impression on you though, Riley."

My boyfriend pointed towards the beds. "Which one?"

I placed my hands on my hips and nodded towards the left one. The guys moved my things, dropping my weekender bag at the end of the empty bed. Grayson pulled me into a hug, then pointed at the door. "I got to get to the west side of campus for my work study pre-semester meeting." He kissed the side of my head, nodding his head towards River and left.

I started to maneuver my suitcases, unzipping one of them and searching inside.

"What are you looking for?" River bent down so that he was eye level with me.

"My sheets. I might as well get something done before this very ominous orientation assembly. I already went to an orientation, so I have no idea what this even is." I grabbed the sheets, moving my luggage to the side. I began to unravel the cheap set of sheets I'd gotten at a thrift store when they were yanked out of my hands and tossed on the bed.

"Well, that was incredibly rude." I narrowed my eyes at River who had his head tilted to the side, arms crossed over his chest so his biceps flexed almost perfectly. He had gotten some of his finger tattoos retouched so the ink looked shiny and new. He took a step towards me, pulling me into him.

His voice was muffled in my neck when he spoke. "I had to sit in a car, in raging traffic, for probably over two hours and I couldn't touch you. I couldn't even circle my thumb on your thigh like I know you like."

I pulled back a little, so that I could see his face and run my fingers over his jaw. "That was your choice, remember?" His green eyes flashed with amusement at my sass.

His hands grabbed my waist, thumbs fiddling with the waist-band of my shorts. "Ah, so you wanted me to sit in the back with my fingers inside that pretty pussy of yours?" His tongue came out and licked at my lips.

A small moan left my throat and River's mouth was on mine before another sound could escape. He tugged at my bottom lip with his teeth, running his palms over my ass to pull me closer to him. My arm instinctively wanted to wrap around his neck and continue this, but I blinked and started to push him away. "I have a roommate that could come in here at any time, not to mention that assembly starts in like an hour."

He didn't let me get far, holding me in place so I was forced to settle against him. "An hour is plenty of time, and if your roommate does come in, that's one hell of a first impression. They'll know you have a boyfriend that takes *very* good care of you." He squeezed my ass, leaning down and running his nose along mine. He dipped his head down lower to kiss my neck.

I couldn't help melting into him the slightest bit. "I'm not having sex with you right now."

He chuckled, the noise causing me to press my thighs together. His laugh was just a tiny bit intoxicating. "Okay, no sex." He moved us so that my bed was behind me. River walked us backwards until my calves hit the mattress, lightly shoving me so I fell onto the bed. He slid his hand up my leg until his fingers hovered between my legs. "I'll keep my cock in my pants if you let me put my tongue in your cunt."

He was sliding my shorts down slowly, almost like he was waiting for me to stop him. I just watched him toss them to the floor and get down on his knees. He pressed his nose against the center of my panties, inhaling deeply as if the scent of my arousal was the only thing that mattered. He pressed his mouth to the material, sucking my clit through my panties. River looked up my body at me, his hands pushing at my inner thighs to keep my legs open.

After this, I would refocus on my plan. I would spend tonight mapping out all the locations I needed to visit and who was on the top of my list to speak with. I would—

My panties were moved to the side and two fingers were gently pushed into me, curling at just the right spot. "So greedy the way you're taking my fingers." He blew air against my clit right before he flicked it with his tongue, sucking it into his mouth and I saw stars.

Chocolate PSD
Bar Mock-Up
Food Packaging Collection
157
157

4
RILEY

I held his face between my legs, hooking my ankles behind his back. River pinched my nipples between his fingers as he toyed with my breasts. He hadn't come up for air for almost twenty minutes and I'd already come twice. His tongue slid over my clit, circling it as his finger pushed into me over and over again. There was a small smile on his face when he looked up at me, taking in my exhausted expression and pleading eyes to let this be the last orgasm.

I was enjoying it, but River had a way of distracting me at the worst possible times. And as much as he thought it was funny, I really didn't want my roommate to wander in and see my boyfriend with his face buried in my pussy with me on the verge of a third orgasm.

"Come for me, gorgeous. One more time and I'll let you up."

He pressed his thumb against my clit and I nearly convulsed when I came against his face. I ran my hands through his hair and tugged, needing something to grasp as my body tensed and relaxed. I caught my breath when the feeling finally passed and River leaned back, moving my panties back into place. He got up from the floor, running a hand over his wet mouth.

"Satisfied?" I asked, using both my hands to lift myself up. My braids hit my back, having long since been removed from my hair tie.

"Oh, devouring your pussy is always satisfying, gorgeous." He smirked, plucking my shorts from the floor, tossing them at me.

I wrinkled my nose at him when I put them on, my shoulders tensing when I heard the sound of the door unlocking.

"What perfect timing." River joked, raising his arms over his head, stretching.

I shoved him back, hoping that I looked somewhat presentable and not like a girl whose boyfriend just eagerly went down on her. I wasn't really sure what sex or anything having to do with sex smelt like, but I sure as hell hoped it wasn't potent.

The door opened and a beautiful girl with short black tight curls and dark skin walked in. She had glasses with thick black rectangular frames perched on her nose and a leopard print head-band with a matching t-shirt dress on that hit right before her knees. A neon yellow fanny pack was hooked around her waist. She rolled in two suitcases and behind her was a man who brought in two more suitcases and a duffel bag. He looked identical to her, right down to the way they both smiled at me.

I waved my hand awkwardly. "Um...hi."

The girl looked from me to River and then back again. A laugh ripped from her throat, followed by a snort. "If I had been alone in this room with Mateo, I would have made the same decision."

We couldn't be that obvious...could we?

She waved nonchalantly towards the empty bed so the guy behind her knew where to put the rest of her stuff. She practically skipped over to me, the friendliest smile on her face. "I'm Corrin Hayes." She looked over her shoulder. "And that brute over there is my brother, Ike."

I cleared my throat. "Oh, um...well, I'm—" She cut me off before I could finish.

"Riley Monroe, yeah, I know who you are." Her dark brown eyes softened, and I didn't know if it was pity or empathy. She flicked her eyes to River. "And River St. James, wow, isn't she a little out of your league?" Corrin shook her head and despite my thoughts just seconds ago, I found myself laughing.

River huffed. "I am inclined to agree with you."

"Cor, can you quit being a fucking pain?" Ike scolded his sister. He ran a hand over his closely buzzed head. "Actually, speaking of Mateo, why aren't they helping you instead of me? I have plans and one of those plans was not helping you move from the north dorms to the east."

Corrin rolled her eyes. "Because mom and dad told you to, that's why. I'm their *favorite*, not to mention I was born two minutes before you, so I'm older and therefore have authority over you."

Ike narrowed his eyes at her, but just shook his head. "I am bringing the last of your bags and then I'm gone." He gave us a small salute. "Good luck with her."

"You have more bags?" I mumbled, looking at the size of the room and more so, the size of the closet.

River pulled me into his side, kissing the top of my head. "I'm going to head back to the house. Call me after the assembly or when you get completely settled, alright?"

"After I call my mom and Marianne, you are next on the list." I said, causing him to swat my ass playfully before he said goodbye to Corrin and left.

I waited a few moments to see if she would speak to me again, but she was giving her full attention to making up her bed. I looked down at my messy sheets and decided to do the same. Corrin's brother had come in, thrown the rest of her bags at her and given me a small wave before he threw his middle finger at his sister while she threw both hers up as well. I had put my black silk pillowcases on the two pillows the school provided and was about to tuck in my top sheet when she spoke next.

"You're human, right?"

I moved my pillows to the head of the bed. "Yeah. Are you?"

She snorted again. "Oh, fuck no." Corrin brought her hand to lips. "Sorry, I didn't mean for that to come out like that. Being a human is fine. I personally like being a witch. My whole family are witches, well except for my dad. My brother would rather focus on his business degree than his metal magic."

I raised my eyebrows. "What kind? Of witch I mean?"

"Fucking dampeners. It would be much better if I showed you. I'm a healing witch, but I also have an affinity for potions and science. I like my magic to come with a lab coat most times, potion chemistry I like to say. The university has a dedicated building for potions on the south part of campus. One of the only places I don't have to wear those stupid dampeners."

I fiddled with one of my braids. "I thought you guys had to wear them all the time."

Corrin looked up at the ceiling. "Any magical student may remove their dampeners for specific classes that pertain to their major or if they are overseen by a professional individual employed by the university within that field of magic that enhances their education." She did a little shimmy. "It's in the handbook. Anything outside of that is grounds for expulsion. Believe me, I'm just a sophomore and I've seen it happen. All it takes is one person to open up their stupid mouth and boom, under investigation for violating the rules and you're out on your ass with no degree in hand."

It was a long shot, but maybe something happened with a student and they got angry at my dad. I couldn't wrap my mind around the thought that something like that could end with my father falling through his office window. I couldn't dismiss any option at this point, then again, I couldn't go around asking every single student if they knew, met or had any suspicions on the matter.

Corrin gasped, startling me out of my thoughts. She was looking down at her phone. "Omg! We are going to be late for the assembly."

"Isn't it just for new students?"

"Yes and no. It's mandatory for new students, but it's open for anyone to go. The university really likes morale, so all the teachers go, faculty, the vice president, sometimes the chancellor. I emphasize *sometimes*, because he only graces us with his presence during graduations or things he deems really important."

I remembered when I was doing a dive into the school, The Mystic Riegan chancellor, Erik Fowler, had a lot of credentials and had been with the school for a while. There wasn't much information on him. My dad never really spoke about him, and based on how little there was to know, I would assume he'd never even met him.

I blinked over at Corrin who was still talking. "There is free food, so obviously I will be in attendance." She grabbed my university ID, shoving it at my chest before I was ushered out the door.

THE AUDITORIUM WAS SLOWLY FILLING UP AS WE FOUND OUR SEATS, PLATES of food in hand. I absentmindedly fiddled with my necklace as I watched everyone filter in, popping a few grapes into my mouth. The room had a high ceiling and three sets of stairs that separated multiple rows of chairs. A few people would look at me and then turn to their friends, who would then also look at me. Some of them would nod and others would contort their faces into that same expression that Corrin had in our room.

I tried to convince myself they were looking past me or maybe I was just imagining the whole thing and really no one was paying me any mind.

"There's your boyfriend's dad." I followed her eyes to a man sitting between a woman I knew was the Dean of the English Department and a tall man who was animatedly speaking on the phone, but I knew he was another Dean of some sort. River's father had dark hair with lines of gray throughout, thick defined eyebrows, and what almost looked like permanent disdain on his face. The scariest part is they had such similar bone structure and facial features that it would be crazy to not think they were related.

I'd never officially met the man. At first, I assumed it was because River just wasn't interested in letting me into that part of his life, but the way he spoke about him had me reconsidering my earlier thoughts. His face almost looked pained and annoyed when his parents came up.

I looked back over at Mr. St. James and internally felt myself wanting to laugh. That man couldn't pick me out of a lineup if he tried.

Corrin leaned into me, swallowing a few bites of her mini muffin. "Does he always look so constipated?"

A laugh bubbled out of me. "I wouldn't know, I've never met him."

She shrugged at this. "I guess it has to be hard sitting on that high pedestal knowing both your kids are circulating in your academic department. River is the dream magic one, right?"

"No, River is a telepath. You're thinking of Asher."

Corrin nodded, tapping the side of her head. "Right. They're both hot, so it's easy to make a mistake."

The doors closed around the auditorium, letting us know that it was about to start as people were finishing finding their seats. "You've met Asher?" I realized I'd said it like I'd *never* met my boyfriend's brother. I'd met Asher, but it was so brief I would have assumed it never happened. The interactions were a simple hi and bye with no eye contact.

River's excuse was that his brother doesn't like anyone. That's why only the bravest students make it out of his classes alive and with good grades.

"Have I met him? Like have I sat with him during his office hours and made small talk? Hell no. He took over one of my English classes during the summer, but apparently, he hates doing that during the fall, well like he hates subbing in for other teachers in general. He likes to stick with his mental magic classes or anything revolving around that, so I wouldn't worry about having him as an instructor." She balled up her napkin and chucked it at my head.

I laughed. "Well, that's good to know, since English is my major and all."

"You must really love writing papers." She leaned back in her chair, chuckling.

The fluorescent lights dimmed a bit and River's dad tapped the microphone in front of him, sending feedback throughout the room. I lowered my voice to a whisper. "So, your boyfriend, Mateo, is in a wolf pack? He's like—"

Corrin placed her hand on her cheek as she stopped me. "They. Not he, they." She adjusted her headband on her head. "Also, not my boyfriend, they're my partner."

I nodded, feeling my cheeks getting a little hot assuming I'd fucked up any potential of having some sort of friend already. "Right, I heard you say that earlier, I'm sorry…"

"You're fine. If you fuck up again, I'll make sure to remind you." She bumped her shoulder against mine before we ceased our conversation to listen.

I wish we had kept talking and shut out the meeting entirely. I thought they would be droning on about what they expect at Mystic Riegan and how they hope we have a hopeful and enlightening year. I didn't think I would start paying attention the moment River's father pointed to the empty chair that sat at the end of the long table at the front of the room. I couldn't make out the name plate from where we were sitting, but Mr. St. James said my father's name and I knew.

My brain short circuited when he started going on about what a great man he was and how what happened was a tragedy. The words started to jumble together, and I could make out things like how he helped so many students and that he could never be replaced. The school was a better place because of my father's hard work. I started to sink further into my seat, like I could feel the eyes on me.

Maybe this was a shit idea. Mom was right and this would be too much. She didn't know why I was really here, but some part of her must have known that this would happen, and I wouldn't have her shoulder to automatically lean on. I felt stiff, like I couldn't even move my fingers to reach for my phone and text River. My eyes burned from the tears that threatened to fall. The fucking overwhelming tears.

I should go home. I should go—

A hand lightly touched my wrist, sliding down to envelop my shaky hand in its warmth. I slid my eyes over to Corrin slowly. She wasn't looking at me, but straight ahead. Her hand had mine tightly trapped as if she was holding me together with every little squeeze she sent in my direction. She turned her head slightly to me, so I could see the softness in her eyes, and I let myself smile at her.

She winked at me before facing forward again.

Chocolate
Bar Mock-Up
PSD
Food Packaging Collection

5
RILEY

"So, you knew my dad?" I asked, spinning my phone on the linoleum table. After the dreaded two hours that was that god awful assembly, Corrin dragged me to Sothis, one of the on-campus coffee shops. She'd ordered and paid for both of us. It was small and had mustard yellow-colored walls and gray tiles along the floor. Pop music played through the speakers at a low volume and the atmosphere screamed casual comfort.

She took a sip of her coffee. "I met with him once. I was having a difficult time since I'd only ever been with witches or just magic users all together, so the school sent me to him during my freshman year." She traced the rim of her coffee cup with her fingernail. "He was the nicest, truly."

I looked over her shoulder, not wanting to look directly at her. "He was the best." I cleared my throat, attempting to answer an earlier question I'd had. "How did you know he was *my* dad? Earlier you said my name like it was obvious who I was."

Corrin pulled at one of her curls. "I'm not always one to gossip, but I will listen to gossip whenever I can. When your dad...." She trailed off, closing her mouth and then opening it up again to continue. "When the accident happened, boy did people talk. I don't know all the details, but I do know people knew he had a daughter, and the social media investigation blew up. People are aggressively invasive."

Right, my dad's *accident*. It wasn't an accident, and I was going to prove it. I pushed my coffee away from me, the smell all of a sudden nauseating. "Well, that's perfect." Sarcasm oozing from each of my words.

She slapped her hand on the table, startling me. "If anyone gives you any shit, bring them to me and I'll fuck their world up. I don't need magic to cause some serious damage."

I pressed my lips together, failing at holding in my laughter. "You met me a few hours ago and you sound like you are ready to go to collegiate war for me."

Corrin shrugged, pushing her glasses up her nose. "It's what I do, babe."

I considered her for a moment, choosing my words carefully. I flung a few of my braids over my shoulder. "Do you know if they're planning on replacing him?"

She clasped her hands together on the table. "I'm not sure. I overheard while I was waiting for my academic advisor that they were going to do interviews, but I don't think they've hired anyone yet." She looked out the window to her right as students walked past, completely engrossed in their own conversations. "They need to though. I don't know how this school is going to fucking survive without a middleman."

I stared intensely at my coffee cup, thinking that if I looked hard enough, I could release all my tension into it. "Do you believe it?"

Corrin tilted her head to the side, her eyebrows turning in with confusion.

"The accident and all that?" I tried to make my voice sound

flighty and nonchalant, but I had a feeling she could see right through that.

She licked her lips, looking around as if she was afraid someone was listening. Her voice got low when she leaned against the table. "I don't, and I'm not the only one." She leaned back, nodding as if she was so secure in her beliefs. "Accidental falling, my ass," she mumbled, scoffing.

My heart wanted to leap out of my chest. I wanted to divulge my thoughts and pick her brain.

No, Riley. Someone was nice to you for two fucking seconds, get a fucking grip.

I opened my mouth to change the subject when my phone vibrated on the table. I brought the screen to my face seeing an incoming text from River.

RIVER

Heard they brought up your dad in the assembly.

I furrowed my brow. Corrin wasn't lying. This school did gossip.

I'm fine. Don't worry.

RIVER

Very convincing. I can come over.

No, I have a whole roommate, River. You can't just show up.

RIVER

Then I'll pick you up. I'll take you out, bring you back home for a nice little massage and then you can stay the night with me.

I rolled my eyes. He was sweet, but I needed to be by myself. Well, as by myself as I could get with a roommate. Corrin seemed like the type that if I told her I wanted my space, she would find a way to make it happen even in our less than private living arrangement.

> Stay put. Seriously. I knew shit like this would happen, so I have to deal.

RIVER

> Oh, look at you…barking orders. You come over and use that mouth for something much better. Then I'll let you ride out your frustration on my cock. We both know I enjoy it when you're a little wild.

My cheeks burned from the heat forming in them.

> Maybe tomorrow. You'll have to sleep alone tonight.

RIVER

> I guess it's just me and my hand. Good thing your taste is still right on the tip of my tongue.

I flicked my eyes up at Corrin, who was looking at her own phone. A text from River came through again.

RIVER

> Call me tomorrow, gorgeous. Love you.

I said I love you back, sending a few red hearts to him and flipped my phone face down for safe measure. It would be just like River to randomly send a picture of his cock just to spite me.

"Ready to get out of here? We can head to the bookstore, grab what we need for the semester." Corrin reached for my cup, pushing her seat back.

"Sure, sounds good."

We both walked out, following the directory outside the coffee shop, towards the bookstore. I could see it in the distance, a tall, rectangular building that had more windows than most of the buildings on this campus.

Corrin opened the door for me, but I paused before walking through. There was another directory next to the bookstore and my eyes focused on the first place noted on the rust-colored sign.

HUMAN/MAGIC LIAISON

I looked over the sign towards the north side of campus. The English, Math and Elemental Magic academic advisors were on the west side so the options to naturally be close to my father's office were dwindling. I could always just ask to see it, snoop around, but there would likely be someone watching me, hovering. I couldn't have that.

"Riley, you good?" Corrin kicked my calf with her black high top covered foot.

I shook my head, plastering a smile on my face. "Yeah, sorry. I'm just a little tired and unsurprisingly exhausted." I pulled out my phone, checking the time. "And it's just midafternoon. Fucking great."

Corrin laughed, reached into her fanny pack, pulling out a folded-up piece of paper. She looked up, searching each of the signs to try to find where she needed to go. I looked over her shoulder, taking her arms and turning her in the direction of the herbs department.

I tapped on my phone, pulling up my email and clicking on the last email from the university that had my finalized class schedule. I scrolled over to see the locations, sighing in relief when I saw that one of them was on the north side. The Mental Magic Department was over there as well, so that made sense since that was my psychology class.

I scrolled up to double-check the rest of my classes when I heard a small gasp. "You're taking general psychology? Me too!" She squealed, pulling me toward one of the bookcases.

"Marianne, I have to go. I have to call my mom." The sun had long gone down and Corrin had taken up video chatting with her partner until she fell asleep with her laptop open.

"I can't believe you're rooming with a witch, that is so cool. I'm stuck with a boring human." I shook my head even though she couldn't see me.

"Let's not forget *you* are also just a boring human," I taunted.

"Don't get smart. That school has already made you incredibly sassy."

I pressed my head further into my pillow. "You sound like River."

"The mind reader better be taking care of you since I'm not there. I have friends in high places if he isn't."

Their relationship had gotten better over time. River really had to prove himself to Marianne, even more so than my parents. He treated it like a challenge, and he was dead set on winning her over. She was always going to be skeptical, but she didn't let out a loud, obnoxious groan every time I would tell her I was going out with him anymore.

I pulled my phone away from my ear and checked the time. "We get it. You are very feisty. I need to call my mom; I will text you tomorrow."

She begrudgingly let me go and I went to click on my mom's number when a text came through.

GRAYSON

Nakakainis ka naman. Napaka killjoy mo talaga. Bakit mo naman kami iniwang dalawa lang ni River?

I blinked, trying to understand what this was. I texted question marks back, fully prepared to use the internet to translate what he was saying.

GRAYSON

Basically, you're a killjoy for deciding not to
hang out tonight, therefore, leaving us to our

own devices.

> Is River standing over your shoulder making
> you type this?

GRAYSON

Not at all.

If I knew my boyfriend at all, he was right there making sure
Grayson said all the right things.

> I'm sure your night would have been very
> dull with me there.

GRAYSON

I think you underestimate how much we
both enjoy your company.

Even though he wasn't here to say that in front of me, something
about that particular statement felt odd. Not in a bad way, but
different than all the other times Grayson had jokingly flirted with
me out in the open.

GRAYSON

Alas I suppose I'll entertain your boyfriend
without you.

> You both are ridiculously needy and should
> acquire more friends.

GRAYSON

I resent that, gorgeous. This is River

I let out a sharp laugh, covering my mouth and looking over to
make sure Corrin didn't wake up.

I rubbed my hand down my face, swiping through my apps to get back to calling my mom. I would give her the rundown on how I was and my classes. I would let her know I missed her. Once I was off the phone, I would pull up the school map and the school administration, setting up a plan on how I was going to get this done.

Before I hit the call button, I went to my photos. I found my favorite picture of me and my dad and lightly traced his face with the tip of my finger, careful not to swipe the picture away. We had taken a tiny mini in-state family trip to the San Diego Zoo. My mom had gotten car sick, so she'd stayed in the hotel room while my dad and I explored the animals. I had a snack in hand, and he had asked one of the staff members to take a picture for us, whispering to me: *mom will be so jealous of us.*

After that trip, I had begged my parents to let me have a lion cub as a pet, which was immediately turned down. I rallied and then asked for a dog. Mom had said no, but my dad was always on the fence. He ultimately sided with his wife. I think that was what made my mom more open to letting Beau into our family, although I hadn't given her much of a choice anyway.

My dad should have come home to me and mom. He should be here, right now, doing the job he loved. The feeling that always motivated me to keep going was raging and my only option was to feed it, hoping it worked out in the end.

Chocolate PSD
Bar Mock-Up
Food Packaging Collection

6
RIVER

"**D**id you send the girlfriend a good morning text?" Grayson inquired, biting into his breakfast burrito he'd woken up early to go pick up. It was from our favorite local place that was highly underrated.

I dipped my hand inside the greasy brown bag and pulled out the one he'd gotten me, nodding. "Of course I did."

"If you would have been more persistent, she would have slept here last night, and we could *all* be headed to school on the first day." He wagged his burrito in my direction, as if he was scolding me.

"She wants to get accustomed to campus life. Who am I to stop her, hmm?"

Grayson shoved the rest of his food in his mouth. "You can be quite persuasive when you want."

I smirked over at him. "True. We both know you just wanted her here so you could attempt to jump into my bed and cuddle with us." I started to open my mouth, about to take a bite of my burrito when I noticed him leaning against my kitchen counter, crossing his arms over his chest.

His deep brown eyes sparkled with that flirty mischief that I knew so well. We had been best friends for as long as I could remember and at some point, during high school, our relationship shifted. Grayson had always been so open about his bisexuality, and I'd admired him for it. I did have the inkling for a fleeting moment that I was bisexual, and I'd kissed him, which shocked both of us one night while we hung out.

He didn't push me away, but he'd simply asked me how I felt about it. I had enjoyed it but knew there was still something gnawing at me. Simply saying that I was bisexual wasn't accurate, and I would be lying to myself if I thought otherwise. I'd still been struggling, trying to figure myself out, and Grayson had been the one to remind me that I didn't need to label myself if I didn't know or if I wasn't ready.

One night I'd snuck out with him to Shamir, a popular gay bar in Oakland, and ended up drinking way too much but also having the most enlightening conversation with a man who explained pansexuality to me in a way that kind of spoke to my soul.

Once I came to that realization, I'd felt a lot lighter, and it even seemed like my powers were more settled and less sporadic once I was comfortable with myself.

Grayson chuckled before shaking his head, licking at his bottom lip. I followed the movement almost like an instinct. The last time Grayson and I had fooled around with each other was a few months before I met Riley, and I'd completely cut that part of our relationship off once she and I had become serious. We could still maintain our friendship without sex. He'd been fine with it, especially since he kind of fell in love with her as well. That was overtly apparent, and I was still trying to wrap my mind around the fact that I was more than *okay* with that fact.

I opened my mind up, letting my powers filter into his. I internally groaned at his thoughts, even though I knew he liked to fuck with me and think things that would antagonize me.

Better put that burrito in your mouth before I replace it with something else.

I pointed my food at him. "Watch your thoughts, buddy. I have a girlfriend."

"I respect that. And I adore her, but that doesn't make my thoughts untrue."

"Actually, it does. I happen to remember that more often than not, you were the one with your mouth full." I raised my eyebrows, taking a large bite of my food. Grayson laughed, using his shadows to reach up and ruffle my hair.

I heard footsteps upstairs, alerting me that my brother was about to barrel downstairs with the most unamused expression in history. I'd lived with him since I was sixteen; I knew my brother like the back of my hand. It was nice that we lived so close to campus and the fact that he didn't make me pay rent, but sometimes I did have the urge to move out. Asher would usually sit me down and explain that once I graduated then he would help me look for a place, a solid job, and anything else I needed. The lighter, more brotherly side of Asher came out probably four times a year, but I looked forward to it. We both cared but we had our own lives and as long as I abided by his house rules, then we were civil enough.

My brother rounded the corner, stopping when he noticed both of us. His green eyes, that matched mine, looked Grayson and I up and down as if he was making sure we were both fully dressed and ready to go. I opened my mouth to say something, but he rushed past me to the fridge, pulling out his overnight oats.

I wrinkled my nose at it. "Well, good morning to you too."

Asher mumbled a form of greeting, letting the fridge close on its own. He had a grey button-down shirt on with black slacks, both of which I knew he'd ironed himself. He had trimmed his beard, so it sat nicely right at his jaw. He placed his food in his lunchbox, throwing the handle over his shoulder. "Am I driving you?"

I shook my head, grabbing my backpack from over near the front door. "Grayson is driving me."

Asher clucked his tongue. "Surprised you aren't driving that death machine of yours." The look he'd given me when I'd parked it in our driveway lived rent free in my mind. We weren't overwhelmingly wealthy, but our parents did well for themselves and we each had ample money in our bank accounts to show for it. I'd used some of my money to purchase my first car, but I'd also paid for motorcycle training and when the time was right I traded my sensible car in for a bike. I had to remind nearly everyone that I was still making straight A's and that I would be extremely careful.

My mom had always been the slight rebel of our family before I came along, so there was a gleam in her eye as if she wanted to know more about the bike. Asher and my dad were disgruntled about the entire thing, but they ultimately shut the fuck up because I'd gone to Mystic Riegan like they'd wanted, majored in mental magic—like they wanted, and this time I did something for me, along with the designs I'd drawn and tattooed myself on my arms and legs.

I scoffed, placing a hand over my heart. "Don't talk about my motorcycle like that. I am the most cautious driver there ever was. Perfect score all around during my license test."

My brother nodded as if he couldn't care less about my defensive words and walked past me, shifting his messenger bag over his head so the strap sat across his chest. "I emailed you my classes this semester and the faculty meetings I have so you'll know when I'll be unavailable."

"How generous of you," I said, sarcastically as he pulled open the door, ignoring me.

"Be nice to your students!" Grayson shouted.

Asher gave my best friend an incredulous look. "I am nice. Maybe they should stop thinking I'm going to turn my chair around, sit in it backwards and speak to them like we're friends."

"Someone slept on the wrong side of their incredibly large bed this morning." I said under my breath. I'd walked into his office enough to notice all the red marks on his students' tests and papers. He was thorough and I suppose fair, but man, could he use a vacation or to get laid. Neither was an easy feat when it came to him.

He sighed, the annoyance brewing in his very being. "Also, I would prefer if dad didn't come to my office hours and talk about how you avoid him anytime you see him on campus."

"Maybe he shouldn't be so fucking needy." My dad hadn't been over to the house in months. He just made things awkward and doted fully on Asher which in all honesty...I preferred. I didn't even know if Asher liked the attention, but I never cared to ask. It was silent around the room, and I hated it, so I changed the subject. "Riley is coming over tonight, so try not to be a dick."

Asher was almost out the door when he turned on his heels. "Why?"

I narrowed my eyes. "She's my girlfriend."

"Doesn't she live on campus now? Go there."

Grayson and I walked around him so we could get outside. "I could, but I don't think her roommate would love bearing witness to all the things I would like to do with her."

Asher locked the front door and then clicked the button on his keys to unlock his car. "I didn't think you cared if someone watched."

"Oh, that's a point to Asher, I think." Grayson said, pointing at my brother. I gave him a shocked look. "I have to give my points out fairly."

The fact that my brother knew things like that about me had me wanting to fall down in a fit of laughter. Asher and I may have had a complicated relationship, but the only reason he was so aware of my sex life was that we'd let a pretty woman share a bed with us before. He was always the *let's think this through* kind of guy and getting him to just shut up and go with the flow was the most difficult task I'd ever been given.

I succeeded, though. I'd succeeded a few times. It didn't happen very much anymore, but I still found myself chuckling as I remembered all the times I had to tell him that I was of legal age, and we triple checked to make sure the girls we were sharing were as well.

I liked to think I'd try anything and everything once and sex in front of other people was something I'd learned I wasn't opposed to early on. I didn't bring up that idea to all my partners, but slowly I would learn their interests and figure out what worked for both of us. I was Riley's first sexual experience, and she was my first virgin, so I treated things delicately. The more time I spent with her, the more times we had sex, she showed me that maybe I didn't have to be *so* delicate.

She liked when I was a little rough and when I grabbed her ass in public, telling her simple but effective dirty things in her ear. Her brown skin would get a red hue from her blush that drove me wild. She didn't mind when I pulled her hair and the nervous, yet excited look she had when she saw my Jacob's Ladder piercing could have been my undoing. She admitted with the most innocent look in her brown eyes that had just a tiny lining of gold near the center, that she liked to turn around and be on top, so that she could watch the silver balls go inside of her and I'm pretty sure I came the minute the words left her mouth.

And then her dad died, and I pulled back for a few months. I was there for her, but anything physical was all her call. I'd been easing us back into our flirty, sexy routine with the most care I could muster.

I walked over to Grayson's car that was parked next to Asher's. "I'll let Riley get to know her roommate more and then I'll ask her if she's okay with me openly fucking her in front of another person because my brother would really appreciate it if I didn't bring her over anymore, even though he has no reason to dislike her except that he has a stick up his ass." I heard Grayson unlock the car, throwing the door open. "Better?"

I heard the words *fucking brat* leave my brother's mind and I wanted to laugh.

I mean he isn't wrong. I thought, sending what Asher said to Grayson's mind. He gave me a look to not provoke the beast.

You are the worst kind of brat, Riv. I heard him say in his head.

"I won't be home anyway, so I actually don't even care. Just keep her out of my stuff, River!" Asher yelled from inside his car. He zoomed out of our driveway and headed towards the school.

"Oh *pare.*" Grayson settled into the driver's seat, looking at me. "I think he likes her."

"That's because you think *everyone* should like her."

"So do you."

I put my backpack on the car floor in front of me and pressed the button to roll my window down slightly. "He just thinks because she's human, she's incredibly fragile, so she needs to find another fragile human to be with. I consider that his version of caring."

"Or maybe he says that 'cause he likes her."

I shoved his shoulder right before he cut on the car. "Shut up."

He hummed, throwing me a lopsided smile. "He is wrong though. She is stupid powerful; how else would she get you to come at her every beck and call?"

I leaned my head against the headrest, turning to lazily look at him. He raised his hand to stop me before I could even get a word out. "I am well aware that I'm not immune to her sorcery either."

7
RILEY

I flicked one of my braids out of my face as I stood in front of the massive building that held most of the mental magic faculty, along with my nine in the morning psychology class. Corrin had woken me up an hour before my alarm when I'd heard her making *pspspsps* noises. I looked around the room for a cat but found that she was talking to her phone screen.

She'd flinched when I groaned at the clock on my desk, finished her call quickly, and rambled on about how Jax was her familiar. Witches were allowed to bring their familiars to the university and drop them off at what she'd called a humane zoo for their soul pets. On the way out of the room and down the hall, she'd explained that as much as she missed Jax, if he was here, she would want to just visit him all the time and take him on cat walks.

If she ever really needed him, he would find his way to her no matter what.

The talk of pets made me bring up a picture of Beau and show him to her, which she'd squealed at and demanded I show her more. I demanded she buy me coffee.

I turned my body to see the building where my dad's office was located. I bit the inside of my cheek, gripping the ends of my checkered flannel with my fingertips. It was breezy this morning, but I knew the sun would be out soon and the breeze would be fully welcomed. I had a gap between this class and my next, which gave me plenty of time to go over the police report I had gotten and printed out yesterday.

Corrin had a class immediately after this, so I could at least be alone.

"Riley, are you coming?" My roommate had her backpack slung over one of her shoulders, waving at me.

I sighed, walking over to her as we followed a bunch of other students inside the building. The classrooms were much bigger than the ones at my community college, especially the general classes that were placed in large auditorium style seating. Corrin pulled me into the third aisle from the front.

I sat down in the swivel chair, watching as students spoke amongst themselves. I overheard one particular conversation that had my ears perking up.

"I hate these stupid changes at the last minute," one girl said.

"This was supposed to be a relatively easy general course. I have my herbs to worry about. For fucks sake," another one replied, pure frustration in their voice.

I furrowed my brow, turning to Corrin. "Do you have any idea what's got everyone so riled up?"

Corrin looked around us, mirroring my expression. She patted the shoulder of the guy next to her, leaning in to talk to him. I waited, rather impatiently, when she turned back to me. Her eyes were a bit wider than before and it was like she wanted to laugh but not from humor. She took out her phone, frantically swiping until she got to her class schedule. I tried to lean over her shoulder and see, but her fingers moved too fast.

"Oh, fuck."

"What? Oh fuck, what?" I tried to grab her phone from her.

"Do you remember when I told you that Asher doesn't like to sub and only likes his mental magic classes?"

"Yes..." I answered slowly, trying to figure out what he had to do with anything.

She pressed her glossed lips together. "Umm, well unfortunately, the incredible Mr. Winslow isn't our professor this semester. The schedule has changed, but at least we get eye candy."

I reached for her phone again, but my hand stopped short of grabbing it when the door opened. I turned my head along with everyone else to see the man walking across the room towards the desk in the middle.

My eyes traveled from his shoes all the way up to his face and *fuck*...was it a face. I had seen Asher St. James before, but I'd never really given him a once over and he'd never truly given me the time of day. Being able to sit here and actually look at him was a tiny bit thrilling even though I was nearly shitting my pants that I would have to spend an hour and thirty minutes with him every Monday and Wednesday.

He was more casual at his house. Fitted joggers and a t-shirt were standard while in the comfort of his own home, but this attire he had on now was almost foreign to me. I hardly recognized him with a fitted button down and slacks. His glasses were rectangular with thin black frames and sat perfectly on his nose, framing his face. His beard was trimmed, and his sleeves were rolled up to his elbows, showing off defined forearms and a few tattoos that I hadn't noticed until right now. Tiny ones that I couldn't make out from where I sat, but it looked like stars and maybe some words in cursive.

He was tall, maybe a few inches taller than River. His hair was almost identical to his brother's, but while River's hair curled at the ends, Asher's hair didn't have a curl at all. It was cut short at the sides and the top was kept longer. He had definitely put something in it to maintain the messy but tame look he was likely not going for, but it was happening.

He hadn't looked over his class yet but just rifled through a few papers in his messenger bag. "I'm sorry to disappoint you if you were hoping to get Mr. Winslow as your professor, but we can't always get what we want. There is still time to drop out and get into another class, so I implore you to do so because I would rather you *want* to be here. If I discover later on that you ignored my warning, then I will have so much fun making it so that you wish you hadn't."

He looked up finally and I let my eyes scan over some of the students who looked as if they were visibly shaken. "I know what they say about me and well…" He chuckled a little to himself. "It's all true. I'm not your friend; I'm not your buddy. I'm your professor. And I have much better things to do with my time than to teach an undergraduate psych course, but if I have to deal with it, so do you."

He started going on about the syllabus that he assumed none of us read over and then I heard giggling above me. Asher abruptly stopped talking, turning his head to find where the noise had come from.

"Something funny?"

The girl behind me opened and closed her mouth, the words escaping her.

"Clearly something is much more entertaining than this class. We should all know what it is." He circled around his desk, leaning back against it.

The girl looked to her friend at her side, who was looking down, hoping that he wouldn't call on her next. "Nothing. It was nothing." Her voice was low as if she was trying to make herself as small as possible.

"How about you come down here and let us all know because it's an early morning and I would love a good laugh." There were a few small snickers from around the room and I was mortified *for* her.

"Mr. St.—" She started to say and as if on cue I heard myself mumble, "Give her a fucking break."

It was like Corrin stopped breathing next to me and I realized what I thought I'd mumbled, was said a little too loudly. I wished I could pull my braids entirely in front of my face to hide, but it was no use. I lifted my eyes to the front of the room to see green eyes staring back. Green eyes that filled with recognition the minute they landed on me.

I had been hoping for an *oh, I know her* sort of expression to develop on his face, but I wasn't so lucky. Asher looked more irritated than delighted to see me. He looked up at the ceiling, scrubbing a hand down his face.

"Miss Monroe, I think it would be wise of you to remember that this is my classroom for the next semester and how I choose to discipline my students is my decision alone. As I said earlier, if you don't like it or my teaching, you are free to leave. You can see the door from where you're sitting; I'm sure you are smart enough to know how to use it." He narrowed his eyes, his tone deep and soul cutting. I wasn't so easily undermined but there was something about him that had me staying in my seat.

"Asher..." His name slipped out of my mouth so easily, it was too late to take it back.

Corrin nearly choked on air and I wanted so badly to kick her from under the table. Asher's eyes flared a little at my addressing him so casually and I wish I could've run out the door without any consequences. It was too late for that.

He tapped his knuckles on his desk before he started to walk up one of the staircases that separated sections of seating. He stopped when he got to my row, placing his hand on the end of the long desk and giving me a smile that was as cold as ice. "A reminder of what's in your syllabus. Address me as Mr. St. James or Sir. Yes, Mr. St. James. No, Mr. St. James. Yes, sir. No, sir. All very simple. Easy enough for you to comprehend?"

I licked my lips, wondering if this is why River didn't like talking about his brother so much. "Yes."

His eyebrows raised expectantly.

I cleared my throat, refusing to look around the room at all the eyes on me. "Yes, *sir*."

Asher's shoulders stiffened a small fraction, but you could have missed it if you weren't looking. I could have sworn his eyes dilated for a moment as he looked me up and down. He let out a harsh breath before he descended down the stairs, demanding we take out our textbooks and flip to chapter one.

I glanced up at the clock above the whiteboard and refrained from letting out a groan. It had only been twenty minutes.

Chocolate PSD
Bar Mock-Up
Food Packaging Collection
157
156

8
GRAYSON

I drummed my fingers against my desk, waiting for my professor to say the two words I loved more than anything.

Class dismissed.

It was only the first day and I was already exhausted. I could have chalked it up to being my senior year, but no, it was simply just the million and one things I constantly felt like I needed to be doing. I didn't dislike school, but I enjoyed my work study much more than any term paper I had to write. The school had given me options to choose from, but the minute I saw the library assistant position, my pencil was checking the box next to it faster than I'd like to admit. My scholarship covered most of the books and housing, while the work study put a major dent in my tuition. Mystic Riegan offered much more to their work study students than most universities in the country.

No one could ever say I didn't work hard at the things I wanted.

My parents had been shocked to say the least when I didn't

exude shifter abilities like they did and even if it skipped a genera-tion or two, they assumed I would just end up a regular human. They hadn't expected me to produce shadows. The last person to do that was my *dakilang lolo*. There was no sign of disappointment growing up, but they didn't exactly know what to do with me. They didn't know how to manage my powers or help me understand them. My parents, well mainly my dad, grew up in the Philippines, where shifters were half the population. He didn't shift much anymore, but I knew if I had presented those powers, he would have done it at least one more time just for me.

My parents tried their best. I decided that burdening them with trying to figure me out wasn't worth it so I went to the library and looked up anything I could about shadow magic. River had bugged me to apply to Mystic Riegan with him, but it was a prestigious university that cost more money than I would let my parents offer, even though they could barely afford it. I never went without, but I knew the university's price tag was lofty. I wanted to go to a school where I could find more shadow wielders, but yet again, I could work hard and do the things I needed to do to get what I desired.

Two years of community college, one transfer application, and a few scholarship papers later, I was here. Here...with my best friend and his girlfriend, who I had the most natural crush on. River was always an open guy who believed in open relationships when neces-sary, but Riley was a little different. I didn't want to tread on toes or fuck up two of the best relationships I had, but *fuck*, there were times when I wanted to cross that line with them.

My phone buzzed in my pocket. I checked the clock on the wall quickly, noting that it was two mins before class was over, before I looked at my phone.

RIVER

lunch?

Sure. Riley coming?

Ever since they'd started dating, our mutual relationship had only flourished, and I'd never questioned its ease. I was always a flirt, but I'd been a bit more subtle about it early on and when Riley would laugh with no nerves or lack of comfortability in sight, I kept going.

River would look on like he was amused by it all. He would make someone think they wanted to run in front a truck if they fucked with her, but it seemed I was bestowed favoritism.

RIVER

I can make that happen.

let me guess, you made a copy of her class schedule, so you are fully aware that she has time to eat with us

RIVER

Don't make it sound weird. She knows I have a copy. Do you want the gorgeous girl to come eat with us or not?

I was about to type something severely inappropriate about eating something else, but I refrained.

yeah, of course.

RIVER

perfect, meet me at Leif's when you get out.

I noticed people getting up around me, letting me know it was time to go and head across campus. I knew River primarily chose Leif's because it was close enough for me to get to the library for my work study shift and for Riley to get to her next class. For a guy that had a stereotypical scary exterior, he was a softie. Besides having tattoos myself, which I guess made me biased, I felt like his only made him more interesting and they were a conversation starter. Especially the ones his clothes tended to cover up.

I still hadn't told Riley that he got her name tattooed on the side of his thigh. It was in cursive mixed in with a few other pieces he had done, so if she did look, it wouldn't jump out at her immediately.

I casually scrolled on my phone until I saw a new email notification. I opened it, assuming it had to do with the start of the new semester. Something I could easily trash. I sighed, tension growing in my shoulders when I read an email from the school about an immediate need to speak about my scholarship and a link for me to be taken to the site that I could make an appointment to discuss it. I looked at the clock on my phone, seeing that there was still time for me to just talk to them in person and get this sorted out before I met up with River.

I shot my best friend a quick text and tried not to let my anxiety get to me. My shadows were raging but I kept them at bay, just like I taught myself.

Chocolate PSD
Bar Mock-Up
Food Packaging Collection

9
RILEY

I'd ignored River's text, my thoughts a frantic mess of *get out of here and head to your dad's office building you idiot* and *did you really get talked down to by your boyfriend's brother?* Corrin had flown past me on the way to her next class and I'd kept my head down when I'd walked by Asher's desk on my way out.

I stood in front of the building that housed my father's office, staring up at it. I tried to picture him coming here, happy and prepared to be the best advocate for students as he could. Those images blurred together into what it looked like minutes before his fall happened. I could never piece it together perfectly because none of it made sense.

I didn't go inside but decided to circle around to the window that he'd supposedly fallen out of. Students paid me no attention as they went inside and others walked past like they had more important things to do. I looked up, squinting to see the window on the fifth floor. It had already been patched up with new glass as if nothing ever happened. I backed up a bit, looking around, wondering if this was where he landed. My mom spared me all of the minute details when it came to his death, but at this point I would rather have every single piece of nauseatingly heartbreaking information than miss out on anything.

I looked around, only seeing a few students sitting on some benches a few feet away and moved my backpack so I could pull out the folded-up police report. I kept it close to my face, roaming my eyes over the information.

He was found on his back, dead at the scene. The time he was found was— eight o'clock at night? I racked my brain trying to remember the night before the police showed up. I remembered him leaving, telling me he had some work to do at the school in the afternoon. I thought it had been annoying since the university had just ended its spring term, but I couldn't wrap my mind around something that would keep him *that* long.

I frowned but looked back over the police report. The officer had reported that my dad smelled like alcohol and that they'd found open bottles of vodka and scotch in his office. He didn't even like fucking scotch. There were no fingerprints or signs of a struggle, so of course they took the easy way out and claimed he was the culprit of his own death. Pressing my lips together, I looked further down the page when a flash of reflecting light hit my eyes.

I blinked, putting my hand up to block it. I shoved the paper back in my bag, walking over to the grass that surrounded the building. I glanced up at the sun and back down to the ground. I turned slightly so my shadow wasn't in the way and that speckle of light shined again. I zeroed in on its location, reaching down and running my hand through the grass. A tiny sting struck my fingertip, as if I'd been cut and pulled back a small fraction. I pressed my lips together repeating my motions but snatching up the object that had broken skin.

I examined the small piece of glass that sat perfectly in the middle of my palm. Dark red lightly splattered part of it, which I assumed was dried blood, but I noticed a dusting of dark blue at one of the edges.

Opening up the front part of my backpack, I dropped it inside.

"What the hell are you doing?" A deep voice that I thought I could avoid for the next day and a half sounded behind me.

I stood up, turning around a little too quickly. Asher's eyebrows were raised as he kept a hand on the strap of his messenger bag.

"Nothing."

He ran his tongue along his front teeth. "It looks like something, or are we going to start off the semester by lying?"

"I—I'm not...I'm not lying. What are *you* doing here?"

He pointed to the building. "I work at this school and my office is in this building. I have some things to get done before my class that isn't filled with a bunch of underclassmen who think the class is an easy A."

I tilted my head to the side. "I'll have you know I don't think the class will be a breeze, especially with you leading the charge."

A short, annoyed laugh left his throat. "I'll take that as a compliment." He tilted his chin towards the space behind me. The small movement gave me a view of his lean neck and the space right under his chin where I noticed a few tiny nicks, like he'd cut himself shaving. "Do you need help figuring out how to get into the building, or do you just enjoy loitering for the hell of it?"

I reared my head back. "It's not a crime to stand around on a college campus."

He placed his hands in his pants pockets, getting closer to me. "You're right, it's not. If that's *all* you were doing, then I would consider letting it go."

"I wasn't..."

He waved his hand, halting my words. "Actually, you can save whatever story you concoct for my brother. I'm sure he would be thrilled to hear what you have to say, as simple and mundane as it may be."

"If the fact that I'm dating your brother makes you uncomfortable, then I'll transfer to a different class, but I don't think that's it nor do I think you'd even admit that, so just let me get through this semester in some form of peace for both our sakes." I spat at him, straightening my spine. "Whatever reason you don't approve of me gets pushed to the back of your mind, kind of like empathy for your students."

He ran a hand through his hair. "I'll leave that to the empaths; they're the experts on all that." He leaned in, his face inches from mine. "I don't care who my brother takes to bed," he scanned my body. "Or who he dates."

I threw my braids over my shoulder, the sun starting to shine a little brighter and work in harmony with the breeze that was still present. "Who's the liar now?"

Our faces were closer than I would have liked, but my shoulders jumped when I felt my phone buzz in the back pocket of my jeans. I ripped my eyes away from Asher to look down to see that River was calling.

Asher cast his gaze down, seeing his brother's picture across my screen. "This interaction has been stimulating to say the least, but *oh no*, looks like you have somewhere to be." A sly smile formed on his face.

I put on my best fake smile. "I'll see you in class, *sir*." I said the last word with more effort than I normally would, making sure since he was so adamant about it that he got what he wanted.

He cleared his throat, his jaw ticking. I walked around him, sliding my finger across the screen to answer my phone.

"I'm so sorry, I'm late." The words rushed out of my mouth as I ran up to River and Grayson. Leif's was a quick walk from where I'd had my altercation with Asher, so I'd only had a matter of minutes to fix my face and attitude.

River patted the place next to him, scooting over. "We ordered for you."

"Did you now?"

Grayson nodded. "Turkey club, no tomatoes, provolone cheese, and extra pickles."

I squinted over at him.

He rolled his eyes, realizing he had forgotten something. "Oh right, we also got you a strawberry milkshake. Apologies if you thought we merely forgot, *trouble*."

River placed his arm behind my neck, letting his fingers roam over my shoulder. "Riley is probably the least problematic human in existence."

"Ah, thanks babe. I appreciate the sentiment." I kissed his cheek.

Grayson stretched, raising his arms above his head. "Never said she was the bad kind of trouble. She's probably the best kind." He winked at me and I shot a glance over at River who smirked and rolled his eyes.

"Is this give Riley flirty compliments day? I'm not complaining, but I don't know how much more of this love fest I can take." I asked, smiling up at the waitress when she handed me my milkshake. She lingered a little longer than I would have liked, eyeing River like I wasn't here before she turned to leave. He paid her no mind as he usually did whenever he caught the eye of an interested individual. I had lost count of how many people had openly propositioned him when I was two feet away.

"What made you late anyway?" River's question had me pulling my eyes away from the waitress and back to him.

"Uh...I ran into your brother." I shifted so my legs were thrown over his and my upper body was so close to him that I could smell his body wash.

Grayson choked on his water. "Excuse me?"

"My brother?" River's eyes widened. "How did that happen?"

I let out a humorless laugh. "Let me preface by saying, he's teaching my psychology class."

River ran a finger over his bottom lip. "That makes sense, since he was bitching about teaching an undergrad course last night. I'm pretty sure I'll never hear the end of this." He balled his hand into a fist, laying his cheek against it. "Oh, man, how was your first class with mean Professor St. James?"

I pulled my milkshake closer to me, taking a long pull from the straw. "He was just the sweetest and a real teddy bear." The sarcasm rolled off my tongue.

"And you ran into him later?" Grayson questioned.

I bit my bottom lip. "Yeah, I was minding my own business and he just assumed I was doing something wrong." It wasn't a lie. I hadn't been doing anything against school policy. I couldn't exactly tell them the specifics, not that even I knew what that was or what I was looking for, but that wasn't the point.

"Did he say something to upset you?" River had turned my face so that I was looking directly at him. His fingers held my chin tight and his deep green eyes told me that his next action depended heavily on what I said next.

"Nothing I couldn't handle. He's just a trip, that's all."

He leaned in, tilting my chin up a little higher so he could brush his lips against mine. His next words were said right at my lips. "Would you like me to help you forget all about that tonight?" His other hand traveled up my leg and cupped my ass. "That little inter-action will be a very distant memory when I'm buried inside of you."

He pecked my lips, moving his kisses to my cheek and then down my neck. It took everything in me to stifle my moan. I looked over to see Grayson with his elbows on the table, fingers interlocked, and his head placed right on top, watching us with this look of appreciation on his face.

River moved his hand to my thigh, walking his fingers to the place between my legs. There was an odd war going on inside of me that was going to tell him to stop, but then there was another part of me—if I was being honest, it was the much bigger part—that wanted to see how long Grayson would sit there and watch. I couldn't wrap my mind around why I wished there wasn't a table between us, so that he could get closer.

The sound of a plate hitting the table had me practically jumping out of River's embrace. The waitress was back with a less than pleasant look on her face. "Anything else?" Her voice was tight as if she was counting the seconds until she could be away from our public display of affection.

We shook our heads, and she was gone before I could even blink. I inhaled the smell of my sandwich, my stomach making a mean rumbling sound.

"Regardless of his sexy offer, you're hanging out tonight," Grayson said, swiping one of his fries through some ketchup and popping it into his mouth.

"Am I now?" I responded, playfully.

River took a sip of his drink. "Yes, Riley. We are going to relax after the first day of classes and watch movies, eat those tiny pretzels you like, and then I'm taking you to my room and fucking you until you can't think straight and coming on my cock like a good girl."

10
RILEY

I'd made it through three classes, including the Intro to Magical History class that I'd forgotten I'd signed up for. I heard Corrin giggling from outside our door before I got inside. She gave me a quick wave and then proceeded to continue speaking.

I threw my backpack on the floor and ducked down, searching for my weekender bag under my bed.

"Mateo, say hi." Corrin squatted down beside me, holding her phone in front of my face. A tan face surrounded by long brown hair that curled right at the nape of their neck looked back at me. A trimmed mustache that formed into a full beard covered the lower half of their face and thick defined eyebrows that framed brown eyes shot up in an amused expression. Mateo smiled, their canines looking more pronounced than most.

I knew a few facts about Corrin's partner: they were Colombian on their dad's side and Mexican on their mom's, they grew up in Mexico until the age of sixteen when they moved to the states. They did college online which made them free for Corrin to talk their ear off whenever she felt like it—while also being free to work at the wolf shifter bar in Mill Valley— and they had something called a knot. I'd read a book where the shifters had them, but once Corrin started going into detail about Mateo's in particular, I shut my ears off.

Mateo looked over their shoulder, nodding at the person behind them, and then looked back at Corrin through the screen. They rolled their eyes, shaking their head. *"Tengo que ir a lidiar con unos idiotas. Te amo. Hablaremos al rato."*

"Te amo." Corrin said back, ending her call. I pulled my weekender bag out, while using every bit of advanced Spanish I'd taken in high school and all those additional online aids I'd used because I thought it would be a good skill to have, to be able to understand and translate.

My roommate put her phone to her chest, smiling to herself like a lovesick puppy. She sighed, looking over at me. "Oh sorry, so they said…"

"I know what they said." I walked over to my dresser and started flinging things into my bag.

Corrin tapped her phone on her chin. "You do?" Her voice screamed intrigue.

"Something about dealing with idiots, they love you and they'll talk to you soon." I shrugged.

"Do you translate everything that they say?" She watched me move around the room, collecting items I needed for my stay with River.

I laughed, stopping in the middle of the room to look at her. "Believe me, if I heard something I didn't want to, you would know." She let out a sharp cackle, pushing her glasses up her nose.

Corrin tapped my bag. "Going home on your first day of class? I'm not judging, I go home a lot, but home for me is also like thirty mins away, thirty-five max."

"No, I'm going to River's. I only have one class tomorrow and it's in the afternoon."

She wiggled her eyebrows. "Ah, going to relieve some of that first day stress, are we?"

I rolled my eyes, adjusting the bag on my shoulder. I made sure I had my phone and my university ID, tucking them into the front pocket of my bag before I did one last look around. Corrin backed up, nearly tripping over my backpack.

"Oh god, sorry, I should have picked that up." I apologized, kneeling down to get it but she beat me to it.

She waved me off, preparing to fling it onto my bed when she stopped. She brought the backpack closer to her, looking it over as if something had caught her eye.

"What's wrong? Are you okay?" I asked, concern lacing my voice.

"I may have to wear these fucking dampeners, but I come from a long line of witches, and I know magic when I feel it."

I felt my eyebrows furrow. "Magic?"

"Mhmm." My eyes widened when she brought my backpack up to her nose and inhaled. She hummed, pulling it back and flicking her eyes to me. She waved her hand around my bag. "Do you mind if I....?" She was asking if she could search it and I shrugged. I was more confused than anything.

She opened the larger section, nearly putting her whole face inside. Her expression showed even more confusion when she came up empty handed. She opened the smaller compartment, rummaging around until she yanked her hand back. She let out a *hmph* and stuck her hand back inside.

I blinked a few times in surprise when she pulled out the tiny glass piece I'd found in the grass. She let my backpack drop to the ground and started inspecting the glass more thoroughly. "Where did you get this?"

I stood so still that I swore I stopped breathing. It was a simple question, and I had a simple answer. What came after that answer was beyond me and I didn't know if I was ready to divulge that to anyone. "Outside."

"Outside where? One of the magic wielder class buildings?"

Suddenly I felt like my braids were too tight and my head was thrumming. "No, just outside one of the other buildings. Is it a big deal or something? It's just a piece of glass."

Corrin crossed her arms over her chest. "Oh, yeah? Why do you have a random ass piece of glass in your backpack, Riley? You could have thrown it away like a productive member of society and prevented a glass hazard, but no you kept it for Hecate knows what reason." She gave the glass another look, her eyes squinting. "Wait, is that blood?"

I placed my hand over my face, groaning. "Corrin, please—."

She placed her palm out, shutting me up. She took in a breath and let it out. "Your blood or someone else's?"

I looked from the glass piece to her. Her expression was hard to read, but it just looked like she wanted to understand before making assumptions. "Someone else's."

"Did you cause this blood?"

"No."

"Whose is it?"

My breath caught in my throat. If I wanted to speak, the words were having a really hard time making their way out. Corrin's face morphed into a look of sympathy when my mouth kept opening and closing. She stepped closer to me, placing a hand on my bicep and squeezing. "Where did you find it, Riley?" Her voice was soft now.

I looked down at the ground, speaking the words to the floor beneath me. "Outside the Department of Mental Magic building and…" I licked my lips, letting the rest of my sentence fall away.

Corrin clucked her tongue. "And you have no idea why this has magic on it?"

My head shot up. "No, I have no idea. I've never seen magic residue before, so I didn't know what that was. I swear." I vaguely knew that some magic produced a small amount of residue after it was expelled, but I didn't know what it looked like or if it wasn't physical remnants, how it felt.

She gave me a small reassuring smile. "I believe you."

It made my heart pound a little harder to hear someone say that.

"It's hard to do anything with these dampeners." She pointed to her earrings, "but I can see about figuring out what kind of magic this is. I'll need to scrape off some of the residue, but that's magical science."

I bit my lip, my nervous energy revving up. She tilted her head to the side. "Do you trust me?"

I heard my phone buzz in my bag. "I might have to now, don't you think?"

Corrin rubbed her lips together. "Perhaps. If this happens to be connected with what I think it's connected with, then I want to help. Like I said before," she sent me a devilish smile, "I don't believe anything that's been said. I prefer the truth and if I can help obtain that, then that's how I'd like to spend my time. It beats homework by a long shot."

My phone buzzed again and then the ringtone for my mom went off. I sighed, nodding at her. "Okay, finding out what kind of magic that is and how strong it is would be a start. It will get me going in some kind of direction."

"It might take me a few days, but I'll let you know when I find something." She placed the glass on her bedside table.

The sound of my ringtone stopped and then a long vibration sounded, letting me know my mom had left a voicemail. "I'd like to keep this a private matter."

"River doesn't know? Or your other boyfriend?"

"No, he doesn't." I scrunched up my face. "Wait, other boy—"

"Whatever, fine, this will be between you and me. I'll tell you something Riley, things like this," she pointed to the sharp transparent shard, "it may seem small, but whatever I get from it might end up bigger than you thought. And secrets like that end up coming out eventually."

11
RILEY

"Yes, mom, the first day was fine. My classes are good and I'm settling alright." I'd talked to my mom once a day since I'd moved in. This phone call was no different, but I'd managed to get her back on track to calling maybe once a week. Twice if she really needed the pick me up or well, if *I* needed it.

Grayson was busy making the popcorn, adding Hershey's Kisses to get all gooey. River had set a bowl out with my favorite tiny pretzels that I'd been stuffing my face with since I got here. My mom hadn't brought up my dad or anything related to him in the few days that we'd talked, but I knew she wanted to.

I'd seen a therapist for a little while, shortly after his death, but I hated it. Therapy was right for some people, but it just wasn't for me. I had Beau and sometimes a girl just wanted her dog and a good book to help the pain fuck off. The minute I'd thought of Beau, I heard his barking in the background.

"Someone wants to say hi to his mom." My mom mumbled

something about switching to video chatting, so I pulled the phone from my ear and waited. I smiled when my screen flashed and my mom's face came into view. I pulled my legs in so I could be more comfortable on the couch.

"How's my favorite boy?" I asked in my baby voice that was reserved just for Beau. A howl escaped from the background. My mom moved the phone so Beau's large face was now in full view. He panted against the screen, his tongue hanging out.

"He has only whined twice since you've been gone and he sleeps in your room every single night. Lays his head right on your pillow." I heard my mom say. Beau stopped panting, side eyeing her as if to say *don't call me out like that* and then looked back at me, smiling.

"It's Beau!" Grayson shouted from behind me, leaning over the couch and smashing his face against mine.

Beau barked again, jumping up and nearly knocking my mom's phone over.

"We both know after Riley, I'm Beau's favorite," River called from the kitchen.

Beau sighed heavily as if anyone but me being his favorite was some kind of sick joke.

"Hey, Mrs. Monroe." Both boys said in unison and my mom moved the phone so that she could look at me again.

"Hey, boys. Fun night in?"

Grayson jumped over the couch, plopping down next to me and grabbed my phone. "Well, your daughter has decided that out of the three movie options we gave her, she wanted to watch none of them and is making us watch a holiday movie in the middle of August."

"I'm not *making* you do anything."

River brought the popcorn and drinks over, placing them on the coffee table. "You would just sigh in agitation the whole night if we went against your wishes, so we are doing everyone a favor."

"Sounds like my daughter," my mom agreed.

"I'm hanging up now. I'll call you soon. Love you, always and always." I laughed, pressing the end call button and throwing my phone on the table.

River found the remote and started to get the TV set up. Grayson leaned back, throwing his arms over the back of the couch. One of his fingers ghosted over the side of my neck and I couldn't help but shiver just a tiny bit. I shifted a little closer to him, but with enough room left so that I could breath.

"I finished that book you recommended," he said, moving one of the pillows out of the way so that River could sit on the couch.

"And what did you think?"

He scratched his jaw. "I didn't know how I would feel about an apocalyptic story where vampires use humans as a blood supply. In the end though, I loved it. I could get into vampire romances. The undead need love just like everybody else."

"What are you guys talking about?" River chuckled, clicking buttons on the remote to find the particular movie I wanted.

"If you read the books I told you about, you would know," I joked, chucking a pillow in his direction.

River swatted it away. "I'm just excited every time you want to try something new because of your books. Just because I don't want to read every single one doesn't mean I don't appreciate them. Please keep reading." He smirked over at me and I squeezed my thighs together. Nothing was more attractive than a man who appreciated his partner's love of books, even if it was just because I randomly send him passages that make me horny, so he knows what to do for later.

Grayson made a move to get up from the couch, motioning for me to switch places with him. "A Riley sandwich is a must."

I stuck my tongue in my cheek scooting over. "I'm a sandwich now?"

"Precisely. This way we equally get you." Grayson looked over at River who had a small smile on his face but said nothing. "Unless that's weird. I can sit in the armchair." He nodded towards the chair that was adjacent to the couch.

I saw that River was looking at me out of the corner of his eye as if he was trying to figure out what my response would be. The couch would seem empty without Grayson here and I liked having them both in my vicinity. "It's not weird. River doesn't mind sharing, do you?" It was meant to come out like a joke, but somehow my voice came off flirtier than I would have liked.

"I do not, gorgeous." He leaned his elbow on the arm on the couch, placing a finger at this temple, narrowing his eyes at me. He placed a hand on my thigh, squeezing.

Grayson settled down next to me, his thigh brushing mine. I leaned forward to grab the popcorn bowl, the smell of butter and chocolate hitting my nostrils. We'd had these movie nights before, but for some reason there was tension in the air that I couldn't shake. It wasn't bad, but it had my skin growing hot. River had his hand on my thigh, but my other thigh was empty and I had half a mind to grab Grayson's hand and place it on my body, but the opening credits of the movie stopped me.

GRAYSON PASSED OUT TWENTY MINUTES BEFORE THE MOVIE ENDED, SO RIVER threw a blanket over him and called it a night. He grabbed my hand and led me upstairs to his room. I sat on his bed, seeing a text from Corrin.

CORRIN

Goods are well taken care of in my little lab at home.

She sent me a picture of the glass shard on top of a table with bottles of multicolored liquids. A few pipettes and beakers were littered around, while what looked like an old school Bunsen burner sat in the corner.

> Thank you. Let me know as soon as you
> have something.

CORRIN

Will do. I don't have class tomorrow, so I'll
be working on it most of the day. I'll update
you when I can.

She sent a winky face and I sighed, wondering if letting one person in was one too many.

I felt hands on my shoulders, squeezing and digging fingers pushed into my skin. "You okay?" River asked, continuing to massage.

"Mhmm." It was all I could say because what he was doing felt way too good.

He removed one of his hands to push my braids away from my neck. Lips hit my skin in gentle, fiery kisses. He gripped my open flannel and pulled back, slowly sliding it down my arms. He continued to kiss my neck, while he moved his hands to my chest, cupping my breasts over my tank top.

River laughed deeply against my skin when he realized I hadn't worn a bra, so he could easily pull and tease my nipples through the material. He held one of my breasts in his hand, continuously teasing and ran his other hand down my stomach. He unbuttoned my pants with one hand and dipped his fingers inside my panties.

I sucked in a breath when he grazed my clit, rubbing the pads of his fingers over it. His lips continued to lick and bite as he ran his fingers over my pussy.

"So wet already." He licked my ear, taking the lobe between his teeth and gently biting down. His fingers slid over my clit, again and again, causing me to lean back against him. I looked down seeing his tattooed covered arm flex and move while he got me off.

I whimpered when he eased two of his fingers inside of me, pumping them in and out. He didn't try to pull my pants off or get me completely naked. He just needed to touch me right now, needed to feel how much he turned me on.

His breath was hot against me. "I need to feel you come on my fingers, gorgeous. Then I'll fuck your sweet little cunt just the way you like."

"Oh, fuck, River, please," I begged, moving the lower half of my body so I could get more friction on my clit. As if he knew just what I wanted, River moved his thumb over my aching clit and played with it. He flicked his thumb over it, while maintaining the rhythm of his thrusting fingers.

"I really need to fuck you, so give me what I want, Riley." He pumped harder and I shut my eyes, feeling my orgasm at its peak. The sound of how wet I was filling my ears each and every time his fingers drove into me sent me over the edge.

River pulled his fingers out when I started to catch my breath. "That's a good girl." I heard him get off the bed and walk around so that he was in front of me. He placed his hand at my face, using his thumb to caress my cheek. "Take it out." He moved his hand down my arm, raising my hand and placing it over where his cock was hard beneath his pants.

I made quick work of his belt, biting my lip when I shimmied his pants down his legs and his cock jutted out. His piercing almost always caught me off guard each time I saw it. I wrapped my hand around him, letting the silver balls run over my palm as I stroked him. He kicked off his pants, watching me intently as I shifted closer to him. Leaning down, I circled my tongue around the head of his cock, peeking up at him.

His breathing was steady, but his hooded green eyes were slowly closing. I pushed myself deeper, feeling the metal on my tongue. I licked the underside of his cock, making sure each part of his piercing was attended to. I sucked him back into my mouth, swirling my tongue around. He placed a hand at the back of my head and started to pump his hips. My eyes began to water, but I kept going, bobbing back and forth.

"Fuck, I really want to come in that sweet mouth of yours," he said, his voice rough. I flattened my tongue, breathing through my nose while he fucked my mouth harder. My eyes flicked over to where his door was. He hadn't closed it all the way and I could have sworn I saw someone. I'd never given much thought to being watched, but it really depended on the person. I had the feeling that I wanted to work River's cock more, sucking harder and going deeper.

Asher wasn't home yet, and Grayson was fast asleep on the couch. Grayson *was* fast asleep on the couch...wasn't he? The idea that he was out there, peeking in, should have made me livid. I *should* have stopped this and marched right over to the door and told him how inappropriate that was. I didn't want to do any of that. I could feel myself getting wetter at the idea that the person at the door was him, watching me swallow his best friend's cock.

I was able to catch my breath when River released me, backing up. He reached behind him, pulling his shirt off in one swift motion. He bent down, taking the waistband of my pants in his grasp and yanking them down my legs, removing my panties as well. He pulled the straps of my tank top down so that it was bunched around my stomach, exposing my breasts to the cool air.

He sucked one of my nipples into his mouth, moving his tongue and turning them into tight peaks. He rubbed and played with one of them, while his mouth worked the other. I threw my head back, moaning.

River reached my face and kissed me, his lips molding to mine. The kiss was deep and aggressive, but I could feel every ounce of love he had for me. His hands gripped my waist, breaking our kiss and flipping me over. He moved my legs so that I was forced to bend them and prop them onto the bed, presenting my ass to him.

He smacked one of my ass cheeks hard, then did the same to the other. I felt a tongue on my pussy, lapping at my wetness. He circled his tongue, burying his face to the point of suffocation. I looked down between my legs as he straightened back up, running a hand down his cock. My thighs trembled when he slid it over my entrance, hitting my clit.

I sighed in relief when he pushed inside of me, holding onto my hips. His piercing rubbed against me, and I nearly bit my tongue with how good it felt. He moved me against him, thrusting in and out. His pelvis slapped against my skin in a resounding rhythm that I could have listened to on repeat.

"Your pussy is fucking perfect. Looks so good filled with my cock." He slammed into me repeatedly, firmly holding my hips.

I held onto his comforter, wanting to rip at the sheets and scream. I snuck a glance over my shoulder, seeing that whoever I'd seen at the door was still there. I had to blink, readjusting my vision, but I could have sworn I saw wisps of shadows wafting over the threshold, clearly confirming my early suspicion. I started to meet River's thrusts, moving my ass against him. I wanted to give my watcher a show.

"Move on my cock, just like that. Fuck, that's a good girl." He halted his movements, letting me fuck him back as he let his hands roam over my back and ass. I arched my back, thrusting backwards and feeling every inch of him slid inside of me just the way I liked. He spanked me once again, pulling out and flipping me back over.

He nestled between my legs, not wasting a second before he slid back inside. He put my legs over his shoulders, hitting me deeper. He slowed his thrusts, moving his hips in a painfully delicious way that had me squirming.

"River, fuck, I can't...please go harder." I begged, holding onto his arms.

"You want me to fuck you harder, gorgeous?" His voice was low and raspy from exertion, but his tone was almost taunting.

"Yes." I breathed out, while he methodically moved his hips so that he was feeding his cock into me at a glacial pace.

"You want me to fuck you so hard that you'll clench that tight cunt around my cock and make a mess on me?"

I didn't have any more words when he thrusted in again and I felt him deeper. I nodded, watching him slide his hand up my body and wrap it around the front of my neck. His other hand fell between my legs, vigorously rubbing my clit while he pounded into me.

My stomach hollowed out and I could feel the orgasm building. River kept going, his hair damp from sweat and every single one of his tattoos on display. I reached out, running my hand down his chest, tracing my fingers over the different lines and loops that decorated his body.

"I want to come inside that pretty pussy so that I'm dripping out of you." His bed creaked from his rapid movements. "You take your pill today?"

"Yes, fuck. Please come inside of me."

He squeezed my neck, slamming into me until I came again and he started to shudder right after me. Our breathing was like a steady melody in the silent room. River let out a relieved sigh, pulling out and leaning over so that he could kiss me. He broke our kiss to place small pecks all over my face that had me giggling until I batted him away.

In all his naked glory, he padded over to his dresser, throwing me a shirt.

"I brought my own clothes, you know." I started to put on his shirt anyway.

He gave me a look of pure adoration, throwing on a pair of boxer briefs and walking over to his side table. He pulled out the silk pillowcase that he bought me for when I stayed over after having a very educational talk about my hair and its needs. I handed him one of his pillows and he slipped it on, tossing it back at me. "I prefer you in my clothes, especially after I've made you come."

I rolled my eyes, getting on the floor to find my bag that I'd put up here before we watched the movie. I needed to pee and clean myself up before we went to bed. I pulled out a fresh pair of underwear, hesitating before I got to the door. I didn't have that feeling that I did before. Whoever was at the door had moved on. If it had been who I thought—who I'd hoped—then maybe a conversation needed to be had.

12
RILEY

I woke up early the next morning, the sun just peeking out. I slid out from under River's arm, my legs a little sore. In the middle of the night, he'd rolled over, kissed me, and asked if he could make me come. That time was slow and with my hands held above my head, while he looked down at me in the dark.

I tiptoed out of the room, my stomach needing food. I'd only eaten nearly all the mini pretzels and most of the popcorn last night and I was in major need of something with substance. I heard gentle snoring coming from downstairs. Grayson was still here, happily snoozing away. That didn't mean he wasn't up last night, watching me get railed by my boyfriend. I pinched the bridge of my nose, making a mental note to find a way to gather enough courage to bring it up in a private conversation.

I let out a sigh before I turned to head down the stairs, when I heard a door open. I turned my head making eye contact with Asher. I swallowed, watching as he slowly closed his bedroom door. His eyes roamed over me, taking in his brother's shirt and my less than put together exterior. There was a tiny glint in his eye that almost looked intrigued but as if practiced, his face went back to vague disinterest.

"Long night?" he asked, the tone in his voice telling me that he didn't actually care.

"No, it was just fine. Thanks."

One side of his mouth pulled into a smile. "I bet it was."

"Excuse me?" My words came out in a harsh whisper.

"In case you need a reminder, I happen to live here too. When I come home at night and hear the tiny whimpers of my brother's girlfriend coming from his bedroom, I think I can assume that the night was more than fine." He stuck his tongue between his teeth, chuckling.

I stood there with my mouth open. "Y—You...you didn't stand there and watch, did you?" Maybe it wasn't Grayson there, maybe I had been wrong.

He licked his lips, whispering, "I came home later than I expected and I'm a respectful person, so I don't like to make a lot of noise if I get in that late. I wasn't expecting to walk by his room and immediately need to tune you out because as much as I've shared with my brother, I'm not really interested in hearing him make you come, Riley."

I wanted to vomit over the fact that my boyfriend's brother and professor used the word *come* in relation to me. "Oh, so it's Riley now?"

He rolled up the sleeves of his button down, giving me another glimpse at his tattoos. "We aren't at school, but if you'd prefer me to call you Miss Monroe from now on, then okay. That's your choice." He leaned his hip against the stair railing, getting closer to me. It made me very, very aware that I only had River's shirt on and nothing else. "Or I could call you little liar, since you have yet to tell me what you were really doing yesterday." His voice was lower now and I could hear my own sharp breathing with the silence that surrounded us, save for Grayson's gentle snoring.

"I'm not a…"

"I'm not really interested and if I ever made it seem like I was, I apologize." He placed a hand on his chest, his eyes narrowing at me. He moved around me to the stairs.

I curled my hand into fists, blowing out a few breaths. I threw my hair over my shoulder and turned to watch as he descended the steps. "Since we aren't in school does that mean I can call you Asher or do I still have to call you *sir*?"

He stopped walking at the second to last stair, turning to look at me. I gave him a triumphant smile even though I was filled with so much anxiety from this little run in. "Or maybe I'll just use Mr. St. James, since I have a feeling that if you had to choose between the other two, you like the latter far too much." I scoffed taking the stairs two at a time, sailing past him.

13
ASHER

I'd learned to control my magic pretty quickly when I was younger, primarily because falling asleep and entering into the dream dimension was not a fun place to be when you were ill-prepared. Oneiromancy wasn't an everyday skill like River's telepathic powers, but it did make me fascinating to almost everyone that my parents would show me off to.

They—mainly my father—would have these parties where he would invite their friends and have them be put in a deep sleep. He would then have me go in and manipulate their dreams. I would go into their minds and see what they saw. I would turn their dreams into nightmares if I wanted to, and you could see it on their faces. I was something my father marveled at, but despite all the *good jobs* and *excellent works* he would throw my way, I still only tolerated the man. There was a time when his love was genuine, I think, but once I came into my powers...that love got twisted and I became a side show act.

I kept River close to me, even though he hated it. I didn't have a terrible childhood, my father didn't hit me or call me bad names, but I wasn't about to have my brother go through the same performative bullshit I did. I made sure I maintained a solid hold on my powers, but I also wanted to dive into the world of mental magic in a different way. I graduated with honors in mental magic from Mystic Riegan, then got my Master's in Education from UC Berkeley. If I was going to help develop someone else's powers, I was going to do it the right way.

I'd had my choices of schools to work at, but I came back to my alma mater and as River liked to point out, right under my dad's thumb. I had my reasons, and they were none of his fucking business.

I sat in my office, taking my glasses off and placing them on my desk. I rubbed my eyes, taking a break from looking over lesson plans for the next week or so. I loved teaching, but sometimes those under-grad shits could really make me rethink my chosen career.

Speaking of a certain undergrad...

I groaned, replaying how well my night had gone when I'd gotten home. Yes, I was met with the sounds of pleasure from both my brother and his girlfriend. They weren't sounds I hadn't heard before, since River was never shy about that kind of thing, nor had he ever learned to fully close a fucking door. None of what I'd come home to bothered me, rattled me. No, it was what I was met with later on that night that stunned me.

I'd been asleep when I somehow catapulted myself into Riley's dreams. They were sporadic and at times a little blurry. I didn't know what I was seeing at first until her face came across my mind, clear as day. I immediately thought it was my own dream and why the fuck was she in them, but then it didn't feel like my mind. Once the chaos of her mind settled, the dream stalled with her sitting on her bed, reading. Her braids cascaded over her shoulders and her brown skin was luminous and all on display from her shorts and tank top.

The sun from her window made the tiny hoop nose ring she had sparkle.

I was gazing at her from the doorway and she looked serene, less antagonizing than how I normally saw her. River chose his partners based on their personalities and how they made him feel. Looks were always something on his mind, but it wasn't a priority for him. I knew how she made *me* feel: she irritated me. I had yet to really understand her personality, and as for her looks...

I shook my head, not letting my mind drift.

I took in the setting and thought about how if I really wanted to, I could ruin this for her. I could make this room a prison, fill it with things she was scared of, pretend to suck all the oxygen from the room. I could make her hate the thought of falling asleep ever again. On the other hand, I could make this dream even more enjoyable.

I could make her slip her own hand between her legs and make her come on her own fingers so hard she might pass out. Or I could have her think they were my fingers and really fuck with her head.

I did neither. I just watched her until I drifted out of her mind and back into my own.

I groaned, running a rough hand through my hair. I didn't care who River dated and she seemed nice enough, but everything happened so fast. They start dating, her dad dies and then she transfers to the school...just like that. I'd questioned my brother about it, but his response was for me to just leave it alone. It was Riley's decision, and he respected that. I could respect her decision as well, while also being suspicious of her.

I knew her dad. He was a nice man who thought the world of this school. He even spoke highly of my brother, which came as a surprise to me since River always did well with moms but not so many dads. Was I wondering about his death till this day? Of course I was. The school had moved on because it had to. I wasn't the police force, nor was I a detective, but he didn't seem like the type to drink too much and fall or even worse throw himself out the window all on his own.

I tapped my fingers along my desk, looking over and peering out my own window.

I put my glasses back on, fingering through the papers in front of me. Riley's name screamed out at me as if it was written in bold red ink, instead of black. The sound of her moaning, the sound of her being pleasured and pleased propelled itself right to the forefront of my mind, which sent a shockwave to my cock.

I took the papers and shoved them to the side.

This wasn't good.

known, but others which have never been known to climb
learn the art as an escape from that somber shadow, so
that the common nettle, the jasmine, and even the jacitara palm
can be seen circling the stems of the cedars and striving to
reach their crowns. Of animal life there was no movement and
a constant movement far above our heads told of that
multitudinous world of snake and monkey, bird and sloth, which
lived in the sunshine, and looked down in wonder at our tiny, dark,
stumbling figures in the obscure depths immeasurably below them.
At dawn and at sunset the howler monkeys screamed together and
the parakeets broke into shrill chatter, but during the hot
hours of the day only the full drone of insects, like the beat of
a distant surf, filled the ear, while nothing moved amid the
solemn vistas of stupendous trunks, fading away into the darkness
which held us in. Once some bandy-legged, lurching creature, an
ant-eater or a bear, scuttled clumsily amid the shadows. It was the
only sign of earth life which I saw in this great Amazonian forest.

And yet there were indications that even human life itself
was not far from us in those mysterious recesses. On the third
day out we were aware of a singular deep throbbing in the air,
rhythmic and solemn, coming and going fitfully throughout the
morning. The two boats were paddling within a few yards
of each other when first we heard it, and our Indians remained
motionless, as if they had been turned to bronze, listening
intently with expressions of terror upon their faces.

"What is it, then?" I asked.

"Drums," said Lord John Roxton, carelessly; "war drums. I have heard
them before."

"Yes, sir, war drums," said Gomez, the half-breed. "Wild Indians,
bravos, not mansos; they watch us every mile of the way; kill us
if they can."

"How do they watch us?" I asked, gazing into the dark,
156

the afternoon of that day, my pocket diary shows me that
Tuesday, August 18th, at least six or seven drums were
throbbing from various points. Sometimes they beat quickly,
sometimes slowly, sometimes in obvious question and answer, one
to the east breaking out in a high staccato rattle, and being
followed after a pause by a deep roll from the north. There was
something indescribably nerve-shaking and menacing in that
constant mutter, which seemed to shape itself into the very
syllables of the half-breed, endlessly repeated, "We will kill
you if we can. We will kill you if we can." No one ever moved in
the silent woods. All the peace and soothing of quiet Nature lay
in that dark curtain of vegetation, but away from behind there
came ever the one message from our fellow-man. "We will kill you
if we can," said the men in the east. "We will kill you if we
can," said the men in the north.

All day the drums rumbled and whispered, while their menace
reflected itself in the faces of our coloured companions. Even the
bold swaggering half-breed seemed cowed. I learned, however,
that day once for all that both Summerlee and Challenger
possessed that highest type of bravery, the bravery of the
scientific mind. Theirs was the spirit which upheld Darwin among
the gauchos of the Argentine or Wallace among the head-hunters
of Malaya. It is decreed by a merciful Nature that the human brain
cannot think of two things simultaneously, so that if it be
engaged in curiosity as to science it has no room for merely
personal considerations. All day amid that incessant and
mysterious menace our two Professors watched every bird upon the
tree, and every shrub upon the bank, with many a sharp wordy
contention, when the snarl of Summerlee came quick upon the deep
growl of Challenger, but with no more sense of danger and no more
reference to drum-beating Indians than if they were seated
together in the smoking-room of the Royal Society's Club in St.
James's Street. Once only did they condescend to discuss them.

"Miranha or Amajuaca cannibals," said Challenger, jerking his
thumb towards the reverberating wood.

"No doubt, sir," Summerlee answered. "Like all such tribes, I
157

Chocolate
PSD
Bar Mock-Up
Good Packaging Collection

14

RILEY

I'd made it through the next two weeks without any mishaps. I couldn't avoid Asher, but he made it a point to never call on me—even when I raised my hand, knowing the answer—and actively looked away from me whenever eye contact could be achieved. I'm pretty sure he scowled in my direction every chance he got.

There were moments when I thought I might have imagined the entire scenario of someone watching River and I. If Grayson had seen something, he was either very good at keeping it to himself or he was way too embarrassed to even bring it up, especially with how natural everything was between the three of us.

I sat in the library after my afternoon class, reading over one of my textbooks. Corrin was continually giving me updates, sending me pictures of different colored liquids and letting me know what it meant. She was close to figuring it out, but with school and her time with Mateo, I wasn't rushing her. She was doing me a favor by *not* asking questions.

My phone vibrated on the table. I snatched it up, looking around the library.

MARIANNE

Why didn't you tell me your boyfriend was having a party?

Marianne and I had been communicating back and forth nonstop since my Asher run in. I ended up having to send her a picture of him—which I'd gotten from River's social media, since Asher was not into having an online presence whatsoever—and she hadn't wasted a second calling me.

"THAT'S HIS BROTHER?!" MARIANNE SHOUTED IN MY EAR. I HAD TO PULL THE phone back just to get the ringing in my ear drum to stop.

"Yes, that's him."

She gasped. "And he's your professor?"

"Didn't I just say this?"

Marianne scoffed and I could just see her throwing her blonde hair over her shoulder, rolling her eyes. "When you said professor, this is not what I pictured. I didn't think you would send me someone fuckable."

I nearly choked on my own spit. "Take that back right now."

She laughed, ignoring me. "I mean, as much as River is growing on me, his brother could I don't know grow in me if you catch my drift."

I was on my way to my afternoon class and tripped over my own feet. "Mare, can you fucking stop. That's gross."

She let out a haughty laugh. "How? Don't you read about this kind of thing?"

"I don't expect this shit to just happen in real life. It's fiction for a reason, you shit."

A few students passed me, giving me weird looks and I ducked my head down.

"Oh, honey, we live in a world where magic and monsters are real. A little teacher-student relations is not going to kill you."

I groaned, pulling open the door to the building that my composition writing course was held in. "If by monsters you mean like shifters...my roommate is dating one and they seem less monstrous than half the people you've dated."

"I resent that." I heard the beep of her car unlocking. "Can't you just like fuck him with disdain or something?"

"Can't you just not ever ask me to fuck my boyfriend's brother ever again?" I heard myself laughing as I said it.

She hummed on the other end, like this was something for her to highly consider. "Fine. River has been good to you so I guess you shouldn't let the hot professor fuck your cute little brains out."

I stopped right outside my classroom, letting people go in front of me so I could finish my call. "I'm sure he'll appreciate that. And by the way, he could be terrible in bed."

Marianne snorted, the rev of her car rattling through the phone. "Riley, I may be a lesbian and not want anything to do with what Asher has going on in his pants, but I promise you...I can tell when someone is a memorable fuck. Which is kind of ironic since I'm sure he would have you forgetting your own name."

In my head, I was giving her the middle finger.

I BLINKED DOWN AT MY PHONE, REALIZING THAT MY FINGERS WERE HOVERING over the screen.

What are you talking about?

MARIANNE
Your boyfriend, you know that guy you're fucking?

> Yes, I am well aware of who he is.

MARIANNE

Next weekend. He's having a party.

> How did you hear about that all the way in Virginia?

MARIANNE

I know people and I'm coming home that weekend anyway.

> When were you going to tell me you were coming home?

MARIANNE

Just now. Keep up, babe. I have to go to class but I love you.

I blew out a breath, thoroughly confused at River having a party and not telling me.

MARIANNE

My mom says your mom is doing good. She had the idea to get her on a dating app, but I shut that down very quickly so don't worry. Also my mom, bless her soul, can't figure out how to send a damn picture so here you go.

A few seconds later a picture of my mom and Beau popped up on my screen. I needed to go home soon, just for a day or two.

I reached into my backpack to pull out my notebook, thinking that getting an early start on homework for next week would keep me from berating my boyfriend with questions. I noticed a crumpled paper at the bottom of my bag. I reached inside, unfolding it and laying it out on the table.

It was the police report I'd been looking at days ago. I hadn't thought about it since I didn't think I needed it anymore. It was all the same information I'd always had, but then my eyes stopped near the bottom.

The witness statement was something I'd either skipped over or just never really looked at all. The statement itself wasn't what was important. They hadn't seen anything that happened, but they did find him and attested to his drinking. That had me rolling my eyes, hard. I dragged my finger over to the witness's name.

Oliver St. James. River's dad.

I gathered my shit, stuffing everything in my backpack. I nearly tripped over my chair as I hustled out to the elevator of the library. I stopped when I heard Grayson's voice. It was low, but I would know him anywhere.

He was speaking more Tagalog than English, which led me to believe he was talking to someone in his family. Grayson wasn't so fluent in Tagalog that he could have full-blown, long-winded conversations, but he knew enough to understand and reply back when necessary.

I looked down one of the aisles, seeing him on the floor. He had his back propped up against one of the shelves. He caught sight of me and tilted his chin up in recognition.

"No. Okay *lang po ako*, Mom." He gave me a look and smiled, rolling his eyes. He looked up at the ceiling, clearly a little frustrated. "Yes. *Plano ko pong umuwi ngayong linggo.*"

He raised a finger in my direction, telling me to wait a minute. He nodded into the phone, listening intently. "Okay, okay, I got you. Love you, Mom. *Ingat ka.*" He blew a kiss into the phone and ended his call. "Sorry about that."

"Don't be. She's your mom, Grayson."

"They're insisting I come home to eat with the family."

"You do love food, so is it really that bad?"

He tilted his head from side to side. "Yes and no. They always send me back to the dorms with food, but then it sits in my mini fridge and goes bad. I can eat, but like that's a lot of fucking food."

I looked over at the elevators, reminding myself of where I needed to go. "Well, let me know when you get back and I'll help you eat it all. As long as your mom makes those little chewy rice cakes she knows I'm obsessed with."

Grayson chuckled. "Biko? She will most certainly be making that, and if not then I'll suggest it." He gave me a tiny smirk. "And yes I am aware of how obsessed you are and how much you can stuff in your mouth."

I wrinkled my nose at him, but moved towards the elevator, smashing my finger on the down button.

"Where are you off to?" he asked, slinging his backpack over his shoulder.

"Um, I just have to go talk to one of my teachers about something, that's all." The lie rolled off so easily.

"I'll walk with you."

"No, you don't have to. I'm sure you have better things to do."

Grayson waved me off, getting into the elevator after me. I watched as the doors closed, running my fingers along my ruby stone that hung around my neck. I didn't believe in crystals or whatever power they might hold, but something about this one made me calmer when I touched it.

I leaned back against the wall, staring at him. "Can I ask you a very awkward question?" While I had him, I might as well get something off my chest.

"The more awkward the better, I say."

I immediately looked down at the floor, letting my eyes bulge out for a minute. "Yeah." I cleared my throat. "Were you asleep the entire time that night?"

Grayson licked his lips, placing one of his hands in his shorts pocket. "What night?"

The elevator stopped letting on a few people and I maneuvered myself to the other side. I moved so close to him that our arms were touching. I lowered my voice. "The night we all hung out. You fell asleep during the movie, so we left you downstairs."

"And?" Grayson countered, looking down at me.

My voice was soft and tentative. "And...I think you might have seen some things."

He placed a hand over his mouth, stifling a laugh. "Seen some things...come on, Riley. You're going to have to be more specific than that." He spoke in my direction, his voice as soft as my own. It was like we were in our own bubble of conversation.

"I don't know how else to put it."

The elevator dinged that we were on the ground floor and everyone walked out ahead of us.

Grayson walked in front of me, but then turned around halting my movements. "I don't think it's so hard. Did I see you and River having sex? See, simple. I'm sure people would kill to watch you guys."

I looked around to make sure no one else heard him. I tugged at one of my braids. "Well...did you?"

He rubbed the back of his neck. "Are you upset?" He wasn't gaslighting me, but he was genuinely asking, while also somehow being cheeky about it.

"That's not an answer."

He ran his finger over his chin, as if he was thinking. He gave me a smile, then smirked. "You and I both know the answer, so asking me is just your way of solidifying something you are fully aware of."

I felt my skin turning hot, remembering him standing there, watching. I couldn't see his face, but I knew he was there.

"The real question you should be asking me is if I'm the kind of guy who likes to stand and watch or would I want to be involved?"

I swallowed hard. It's like he'd been in my head and considered every thought I'd ever had about the situation. "And your answer would be?"

He shrugged, walking backwards. "That's a discussion meant for when your boyfriend is around, don't you think?" He gave me a quick salute.

I watched him walk away, shaking my head at how easy, but unnerving that was. I had kind of gotten my answer, but I was left questioning myself. Was it a violation of my privacy that Grayson had stood there and watched, sure...but did I maybe, sort of, want it to happen again. It felt only fair that River should be a part of this conversation, but there was something I had to do right now and without Grayson hovering, I beelined for the Department of Mental Magic.

Chocolate.PSD
Bar Mock-Up
Food Packaging Collection
157

15
RIVER

"How are classes?" My brother asked me, balling up his napkin and throwing it into the paper bag. We occasionally had lunch together, even though I would much rather be eating with my girlfriend, but usually during these lunches he was less of an ass than usual.

He'd gotten us subs from one of our favorite places in the bay area and paid, so I wasn't going to complain. I cracked my knuckles, leaning back in my chair. "They're fine. Don't tell me you've met with all my teachers and asked them how I'm doing?"

Asher gave me an incredulous look. "Why the fuck would I do that?"

"You did it when I was in high school."

"You had a lot less discipline in high school, I had to keep you on track."

I scoffed. "I wasn't that bad. This coming from the guy who fucks with his students while they're daydreaming."

Asher pointed at me. "I only do that when it's totally necessary. I won't have mediocrity in my classroom or sleeping shits who think it's nap time."

My dampener made it impossible to send him the multiple wildly funny thoughts that formed in my head, so I would hold off until we were home.

"River, dad talked to your academic advisor, and you've got a meeting with him."

I nearly choked on the small sip of my soda. "With dad?"

"Yes, with dad."

"Lemme guess, this is the only way he could get me to sit down and legitimately talk to him?" It was deviously perfect. My dad, being the dean of the entire department, had so much sway with the advisors. At Mystic Riegan, missing meetings without sufficient reasoning looked bad on your entire school profile. Most students would be over the fucking moon to have a one on one with the dean of their chosen major and I just so happened to be the chosen few that hated it.

"You do use his money, River."

"That shit doesn't work on me. I've told you before I don't want it." My dad would never threaten to take it away though, because that kind of talk was futile. My mom wanted us taken care of regardless of our relationship with her husband. Our dad loved her, so keeping her happy was his first goal in life and then we came right after that, begrudgingly so. Asher could have whatever kind of relationship he wanted with the man; I was good at doing exactly what I've always done.

My dad tried to make me some kind of party favor when I was around ten, right when my powers had decided to make a full appearance. I remembered all those people in our living room, waiting to see what I could do as if they were used to this shit or something. My dad had even tried to give me this foul-smelling drink to help enhance my powers, open my mind up more. I'd spit it out the minute it hit my tongue.

Asher had been away at Mystic Riegan getting his undergrad before that and he'd come home to a house full of strangers. He kicked them all out and he and our dad had a very angry conversation in our study.

He lived at home, driving back and forth, monitoring me and our dad after that. Eventually, he moved out...taking me with him while he went to get his Master's. I moved in with Asher because it sounded better than living at home, and he basically had my stuff packed and moved before I could really give an answer.

"That's all fine and well, but a few minutes of lackluster conversation won't hurt. Just give him monosyllabic answers and call it a day." My brother made it sound so easy.

"Those answers won't be good enough and he'll make me want to throat punch him, Asher. I don't know how you stand him."

Asher shook his head, taking my empty food wrappings and throwing them in the bag as well. "I don't, I assure you. He is kind of my boss though, so some kind of respect is in order."

"He wouldn't be if you had just gone to another school," I mumbled, knowing that we'd had this conversation numerous times already.

Asher sighed, throwing away our trash.

"He's going to use mom as some kind of sympathy calling card and then just because of her, try to ask me questions that show some sort of interest in my life!" I scoffed, feeling my voice getting louder and my chest felt tight. "I don't need him knowing about what I do in my free time or anything to do with Riley. She hasn't said much about meeting him, and I prefer it that way. Knowing our dad, he'd say some wild shit about hers and I'd have to kill him because he hurt her feelings." I could have flipped over Asher's desk if I thought he wouldn't scream at me to calm the hell down. "You want me to be nice to that guy?"

Asher slammed his hands on his desk, grabbing my attention.

"Not so loud, alright." He widened his eyes at me from behind his glasses. "I get it okay. Go to the meeting with him or don't go to the meeting with him, that's your choice, River. I'm not the one you're upset with, so lose the fucking attitude."

I leaned my head back, looking up and taking a few deep breaths. "Sorry."

Asher smacked his lips together. "Speaking of Riley..."

"Oh fuck, not you too."

My brother got up and circled around his desk, before propping himself up against it. He crossed his arms over his chest, giving me a stern look. "She went to community college before this, right?"

I furrowed my eyebrows. "Your point?"

"I'm just saying it's kind of odd that she was just fine doing that and then suddenly she wants to transfer to a much larger university. You even told me she had no interest in Mystic Riegan whatsoever."

"People change their fucking minds, Asher. I do it all the time and you don't question *me*."

Asher rubbed his temples. "I don't question you because half the time it gets me nowhere. And you also find a way to divert the conversation in your favor."

"It's a skill I should add to my resume."

Asher pointed a finger at me. "Think about it, River. Why would she want to attend a university that her dad worked at, that he died at. It feels very morbid to me, and she doesn't seem like the type to want to converse with the dead, perform a seance, so..."

I laughed a little at how ridiculous he was. My brother could go to lengths to make a good situation feel like a bad one. He could find the tiniest thing wrong with someone and blow it up, creating a spectacle from it. I got up from the chair, grabbing his shoulder and shaking him. "Maybe she just wants to feel closer to him, who knows. I don't ask because it's not my business. You forget that not everyone has a messed-up relationship with their father."

He hummed, giving me a look that told me he wasn't really

convinced. "Just be vigilant, okay? Also close your fucking door or tell her to be quieter."

I snorted out a laugh. "I will never tell her to be quieter, but I will highly consider the other thing you said." I placed my hand on the doorknob but stopped before I turned it. "We both know you listened for just a minute, so please wipe that look of superiority off your face. Thanks for lunch."

I threw the door open, walking out without paying attention and running into a body.

"Fuck, I'm sorry, I—," I reared my head back in shock at who I'd collided with. "Riley?"

16
RILEY

My shoulders tensed when I saw River looking back at me as if he had a million questions. I looked over his shoulder to see Asher appear out of his office, leaning against the threshold of the door. If he was already suspicious of me before, this would add another thing to his list that I'm sure he was building.

"Uh, hey," I said, my t-shirt immediately feeling a little too tight, even though it was made of the most breathable material.

"What are you doing here?" River asked, his face the look of pure innocence.

I'd looked at the names associated with each floor and found Mr. St. James. He was one floor down from my dad, so if I could accomplish two things at once then today would be a success in my book. I was the most confident and determined I'd ever been, planning to march right into his office, ask to speak to him with urgency and hope I could get moved to the front of whatever waitlist he had.

What I had not planned for was running into River and the last person I wanted to see.

I looked over River's shoulder to see their dad's office staring me right in the face.

"Yes, what *are* you doing here, Miss Monroe?" Asher repeated, but his tone was more accusatory as if he was just begging me to fuck up.

I rubbed my lips together, thinking through my options. "I came to talk to Mr. St. James about something for class."

River's mouth pulled up in an amused manner. "Wait, you make her call you Mr. St. James? Asher, you really do take yourself too seriously."

Asher ran his tongue over his front teeth. "I don't have office hours today. I know that and you know that."

I gave a casual one shoulder shrug. "I thought maybe you'd make an exception for me."

"Unfortunately, I'm not one for favoritism. You'll have to come by on my regular days like everyone else, but I don't think you will because I don't think that's why you're actually here." His eyes never left my face, as if he was trying to intimidate me with just his piercing stare alone. I wouldn't say the look made me feel small, but I also wouldn't say it did nothing for me.

River snapped his fingers in front of his brother's face. "Give it a rest, Asher." He shook his head, giving me his full attention. "You all done for the day?"

I nodded, knowing that Asher was still staring at me.

"Good, let me walk you back to your dorm." He started to walk past me but swiftly turned around on his heels. "Forgot my bag."

When River was out of sight, Asher stepped up to me, making sure there was no space between us. He leaned down, so that his words could not be misconstrued. "As flattered as I am that you've made me a part of whatever it is you're doing here, *don't* do it again. My brother may be so infatuated with you, but luckily, I am not. Strike two, little liar."

"I'm not doing anything. It's not a crime to want *help* from my teacher. Is it, *sir*?"

His jaw ticked, but he didn't say anything else. He moved away from me when River returned, giving his brother a tight smile. Asher went back into his office, slamming the door. River took my hand and walked us to the elevator. I turned my head, seeing his father come out of his office right as we entered, and I let out a sigh, almost cursing under my breath.

I would need a new strategy.

17
RILEY

River gave me room in front of the door to my dorm so that I could tap my keycard. He followed me inside, sitting down on my bed. Corrin wasn't here, so I slipped my phone out of my pocket checking on any messages from her. I had one from my mom, which I would answer later, but nothing from Corrin. I closed my eyes, holding my phone so tight that I felt a cramp in my hand.

"Lucky you with no class tomorrow." River kicked his shoes off, laying back on my bed.

I blinked, bringing myself back into the present. "I still have homework." I walked over to my dresser, picking up the one picture I'd brought with me of me and my parents. It was in a frame that I'd bought at a craft store because I thought it was cute. I'd had to cut the picture down to make it fit, but it was in the shape of a heart, and I loved it regardless.

"Still, I wish I could hang out with you tonight, but I idiotically decided to take a night class."

I swiped a tear from under my eye and focused on him. "I can see the appeal of night classes.

"Advanced Telepathy is a much easier class to grasp in the evening. I think my mind is a little more subdued."

I walked over to him. He instantly sat up, swinging his legs off the bed and pulling me so I was standing in between them. "Hopefully not so subdued that you fall asleep. You're supposed to be graduating soon."

He gave me a tiny smile, cupping the side of my face. I leaned into his touch, shuddering at the instant comfort he gave me. "What's wrong, gorgeous?"

My eyes were half closed, but then they shot open. "What do you mean?"

"Well, your cheek is a little wet, so I'm going to assume something is bothering you."

Fuck, I thought I had caught the tears before they could propel themselves out of my fucking eyes. "A lot on my mind, that's all. Nothing I can't handle."

River slid his hand down my arm, the cold metal of his power dampening ring cooling parts of my skin. "Is this about your dad?"

I reared my head back, stepping away from him. "Why would you say that? Did your brother say something?"

He raised his hands, telling me he was trying to come at this delicately. "He might have mentioned something, but whatever you tell me...I'm on your side. Being here can't be easy and if you want to talk about it then I'm here. I'm always here."

I sighed, feeling the heavy weight that had landed in my chest subside. I couldn't talk about this because then it would make me want to divulge everything to him, and I wanted all my facts straight. I didn't want loose ends and plot holes. I didn't like my stories with them, so I didn't want them in my actual life.

I rushed back over to him, leaning down and kissing him. He was the best and I understood why nearly every person fell in love with him. He was insanely good looking, but he had a heart big enough for everyone he cared about. As much as he thought with his cock most of the time, he knew when to turn down the heat and just let it simmer so he could focus.

I hummed against his mouth, changing the subject. "So, a party, huh?"

He raised one of his eyebrows. "What?"

"Marianne texted me and told me you were having a party. I was a little confused since that was the first I was hearing about it."

River scrubbed a hand down his face. "I was going to tell you. Well, really I was just going to pick you up and bring you over. I didn't think I needed to invite my girlfriend to my own party." He rolled his eyes, his tone filled with humor.

"And what if I had plans?"

"Bring your plans along." He stood up, holding me close to him. "A big party downstairs, we go sneak off and have our own very sweaty, naked, private party alone upstairs."

I giggled when his lips ghosted over my jaw and towards my ear. With all the feelings about River, my dad and all the things I still didn't know, I let my mind drift. I didn't realize what I was saying until the words were out of my mouth. "And what about Grayson?"

River lifted his head to look at me. I thought I would see a hint of annoyance or even jealousy at the idea that I just brought up his best friend while he was attempting to seduce and flirt. I didn't see any of that when I looked into his eyes. I saw that same twinkle of something familiar that made my heart speed up. I saw mischief.

"I'm sure Grayson can take care of himself."

I broke our eye contact, looking down at the ground. "Oh yeah, of course. I don't know why I said that." I could have let the floor swallow me whole at any moment now.

River crooked his finger, tilting my chin up to look at him again. "Riley..."

"I think..." I paused, rephrasing. "I *know* he was watching us the other night and I think we should all talk about it." My voice trembled a tiny bit towards the end as if I was losing my confidence. I really didn't know another time when a topic like this could be appropriately brought up.

He cocked his head to the side. "Would you like me to talk to him myself? If you feel some type of way about it, I promise he'll get the message." His eyes had turned a little dark as if he was ready to ruin his friendship for me.

"N—no...don't. I mean, I don't...feel some kind of way about it. I mean, well, I feel something about it..." I could hear myself rambling, but the words were just tumbling out until he hummed appreciatively, as if he understood.

"Maybe we do need to talk about it then." River gave me a side smile that would have melted my insides if I wasn't a little taken aback. His free hand had traveled to my waist, under my shirt and his fingers were tracing little circles against my skin. "Together." He still held my chin, but he gently lifted his thumb to follow the curve of my lower lip.

"You aren't upset that I'm not, I don't know, *more* upset about it."

"Mmm...no. If you were uncomfortable then I'd deal with it, but clearly you have something else on your mind and discomfort is not the word I'd use for how you felt about being watched." He leaned down, speaking against my lips. "I'm more than willing to give you everything you want and more, gorgeous." His words implied so much more than I was prepared for.

I reached down, placing my hand over his, stopping his intoxicating movements. "Have you and Grayson ever..."

His shoulders moved as he laughed lightly, withdrawing his face from its place so close to mine. "Yes. Is that a problem?"

I plunged my teeth into my bottom lip. "No, not a problem at all. I've maybe actually thought about it...if you both had..." I shook my head when he grinned over at me. I pressed my lips together. "Did you guys get together when we started..."

"No, no, what we did, what we had was back in high school and a few times here and there before I met you." He quickly added. "He's my best friend and I love him. Do I still have a connection with him that is special to me? Yeah, but I would *never* do that to you. The fact that he cares about you just as much as I do is really a bonus." I found myself liking that piece of information. Yes, Grayson cared about me, but I enjoyed knowing that they cared about each other. That their relationship could go beyond friendship, yet if friendship was all they desired they would be okay. River wanted all the good and happy things for me, but I wanted the same for them, for both of them. Perhaps our little talk needed to be about more than just me.

I nodded, pulling away a little, but he didn't ease up his hold on me. "If you want to change things, Riley, all you have to do is say the word and you can have it all. Me and him both need you to say what you want out loud and mean it. How about tomorrow after my class and his work study, we sit and figure this out?"

I pursed my lips. "You make this sound so easy."

River shrugged, reaching up and grabbing the back of my head with both his hands. "You won't let me read your mind, so you're going to have to use your words. You know how to do that, don't you?" He pressed his forehead to mine and I nodded, swaying a little bit.

"That's my good girl." He kissed me, licking at my lips and taking my bottom lip between his teeth and pulling enough to make me whimper. "I'll pick you up tomorrow afternoon."

He grabbed his bag and walked out the door without another look over his shoulder. I inhaled deeply and my exhale came out shaky but filled with just a miniscule bit of excitement I didn't quite comprehend. That was a tomorrow issue, but today I'd missed my opportunity to speak to Oliver St. James. That could also be tomorrow's issue.

I took out my phone, sending a reply text to my mom.

> Sorry for the late reply. Yes, I'm planning to come home this weekend.

I hadn't thought about coming home fully, until I'd read her text and saw that she'd asked. Her response came quicker than I thought it would.

MOM

Perfect, I haven't touched your room, so it's all ready for you.

Okay, I lied. I washed your sheets, but that's because Beau left dog hair everywhere.

He misses you.

I miss you too. I'll also get your favorite little gummy bears from that convenience store that looks unsafe, but you always say it's fine.

I chuckled to myself, remembering that the only reason why I loved those gummy bears was because of my dad. I made him take me back to that place after I'd run out and my mom had a field day when she found out what this place looked like and that my dad had taken their seven-year-old daughter there.

My vision started to get hazy when the tears began to take hold, but Corrin's name on my screen stopped them. I clicked to open her text.

CORRIN

You need to get over to my house. I'm sending you the address.

Chocolate PSD
Bar Mock-Up
Smart Packaging Collection

18
RILEY

Traffic was worse than I thought, so instead of an easy thirty minute ride, I'd spent the last forty to fifty minutes in the backseat of my rideshare trying not to fidget. Corrin couldn't have all the answers, but she had *something,* which made me both nervous and giddy all at the same time. The fact that she'd said so little about this "lab" that she had at her house had me a little on edge, but I had decided to trust her, so I had to deal with what came with that trust.

Corrin lived in a neighborhood in one of the smaller towns called Seiros, closer to the water. We passed more condos than full blown homes as we drove by but regardless, they were nice, many of them with gardens planted out front or wrap around fences. We pulled up to her concrete driveway, just as her front door was opening.

Her house was the color of the ocean with shingle roofing and way too many wind chimes out front. The breeze that the water blew in had them all moving musically. She was clothed in jean overall shorts and a bralette when she ran over to me barefoot. Her tight curls were in a multitude of twists on her head, pushed away from her face with a silk headband.

"Finally!" she yelped, grabbing my hand and rushing back inside.

The door slammed behind us and I looked at the shoes next to the front door, taking that as my cue to remove my own.

"What did I tell you about tracking dirt into this house?" A stern voice that made me want to stand up even straighter asked.

"Sorry, sorry, I know, geez." Corrin turned around and slipped on her flip flops that were sitting by the door. "It's like she knows every-thing," my roommate whispered.

The woman whose voice I'd heard stepped out from around a corner, wiping her hands on a kitchen towel. "I do know everything or really it's that you are oh, so predictable." She took the towel and lightly smacked Corrin with it.

"Riley, this is my mom." Corrin pointed her thumb towards the woman, who was beautiful and tall. Her mom mirrored her dark skin and texture of hair. Her hair was also in twists, but they were much longer than her daughters. She had one stud in each nostril and an eyebrow piercing.

I smiled at the woman, who reciprocated. "It's nice to meet you."

"Corrin! Get this damn cat out of here! He's trying to eat the food!" A man yelled from what I could only assume was the kitchen.

Corrin rolled her eyes, stifling a laugh. "Jax! Stop bothering daddy and come here!" The sound of small paws rounding the corner sounded. An orange tabby circled around Corrin's feet, rubbing up against her ankles and purring. His little nose leaned in to sniff me. He looked up at Corrin and gave the cat version of a shrug then went to inspect my shoes.

"He says you're okay to stay and he trusts you," Corrin explained.

"Who?"

"The little heathen over there." Her mom wagged a finger at Jax. The cat turned its head up at us and trotted out of the room.

"Go to my room, Jax!" Corrin yelled, shaking her head. "He

doesn't love being told what to do, so I'll likely find a tiny pile of shit on my bed."

Footsteps sounded and a dark-skinned man appeared with the kindest eyes I'd ever seen. His curls were cut close to his head, but you could still see where they made tiny spirals. "I need to go get some basil from out back and the food should be ready soon. Ah, this must be Riley."

The stunned look on my face at their familiar knowledge of me must have been funny. Corrin's mom grabbed her daughter's shoulder and shook it. "This one collects friends like umm, what was that one show, that monster collector thing…"

"It's called Pokemon, Mom. We had a very long discussion about it where you pretended to listen for the sake of my happiness," Ike offered, walking through the backdoor. He looked over at his sister expectantly.

Corrin rocked back and forth on her feet. "Okay, well we have to go." She gripped my forearm. Before she could drag me away, her mom stepped towards me.

"Can I?" She pointed to my necklace.

"S-sure," I hesitated, but felt no reason to be alarmed.

Her mom gently picked up the ruby gem, carefully not to tug on the chain and ran her thumb over it. "Beautiful craftsmanship."

I let myself smile a little. "It was a gift from my mom." I let my eyes look around a little more, noticing the crystals that decorated the house. It wasn't an excessive amount, but it was more than I'd ever seen. They all had different shapes and sizes, some were hanging up, while others adorned tables.

"That's…interesting. Your mother has quite the eye." Her smile was warm when she let the gem fall back against my chest.

"Ugh mom, lets not weird her out, okay," Corrin scolded, throwing her brother a menacing look when he cleared his throat as if to tell her to hurry up.

Her mom threw a look to her dad. "I do not weird people out."

He scrunched up his face in thought. "Only sometimes."

Corrin pulled me away from them, throwing a lackluster wave over her shoulder. "Oh, um, it was nice to meet you both." I was able to shout before I was led out the back door and into a shed that was much bigger on the inside than on the outside.

I looked around at the scientific contraptions I was seeing. There were handcrafted mortar and pestles but also shiny, glass beakers and test tubes. She had been right when she'd claimed potion chemistry. I saw my tiny glass shard sitting on a piece of weighing paper and then realized Ike was in the room.

Corrin followed my eyes and flinched a little. "Okay, don't be mad."

"Corrin.... why would I be mad?"

"So, Ike doesn't like to knock or make himself known when he enters my space." She threw him a look of annoyance. "I was working and he saw what I was doing, so he asked about it and he likes to blab to our parents when I'm lying, therefore I was forced to tell the truth. You do not want to see my mom when she's angry, all the crystals in the house go nuts." She took a deep breath when she was finished.

I slowly pressed my lips together, running my hands down my braids and tugging at the ends. "You told him?"

Ike hummed. "Yes, but what she knows isn't a lot, so really it's almost like I know nothing at all."

"As much as I hate to say this, you'll want him in on it. Ike is like the best researcher. Future corporate analyst over here, who also happens to be the guy who used his magic to form random metal into armor when he used to LARP at age twelve." She stuck her tongue out at him and he blew out an annoyed breath, looking back at me.

"What exactly did she tell you?" I asked, more concerned with that fact more than anything else.

Ike pulled out a chair and sat down. "She told me your dad was the guy that died over the summer, that you don't think it was an accident and neither does she, and you found this glass piece with magic on it and hope that it will lead you to something that will avenge your dad's death."

My mouth dropped open, my eyes flicking over to Corrin who was smiling at me with her lips pressed together. "Oh yeah, she didn't tell you *anything* at all." I made sure the sarcasm was loud and obnoxious.

Corrin sighed, "I'm sorry, Riley. I do promise you can trust me, well, you can now trust *us*. I should have asked you before I got him involved, but on the upside, he did help me figure out what I asked you over for." She didn't make a move to get closer to me, letting me have my space.

I chewed on the inside of my cheek, mulling over my thoughts. I jumped a little when Jax rubbed his body against my ankles. I bent down to pet him, missing my own furry companion. I used my index finger to scratch underneath his chin and his little eyes clearly told me to forgive his mom.

I straightened and walked over to her. "Fine, all is forgiven for now. You're on friend probation."

Corrin clapped. "I'll take it!"

"Now what's going on? What did you find out?"

Corrin pulled out her stool from underneath the table, taking tweezers and plucking the glass piece up. "I had already told you that there was magical residue on this and what I found confirmed it, but it's not just one piece of magic."

"One piece of magic?"

Ike came up behind us. "She means it's not just one magical skill. The residue has remnants of telekinesis, but the person that used it isn't simply telekinetic."

Corrin put the glass piece back on the weighing paper, swiveling on her stool. Her brown eyes were wide with intrigue. "I will tell you I tried to pull some of the other powers out. There is a method where I drop the glass into a concoction that I created. It would be kind of like water and oil, instantly separating so that I could get a better look, but...."

"It burned her." Ike finished; his voice was softer.

"What?!" I pressed, reaching for her hands to find where she was hurt.

Corrin slapped my hands away. "I'm a healing witch, I'm totally fine. Shit, hurt like a bitch though. I dropped the glass in there and it flew out landing right back on the table and the boiling water just kind of shot out, landed all over my fucking hand."

I placed my hand over my heart. "I'm sorry. I shouldn't have asked you to do any of this."

My roommate giggled. "Seriously calm down. As much as it hurt, it was fascinating. If this magic is angry, I would kill to see who its owner is. Magic is a bond and the more emotions you put into it, the more it grows, shapes and forms."

I tried to laugh with her, but a realization stopped me. "So telekinesis would likely mean my dad was pushed..."

Corrin's voice got small. "Seems that way."

I sent a half-hearted smile in her direction, happy that at least I was getting some truth from this.

"We can knock out shifters as your list of suspects. Their ability to change takes over way too much of their DNA, they wouldn't be able to take on any other powers," Ike explained, when I'm sure my face was confused.

"I'm guessing it couldn't be a student either. I mean, if it holds more powers than any normal magic wielder has, no student could do something like that. Isn't that the whole reason they come to Mystic Riegan, to enhance and learn?" I offered, chewing on the inside of my cheek.

Corrin tapped her fingernails on the table. "Sort of. Not all on their own. If you have a teacher that's willing to help you, mold you and pretty much manipulate you then sure it can happen. You are usually learning your inherent skill and maybe something additional that offsets what you already have, but not an entire array of powers. No one wants to entrust that much power to a fucking twenty-year-old. Highly unlikely, but sure, why not. I will say my guess isn't a student, but faculty or even higher."

My mind went back to River's dad being named as a witness on the police report. I hated thinking the worst, but I had to look at all the options.

"I wouldn't completely say they are out of the equation in some way, Corrin. Tell her." Ike nudged his sister's shoulder.

Corrin played with her earlobe as if she was trying to decide how to say what she wanted. "A few witches are missing."

"Missing?" I noticed another stool underneath the table, so I pulled that out and sat down.

"Yeah, we don't know if it's super serious or something; I mean it's college, people go off and do whatever they want, but it's a little alarming." She tried to laugh it off, but I could tell she was concerned.

"What's a few?"

Ike blew out a breath. "Two so far. Not enough to make the coven on high alert, but two too many to not go out with a buddy at night kind of thing."

"And is the school doing anything?"

Ike and Corrin both rolled their eyes. "The school doesn't want to cause a fuss about it. We just know because people talk, especially witches and since it's my own coven, well, I'm kind of privy to that information."

I reached for the weighing paper, sliding it and the glass shard over to me, prepared to put it in my bag. "Okay, you've done enough. I didn't want to put anyone at risk of something and this just solidified that."

Corrin pressed her fingers to the other side of the paper, sliding it back over. "I want to help. If it isn't a little scary then it's not worth the risk." She took her glasses off, handing them to her brother for him to use his shirt to clean them for her.

"What my sister is saying is that you're stuck with her." Ike laughed, shaking his head as he lifted his shirt and cleaned each lens.

"Which means I guess you're stuck with both of us." Corrin snatched her glasses from him, smiling.

A knock sounded at the door and Jax jumped into Corrin's lap. Her mom peeked her head in. "Food's ready. Are you staying for dinner, Riley?"

I scratched my head but heard my stomach grumble. "Um, yeah. I would like that."

Corrin lifted her cat up and made a *pspsps* sound. "Are you ready for dinner, baby Jax?"

I followed them out of the shed, stopping when a spotted bird came flying at us, landing on Ike's shoulder. Ike looked at the bird and smiled. "This is Ted."

Corrin cackled. "Only you would name your familiar Ted." Ted made a noise at her and flew into the house when she opened the door. It smelled like a dream when I stepped inside.

"You said on the day we met that your dad wasn't a witch, right?" I knew she had mentioned a long line of witches in her family.

Ike answered, "Dad is a shifter."

"Hence why he and Mateo get along so well. Well, he tolerates them. My dad isn't thrilled they work in a bar." Corrin placed Jax down, rubbing her hands together as cat fur floated off them. "Mom's witch bloodline is super strong, so it pushed Dad's shifter lineage right out the way."

Ike let me go ahead of him so we could wash our hands and head into the dining room. "What kind of witch is your mom?"

"Isn't it obvious?" Corrin laughed, waving her hand around the room. "She's a crystal witch."

Chocolate PSD
Bar Mock-Up
Food Packaging Collection

19
GRAYSON

I unlocked the front door with the spare key River had given me and headed straight for the living room. I dropped my bag on the ground, hearing a noise and turning around. Footsteps sounded upstairs followed by a door closing.

"River, that you?" Asher asked from the top of the stairs.

"Nope, just me."

I heard him sigh, descending the stairs. He had a simple t-shirt on and a pair of dark straight legged jeans. I took a step back, creating an L with both my hands, turning one of them sideways so each point could touch and I was looking through my makeshift square. "Damn, don't you clean up nice, professor."

He grabbed his keys from the entryway table. "You never get less annoying, do you?"

I shrugged. "All part of my charm."

"Charm is not the word I'd use." He waved his hand at me. "What are you doing here?"

"I'm waiting on River to get here."

"Just River?" He lifted an eyebrow at me.

"Riley is coming too, if you must know." I was hoping she'd be coming in more ways than one if tonight went well.

He clucked his tongue, preparing to head out the door.

"You know, you didn't like me at first and then well, you learned to tolerate me. Maybe you'll eventually do the same with her," I offered, falling back onto the couch and placing my hands behind my head.

He ran a hand through his hair, the overhead light reflecting off his glasses. "I don't dislike you, Grayson. I never have. Just because you are annoying doesn't mean you aren't a good ally to my brother. Did I think you two would start fucking? Of course not, but I can't stop my brother from being who he is and liking who he likes. It's not my place to label the little asshole something that he's not."

A laugh bubbled out of my throat. "You knew we were fucking?"

He let out a heavy sigh and narrowed his eyes at me. "How many times do I have to keep telling you guys, my brother never learns to close a fucking door. Also, you make noises just the same as she does, so at least River seems to know what he's doing."

He closed the door behind him and all I could do was laugh. He wasn't wrong. River did know what he was doing, but so did I. My best friend wasn't selfish when it came to letting others take the lead, at least when it came to me. I opened my bag and double checked that I had stuff for my weekend with my parents. They had gotten the email about my scholarship as well and that was the longest conversation of my life. It was all settled now and I was back on track. My parents didn't need to worry about me.

Chocolate PSD
Bar Mock-Up
Packaging Collection
157
156

20
RILEY

The air was nice and warm this time of night, although the wind whipped a little too much for my liking on the back of River's bike. I placed everything I needed in a backpack instead of my normal bag to make the ride easier, but no matter how many times I rode on the back of his motorcycle, it never became a natural sensation.

He parked as close to Grayson's car as possible, needing to keep Asher's space empty. I hoped off, steadying myself now that I was back on the ground. I unclasped my helmet, holding it against me. River flipped up the visor of his own helmet, giving me a look that said *are you okay?* I gave him a thumbs up and he proceeded to take off his helmet, grabbing mine as well.

The ride over here numbed my thoughts, which I was grateful for. Neither River nor Grayson would let tonight, or any night, turn out badly, but this was territory I didn't think I'd ever be in. I took a deep breath and grabbed River's hand when he offered it.

Grayson was already waiting inside when we entered, giving us a big smile.

"Finally. What took you so long?"

River tossed his keys on the entryway table. "I still abide by the speed limits." Grayson raised one of his eyebrows causing River to give him a middle finger. "I abide by the speed limits sometimes, is that better? They are suggestions at minimum."

I jumped onto the couch, throwing my backpack next to Grayson's duffle. "Did you miss us or something?"

Grayson tapped my nose ring. "I always miss you."

I pressed my lips together, readjusting my slouchy crop top and settling back on the couch. River came to sit down next to me, turning his body so he could face us. The room got quiet and the tension was almost like a physical entity in the room with us. I could hear myself breathing and I needed someone to say something... soon.

River cleared his throat, moving his eyes to Grayson. "Did you watch Riley and me have sex?"

I nearly choked on air.

Grayson sucked his teeth, placing his elbow on the armrest. "Starting off strong, are we?"

"Rip the band aid off," River said, never looking away from him. He placed his hand on my leg, squeezing.

"Okay." Grayson looked over at me, a tiny hint of smile on his lips before looking back at River. "Yeah, I did. Not the whole thing, but some of it."

I stared down at my hands. "I know I'm supposed to be really angry about that or something, but I'm not."

"How *do* you feel, Riley?" River asked, his voice was deep but careful.

"I liked it...I think."

River laughed softly. "No, no. No 'I think'. We aren't going anywhere while you consider things. Did you like it?"

I swallowed, taking all my thoughts so far into account. "I did. I liked it." I let out a heavy breath. "I liked it a lot."

River nodded, moving his hand up and down my leg. "What do you think that means for you? Where do you want to go from here?"

"Don't tell us what we want to hear either," Grayson added, rubbing his fingers over his mouth.

"I knew you were there and I…I liked you seeing me like that. I just wish that you could…" I pulled my legs up and close to my chest, feeling happy about being open for just a small moment, but I wanted to close myself off again.

"Wish I could, what?" Grayson pressed.

I turned my head to look at him. "You told me that the question I should focus on was if you were the type that just likes to watch or would you want to be involved. Well, I'm asking you, which is it?"

Grayson pressed his tongue into his cheek, flicking his eyes to River. I looked at my boyfriend who gave nothing away but simply nodded his head towards me. Grayson put his hand on my knee. "You want me to be honest?"

"Yes."

His lips melted into a smirk that had my heart thumping and heat coursing through my body. "I don't mind standing back and watching you because, fuck, are you something to watch. I liked watching you gag on his cock and how your pussy just took every single thrust beautifully. I won't complain if that's how you want things to be Riley. I'll be happy to jerk off watching you get fucked whenever you want, but that's not all I want."

"Hmm, and what is it that *you* want, Grayson?" River asked scooting closer to me, moving my braids over my shoulder so that he could stroke my pulse point with his thumb.

"I want to be involved. Maybe not all the time, but I want to share you sometimes." He moved his hand to my shoulder, moving my braids and touching the other side of my neck.

River leaned down to speak in my ear. "Now is the time to use your words, gorgeous. You say no and we'll stop and move on. We can watch a movie or I'll take you back to the dorms." He reached up and turned my head so that I was looking at him while his eyes bore into my own. "If you say yes...if you say you want both of us, our hands, our mouths and both our cocks to make you feel good, then we'll do whatever you say. We'll spend all night making you come."

I slowly moved my legs down and tried to keep my sharp breathing in check. My cheeks felt hot and I could feel so much wetness pooling between my legs I was almost embarrassed. I wanted him to kiss me, but all he did was wait.

My lips were drier than normal, so I stuck my tongue out and licked them. River's eyes watched the movement, never letting up on the way his thumb stroked my neck. "It's okay to be greedy, saying you want both of us, gorgeous."

"I do..." I started, tentatively placing each of my hands on their legs. "I do want both of you. I want you both to touch me, but I also want you to want each other."

River lost his bravado for a moment but rallied. He stopped touching my neck and moved his hand to my thigh, sliding it so close to where I was aching and then back down to right above my knee.

"What gave her that idea, hmm?" Grayson said playfully.

"She asked, so I was honest."

I squeezed their legs, getting them to look at me. "I still want you both regardless, but if at some point you just so happen to kiss or find yourselves wanting to fuck each other, then I want it to happen."

River slid his hand up my leg again, stopping right between my legs. "That's what you want?"

"You're being honest with us?" Grayson kept looking from where my hand was on his leg to my face like if he looked too long at one, then the other would cease to exist.

"You want to make me happy, then I want you to be happy too." I erased any sort of modesty from my mind and moved my hands so that my fingers ran over the hardened cocks that were pressed against their pants. "You want to make me happy, don't you?" I bit one corner of my lower lip, batting my eyelashes.

I didn't know when I'd got so brazen in a matter of minutes, but I kept telling myself that I'd wanted this to happen for a while now and I was finally ready and willing to ask for it. I knew for a fact they were equally ready to give it to me.

"Fuck, happy. I'm prepared to make you scream, gorgeous." River kissed me, while I rubbed my hand across the shape of him. He groaned into my mouth, breaking the kiss and turning my head.

Grayson took one of my braids and slid his fingers down it, twirling the end. He leaned in and the fact that River was watching so intently, had me fidgeting to get his hands to touch me more. Grayson's lips barely touched mine. "I'll be as gentle as you want, *aking sinta.*"

I was so used to him calling me trouble that the new name caught me off guard, but now wasn't the time for me to ask what it meant. The smile he had disappeared when his lips crashed against mine and his tongue tangled with my own. I moaned against him; things were going from almost a slow motion to hyper speed. I was trying to wrap my mind around where their hands were and where to place mine now that we were really going for this.

In my mind this was simple and easy, especially when it was *all* in my head. I could just blink it away when I was done. I needed to just let go and let this moment between the three of us happen, just like I'd envisioned. I had rubbed them over their pants and they both seemed to enjoy that, I could handle anything else...right?

Right...? Fuck...I could feel the panic starting to make a home in my chest.

River's hands moved towards the waistband of my pants and Grayson's lips explored the side of my neck, but the confidence I'd had no more than a few minutes ago was waning thin, preparing to snap, ceasing to exist.

I wasn't uncomfortable with them, but I had no idea how overwhelming this was until I was right here sandwiched between them, facing my wildly forward behavior. I wanted their hands. I wanted their mouths. What I didn't want was to feel like I wasn't fully present with them, like I couldn't even enjoy it myself. Everything felt good, but my head could be a real cock block sometimes.

River's hands went to unbutton my pants, when I pulled away from Grayson looking into his dark brown eyes that had so much lust and desire swimming in them. He leaned in for a kiss, but I leaned back, shaking my head a little.

"What's wrong?" Grayson asked, his expression instantly turning into one of concern.

"Woah, what happened?" River's hands stopped touching me and they both backed off, nearly flying to opposite ends of the couch. His voice was full of worry, and I watched as they glanced quickly at each other, then back at me.

I took a deep breath, letting out what I hoped was a playful laugh. I shook my head, faster than I would have liked and awkwardly patted their legs. "Nothing, just a little in my head stuff, that's all. Don't be concerned about it. We can get back to...."

My voice trailed off when I saw River's eyebrows turn inward. He pulled his lips in and dipped his head down to really focus on me. "Most everything you do concerns me, gorgeous. You can be in your head about anything else, but not this."

I shifted my gaze to Grayson, who was leaning back against the arm of the couch. "Do you want to talk about it?"

I huffed. "There is nothing to talk about."

River nodded slowly, clucking his tongue. He turned so that he was facing the TV, reaching for the remote on the coffee table. "Okay, fine. We are ready to talk about whatever made you hesitate and want to stop whenever you are, only then can we consider continuing. For now, you can pick a movie you'd like to watch." He dangled the remote in front of me, the most casual look on his face.

I gaped at him, waiting for Grayson to say something, at least in my defense, but he said nothing. I was still turned on, but I also kind of wanted to laugh at the current situation and what I'd just done to the mood. I felt like I could breathe a little bit more now even though I was frustrated as hell at the predicament I'd currently placed myself in.

I stood up abruptly, gaining their immediate attention. "I'll be back."

"Where are you going?" Grayson called, when I'd made it to the stairs.

"I'll be back, okay." I repeated, taking the stairs two at a time until I was pushing open River's bedroom door and collapsing on his bed.

I would assume most people in my position would think I was an idiot for ruining the moment. I had two guys that thought the world of me and wanted to make me feel good in any and every way possible. The dynamics of a threesome were difficult to wrap my brain around since I'd only ever watched them on the internet or read about them, but the thought of being with River and Grayson had me wanting to explore those dynamics. I didn't understand why I was subconsciously creating this rift in whatever tonight could have been.

Watching a movie and just doing things the way we used to would probably be for the best. They would happily put their needs aside just so that I was comfortable, but I had needs too. And I really, really wanted them. I just...fuck...

A knock sounded at the door and it opened slowly. River poked his head in, a tiny smile peeking out from the corner of his lips. "Hi."

I pulled myself into a sitting position on his bed, grabbing one of his pillows and hugging it to my chest. "Hi."

His eyes darted around his room. "Can I come in?"

"It is your room, ya know."

He chuckled softly. "Mhmm, but if you want your space then I understand. Reading your mind would make this a hell of a lot easier to proceed."

I brought my chin down on top of the pillow. "You said you wouldn't do that, remember?"

He pushed the door open more, raising his hands up. "I know. And I won't. It's just me now, gorgeous, so can you at least tell me what's going on in that head of yours."

I chewed on my bottom lip. "Does he hate me? Do you?"

River's face contorted into utter confusion. He closed the door behind him and rushed over to the bed, sitting beside me. "One, we could never hate you. And two, what the hell are you talking about?"

I groaned, letting my face fall into the soft cotton of the pillow. My voice was muffled when I answered. "You guys were so ready for this. *I* was so ready for this, and I just fucked it up by freaking out." I lifted my head up and looked at him. "I liked it, I didn't want it to stop. My head, it just...I don't really know what I'm doing, River."

River licked his lips, running his fingertips across his forehead as if he was trying to understand what I was saying. He was considering my feelings and what all transpired downstairs. His smile that showed his dimples made an appearance. "There is no *were*; we are *still* very ready for this. Let's just settle that first. You fucked up nothing, Riley, as you can see I'm here trying to understand and Grayson is downstairs trying to figure out how many snacks he can get delivered so that you'll want to be in the same room with us again."

I snorted. "He is not."

River rolled his eyes. "You underestimate our affection for you."

I threw the pillow at him and ran a hand down my face. "I don't want you guys to think you did anything wrong." I turned, bending my knee so I could prop it up on the bed and look at him straight on.

River flicked his eyes over to the door and then back at me. "Don't worry, he knows that now." I knew he had just used his powers to tell Grayson what I'd said through his mind. I opened my mouth, but he cut me off. "He's not up here talking to you, so he deserves to know that you don't hate him, just like we don't hate you."

I hummed. "I just....in theory this was a good idea. I couldn't help but imagine this moment sometimes and well, when it became reality, it was a little too real, I guess. I wasn't lying when I said I wanted you guys to touch me and for you to touch each other. I want you to be happy while also…" I fingered the end of one of my braids. "Making me happy."

River rubbed the back of his neck, looking up at the ceiling. "Believe me, baby, we want to touch you. We want you to lean into that touch so much you are begging us to never stop. We want to make you happy, so let's rewind and tell me what made you unhappy. Or actually let's go back to something you said earlier." He placed his hand gently on my knee. "You said that you didn't really know what you were doing. From where I was sitting, you were doing just fine, but clearly you think otherwise."

I placed my head in my hands, refusing to speak. I squealed when I felt hands gripping my thighs and pulling me across the bed. I peeked between my fingers, noticing River's face much closer than it was before.

"If you want me to leave, I can, gorgeous. Just say the word."

I dropped my hands, sighing. "No, don't."

He reached up and grazed his knuckles along my cheek, remaining quiet.

"I just meant that…I…we…" I took a deep breath and mentally counted to five. "You're the only person I've ever been with. I only know how to be with you in that way and you know how I like things, you know how to make me feel good, you were…my first." I could feel my nerves increasing from being so open. River had made our first time together an experience filled with a million kisses and way too many *that's what she said* jokes that had me laughing and forgetting my nerves all together. He stopped when I needed him to, going slow at first and checking in whenever I'd tense up or have an ounce of hesitation on my face.

River was all smooth talk and no filter, but in that moment, he was sweeter than I'd ever seen him. He was pleasantly surprised that an hour later I was climbing on top of him and begging for him to let me be on top, which he eagerly obliged, watching me guide him where I wanted him. I went at my own pace, while he sat back and let me seek my own pleasure. That was always his goal.

I trusted him. With my heart and with my body.

I wanted to trust Grayson too, but that was proving difficult.

My boyfriend's laughter was soft, and he had this charming way of making any situation comfortably casual. "I was and that's an experience you and I share that is private to just us. I like knowing that I got to understand your body, Riley. You trust me enough to let out sounds you would probably think are embarrassing and you feel confident enough to tell me what you like or don't like when we're having sex so that your orgasms are authentic and utterly perfect."

I nodded. "You and I are really good together. I just...I want that same energy with Grayson."

River kissed my forehead. "I don't think you could recreate what *we* have with Grayson, but I do think you need to have your own thing beyond your friendship. The same sexual comfort you feel with me, you need to feel that with him and maybe...."

I tilted my head to the side. "What?"

"Maybe me being right there next to you isn't allowing you to do what you need to do."

I chewed the inside of my cheek. "What are you talking about?"

He gripped my knee, jostling it from side to side. "If you're up for it, how about you go downstairs and be alone with him. Have a little date or whatever."

A laugh erupted from my throat. "You want me to go and be seduced by your best friend?"

He laughed, running a hand through his hair. "Don't sell yourself short, gorgeous. You can be very seductive when you aren't even trying. You want *us* to touch you, but you only really know what it means to be touched by *me*. You've made it clear you want to have sex with both of us, but you've never really given yourself the chance to view Grayson in that way, so maybe it's time you did." He got off the bed, my eyes following him. "I won't bother you, although I may creep in from time to time." He winked at me. "Only in Grayson's mind though."

I licked my lips, jumping off the bed and pacing. "And if something happens...like things that don't involve clothes?"

River pressed his lips together, hard. His eyes were crinkling at the corners a bit, which told me he was trying to stop himself from laughing. "I would assume you want him to do all those things..."

"Ugh, River it's not funny..." My voice was anything but serious. I nearly wanted to laugh myself due to the fact that this situation was very high on the list of bizarre things to ever happen to someone.

My boyfriend gripped my shoulders, sliding his hands down my arms. "I'm sorry, I'm sorry. If you want to kiss him, then do it. If you want to explore more than that, then go for it. If this is the way that makes you comfortable, full of that sexy confidence I know you have and in return, at a later time, I get to make you come and then watch him also make you come, then by all means please get your ass downstairs."

I lightly shoved him back. "Okay, okay. I'm going to go downstairs, happy?"

River tapped his chin. "Hmm...will going downstairs make *you* happy? Remove me from the equation. Would you be happy to go spend this specific kind of alone time with him if I wasn't your boyfriend and he wasn't my best friend?"

I furrowed my eyebrows considering this. I liked Grayson...a lot. He listened to me. He knew nearly all of my favorite books and laughed at all of my jokes even when they weren't funny. He could actually discuss book to movie adaptations and even have shouting matches with me on why our fan cast was better than the others.

"Yeah...I would."

River squinted at me, giving me one solid nod. He sauntered over to his bed, laying down and placing one of his arms behind his head. "Hmph, I had a feeling. Just take a minute and go downstairs when you're ready, unless you've changed your mind because I can tell him to fuck off and go home."

I hurried over to him and gave him a long kiss that left me a little breathless. "No! Don't do that. I want this.... I want you *and* I want him." I backed away, pushing my braids over my shoulder when I turned around.

"Oh and gorgeous?" River called before I could open the door.

I looked over my shoulder, curious.

He gave me an innocent smile. "Your pleasure turns me on, so if anything does happen, be loud for me, alright?"

Chocolate .PSD
Bar Mock-Up
Good Packaging Collection
157
156

21
GRAYSON

I had changed my sitting position on the couch five times before she came downstairs. Her footsteps were soft and tentative, but the look she gave me when she entered the living room was one of pure determination. It was fucking cute, and I couldn't help but smile at her. Riley looked back at the stairs, took a breath and then walked over to the couch.

"Can I sit down?" she asked, and I gave her a skeptical look but swung my arm out in front of me.

"Of course you can."

I let my arm hang over the back of the couch after I made sure she was comfortable. Riley tucked her legs under her thighs, focusing on me. I cleared my throat when she didn't say anything after a beat. "I've heard twenty questions is a nice way to get to know someone."

She rolled her eyes, and I zeroed in on the gold coloring that highlighted her pupils. "I already know you."

I hummed. "Clearly that's not enough, now is it? We can start with how school is, how you like campus? Or we can talk about how my mom used to like River more than me, but now I think she likes you more than both of us combined. No, wait, we can start with the fact that you keep recommending series to me that aren't complete and making me invested in a story when I have no idea when the next one is coming out."

"Grayson..." She started interlocking her fingers, fidgeting. A tiny laugh escaped her lips which settled the nerves in my stomach for at least a moment.

I chuckled, shaking my head. "I already got the run down from your very thoughtful boyfriend, so don't worry. I know lots of wonderfully normal things about you. You'd be surprised at all the information I've retained over the past year, especially since River never shuts up about you." I pulled one corner of my bottom lip into my mouth, letting my voice get low. "I am sorry if we went a little too fast. Or maybe if it was just me."

She scooted closer to me on the couch. "No, you guys are great. I guess I feel like I know you like my friend or like a guy I've thought about kissing while my boyfriend watches with hearts for eyes. It's a little nerve wracking to jump from friends to...." She motioned towards the couch and everything that almost transpired here, letting her words fall away.

"I suppose it is quite different when it's reality and not fiction."

Her eyes sparkled when I mentioned anything to do with books. Riley pointed her index finger at me. "Hey now, you're the one who isn't a fan of friends to lovers."

I waved her off, noticing her body relaxing. "I'll make the world's biggest exception if that means I get to make you happy."

She leaned against the back of the couch, her cheeks turning a slight reddish color. "One thing you and River have in common, you sure can flirt with the best of them."

"I can flirt less if you'd like."

She bit her lower lip, as she tucked one of her braids behind her ear. "Please don't." She traced her finger along the top of the couch. "You can actually flirt a little more if you want."

I wanted to move closer to her, minimize the small amount of distance there still was between us, but I wanted her to make the move. If she wanted to kiss me or anything else for that matter, I wanted her to ask for it. I fucking wanted her to need it. I sure as shit knew I needed it. It surprised me that she couldn't hear how loud my heart was thudding in my chest.

I'd been raised by a woman that held me to a higher standard, and she taught me to treat women with respect and honor the boundaries they set. Although, if Riley wanted me to disrespect her in all the filthy ways that were tumbling around in my head, I would be honored to oblige her. It was a little thrilling knowing River was upstairs probably listening to music to try to distract himself from seeping into my mind to hear my thoughts and lurking in the back of my mind so he wouldn't be left out.

I laughed softly to myself which caused her to give me a confused look.

"What's so funny?" Riley questioned, shuffling on her knees so that she was even closer to me.

"Oh, nothing. Just thinking."

She giggled, leaning forward and poking me between my ribs. "No fair. You are making that face, so be a good boy and just tell me." She let out one more tiny laugh but stopped when my breath caught.

The only person who called me that was her boyfriend and that was way before they ever started dating. It wasn't something I liked all the time, but coming from her lips, fuck it made my dick hard. I blinked, attempting to get rid of my increasingly dirty thoughts so that I could solely focus on her.

"Riley, I..." I started but she cut me off.

"Is that something you like?" she asked, the curiosity in her voice and the eagerness in her eyes had me wanting to fold far too quickly.

I cleared my throat, feeling the need to back up and give her more space. All I wanted to do was be closer to her, but I didn't want her to think I was being pushy. If she retreated and wanted to sit here and talk to me about her classes or show me the ten million photos I knew she had on her phone of Beau then I would accept that. Her body language told me something different, but I needed her to be completely sure before I put my hands on her and had her begging me to make her come.

I ran my index finger over my top lip, eyeing her. "Sometimes."

She nodded casually. "Does River call you that?"

I raised one of my eyebrows. "He has, yeah."

"Have you ever called him that?"

I laughed, shaking my head. "No, umm, your boyfriend isn't the type that likes that kind of thing. River loves to give praise and your orgasm is enough for him to know he's been the perfect boy. I'm sure you're very aware of that." I moved my foot up so I could lightly hit the side of her leg.

She moved even closer to me, so close that I had my back to the arm of the couch and her knees were touching my thigh. Riley pressed her lips together, the space between her eyebrows working overtime, which told me she was thinking through her next words.

"Would you like me to call you that? Or is that something you like when River does it?"

I swallowed, reaching my hand out and tracing my fingers along the back of her hand. I barely touched her skin, but her breath hitched. "I'll be your good boy anytime you want, *aking sinta*."

She tilted her head to the side and I knew the need to ask me what that meant was on the tip of her tongue. Before she could even open her mouth, I continued. "Considering what I want is very thoughtful of you, but I'm more interested in what *you* want."

She moved her hand so that our fingers could weave together. "I've told you both what I want."

I groaned, not from annoyance, but from how adorable she could be when she was shying away from what I actually meant. "Do you want to keep talking? I can do that all night if it's what you want. Do you want me to kiss you? I could kiss you until you can't feel your lips anymore. Do you want me to touch you? If that's what you want, then where? Do you like slow caresses or do you like it a little rough? I might like to be a good boy at times, but do you like to be a good girl? What. Do. You. Want?"

Her eyes were wide and I almost thought I'd fucked this up, moved too fast. Her mouth had dropped open just a tiny bit and her breathing was even, if not a bit harsh. I could be forward, but damn River's uncontrollably filthy mouth had somehow found its way to me and I'd just spewed all that out as if it was nothing.

Riley squeezed my hand, her fingers tightening. Her voice was a little shaky when she spoke. "I like when River calls me a good girl and I wouldn't mind if you did it too."

I licked my lips. "I'll keep that in mind."

I watched as her hand shot out towards my face, running her fingers through my hair. She cupped the back of my neck, then slid her hand around the side, using her thumb to trace my jaw and then the pad of her finger found my lower lip. Her eyes looked a little far away, like she was contemplating her options. Riley closed her eyes before dropping her hand down to my chest, splaying her fingers out across my shirt.

"I want you to kiss me."

I gently grabbed her wrist, bringing her knuckles to my lips. I placed a soft kiss on them, before smiling at her. "That's what you want?"

She brought her bottom lip into her mouth with her teeth, nodding.

Her body started to lean in more, but she was doing it so slowly, like she wanted me to take the hint and go the extra distance. I would happily oblige her. I quickly grabbed the side of her face and closed the space between us, kissing her. Her mouth opened automatically and a soft moan escaped her throat. I wasn't rough with my kiss, but I let my lips learn hers. I had started this kiss, but I was letting her decide how we moved.

Her tongue licked at my lips and found its way into my mouth.

My tongue danced with hers as if it was the most natural thing in the world. She took hold of my shirt, pulling me into her, like she was pleading for more without having to say a word.

I broke the kiss, sitting up straighter and grabbing her waist. I turned my body so that I was parallel to the back of the couch, taking her with me and helping swing her leg over so she was straddling me. "Comfortable?" I asked, my hands at her waist.

"Very much so." She had a playful tone to her voice as she wiggled on my lap. I held down a groan at the way she rubbed against me. She tossed her braids over her shoulder, her nose ring glinting in the overhead living room light. Riley brought her hands around the back of my neck and shifted her hips forward so that her core grinded against my cock that was quite literally crying in its confinement.

I leaned forward, capturing her lips and continuing to kiss her. Her mouth opened for me more and she pressed her chest against mine harder. She played with my hair and grazed her teeth against my bottom lip. Her body moved against me in a rhythm that I assumed felt good to her because little whimpers and moans came from her mouth as we kissed.

I pulled back a bit, running my nose along hers. "Does that feel good? Grinding that perfect body against me."

She looked down at what she was doing, stopping for a moment. It was as if she suddenly realized how into this she was, how turned on she had to be. "Fuck, I'm sorry."

My brows furrowed, holding her in place when she tried to jump off me. "Sorry? Whatever the fuck for? If you don't like what you're doing, then we can try something else." I grabbed the side of her face, bringing her down to kiss me. "I can be good and just let you get yourself off if that's what you want. I'll even beg you to do it."

She giggled, the tension in her shoulders simmering. "It did feel good."

"I want to do what you like. I'll be a good boy and let you grind on my cock, if you'll be a good girl and let me watch you come," I whispered, letting my fingers fiddle with the hem of her shirt.

She sucked in a breath, her eyes dilating and her thighs tensed. Riley bent down to kiss me, her hips rotating. She went harder against my lap, making sure her covered pussy collided with my cock. Dry humping was something I hadn't done in a long time, but I'd forgotten how intense it felt. It was frustrating since there was a layer of clothing in the way, but that layer was what made it hot.

Riley grabbed one of my hands, never breaking our kiss and brought it to her chest. She placed my hand over one of her breasts, as if she was telling me that this was what she liked, this would get her off. I palmed her breast, using my other hand to help guide her and keep her rhythm. I removed my lips from hers so that I could trail my kiss down her neck. She held onto my shoulders tightly as she continued to chase her orgasm.

My mouth found her ear. "Keep going, keep doing what feels good."

"Fuck...fuck..." Her words came out a little choked and breathless. I kneaded her breast in my hand, wanting to fuck up against her, but this moment was hers. She closed her eyes, rubbing her core against me hard and in short motions as her body shuddered. Her shoulders started to slump and she sighed, tucking her face into my neck.

Her lips found my pulse point and the kiss she placed there was like a tiny fire.

I rubbed her back, feeling her heart thudding against my own chest when she fell against me. "You did so fucking good. What else do you like?"

She choked out a laugh, bringing her body away from me. "I like a lot of things, Grayson."

I hummed, placing my index finger in the middle of her chest and sliding it down her body. *"Kaya pa kitang dalhin sa langit gamit ang dila ko. Yun ba ang gusto mo?"*

Her eyes searched my face. I knew she didn't understand, but she was starting to play with the hem of my shirt, letting her fingers find their way under and touch my skin. She was smart enough to know that I would only say good things to her.

I watched as her hands explored and her mind worked. "I asked if you wanted my tongue on you, to make you feel good."

Her hips started to move against me again and she licked her lips. "Yes, please."

"Good because I've been dying to taste that pussy." I hooked my arm around her and swiftly moved her onto the couch, letting her get comfortable. I got down on the ground, flicking my eyes up at her when my fingers found the buttons of her pants. I undid them one by one and yanked them off her legs. I gripped her thighs, pulling her forward so that her pussy was closer to me.

I could feel her body shiver, but the look in her eyes told me it wasn't from nerves, but from sheer excitement. She tilted her head up and over to the stairs. My hand hovered near where I was about to move her panties over. "We can stop if you want."

"Don't stop. I like knowing he's up there. I also like it being just you and me." She inhaled a deep breath, bringing her hand to her panties and moving them over so I could take in her glistening cunt.

"Spread your legs wider for me."

She did as she was told, making sure her panties stayed in place. I brought my hand to her pussy, using my fingers to open her up. "This pussy is so pretty. I bet it's even prettier after it's been taken care of." I pressed my index finger inside of her, watching her toes curl. "Do you like more fingers, *aking sinta*?"

She blew out a shaky breath. "Y- yes."

I curled my finger, pumping it inside of her. I added another, being slow and deliberate. I made sure to pay attention to her every move, each time she moaned over what I was doing. I brought my face toward her center, inhaling the scent of her arousal and all I wanted to do was make her scream so loud, River's neighbors would be concerned.

I flicked my tongue across her clit and she jolted.

"Oh fuck," she cried out, her fingernails clawing at the couch cushions.

I gave her a tentative lick again, over and over, teasing her. She reached down, gripping my hair and tried to get me to use my entire mouth. "Say what you want, Riley and I'll give it to you. I'm your good boy, remember?"

She pressed her lips together. "Put your mouth on me, please. I want you to make me come."

I moved my fingers inside of her a little faster. "You want me to eat your pretty pussy so that you soak this couch and come so loud that your boyfriend can come down here and tell you what a good girl you've been?" My fingers kept moving and I shot my tongue out, licking her completely, circling her clit. My shadows crept out, moving up her legs and caressing her skin.

Her mouth dropped open and she spread her legs wider. "Yes, I want that, please. I want your tongue."

I smirked up at her, finally starting to devour her. I took her clit into my mouth, sucking it and fucking her with my fingers. I heard the sounds of how wet she was each time I pumped into her, her arousal coating the inside of her thighs. She was watching me, her eyes heavy and hooded. She bit down on her bottom lip so hard that it was starting to lose its color.

I willed my shadows to move up her body and under her shirt so they could tease her breasts and play with her nipples. They wrapped around her legs, keeping them open for me. She whimpered as my powers and I worked in tandem to get her off. She tasted like a fucking dream and she was coating my mouth and chin in how much she was enjoying this. My shadows moved further up, over her neck and her eyes rolled back.

"A-another finger..." she coaxed, stuttering a bit.

I stretched her with another one of my fingers and her body melted into the couch. Her tight pussy looked so fucking perfect filled up and I could have watched my fingers work her over for hours if I wasn't needy to have her clit in my mouth.

Her thigh muscles tensed and her breaths were coming out shallow. I pulled my mouth away from her dripping pussy. "Come for me, come on my face." I brought my mouth back to her, her clit my main focus. My fingers drove into her until she let out a loud cry, holding onto my hair so tight, my scalp was burning.

I pressed a kiss to her pussy and then to both her inner thighs. I wiped a hand down my mouth, moving up her body and grabbing her face. "You okay?"

Her brown eyes looked a little dazed, but she nodded. "Okay doesn't really cover it."

I smiled at her before letting my lips graze hers. She opened her mouth for a full kiss, tugging at my shirt. Her kiss was desperate and wanting, I could feel that she wasn't fully prepared to come down from her orgasm just yet.

Riley nuzzled her nose against mine. I groaned when her hand slid down the front of my pants, gripping my hardened cock.

I tapped her nose ring. "What are you doing, *aking sinta*?"

She hummed, rubbing me now. "I think..." She stopped, giving a small shake of her head. "No, I don't *think*. I know." She had the most determined yet lust-filled eyes I'd ever seen.

"You know what?"

"I *know* I want you to tell River to get down here."

Chocolate PSD
Hair Mock-Up
Good Packaging Collection
157
156

22
RILEY

Grayson kissed up my neck, biting at my earlobe. "I made that pussy needy, hmm?"

I gave him a playful smile when he pulled back to look at me. He flicked his eyes towards the stairs then back at me. His lips found mine and his hand slid between my legs, rubbing two of his fingers over my clit. Small sounds escaped my mouth as I moved with his hand, tasting myself on him as I kissed him back.

I heard footsteps descending the stairs, breaking my kiss with Grayson to see River strolling into the living room. His face was glowing with a grin that would have put the Cheshire Cat to shame. His green eyes moved from both our faces to where Grayson still had his hand between my legs. He licked his lips, crossing his arms over his chest.

"Looks like you two had fun." He cocked his head to the side.

I felt my cheeks getting hot.

He ran a hand through his hair, his shirt lifting up so I could see the tattoos that hid beneath. "You told him to tell me to come down here?" River stepped further into the room, leaning his body against the couch.

I started to sit up causing Grayson to move his hand. I let my legs close, nodding up at River.

"And why is that, gorgeous?"

I narrowed my eyes at him. "You know why." I could feel myself wanting to rub my thighs together, get some kind of friction going because with both of them in the room....it was making me antsy.

River looked up at the ceiling, chuckling. "Ah, but I love to hear you say it. I can see how much you want it, so just open that mouth and *tell me*." His eyes bore into mine and fuck, if his voice didn't go down an octave. I swore I felt Grayson stiffen next to me as if River had him feeling the same way.

"I *know* I want you both."

River's eyes sparkled with this kind of sexy pride that had my confidence overflowing. He walked over so that he could lean over me, cupping my chin and placing his thumb at my bottom lip. "Such a good girl. You sounded so fucking perfect when he made you come. I almost started stroking my cock because of it." He kissed me and I placed my hand on the front of his pants, finding the shape of him and rubbing.

River ripped his mouth away from me and continued to let me touch him, while he reached his hand out and started to mirror my actions, but to Grayson. I looked over at them, wetness pooling between my legs as I stared at my boyfriend stroking his best friend's cock over his pants. "You made her come like such a good boy. I should have told her all the things that tongue could do. You've made her all greedy now."

Grayson groaned, flexing his hips.

River stepped back, getting onto his knees before me. "Tonight, you're ours, gorgeous."

I looked over at Grayson who was already moving his fingers

along my arm and up my shoulder. "What you said early...about being as gentle as I want..."

Grayson leaned in to kiss my neck. "I meant it..." he started, but I cut him off.

"Don't. I don't want fucking gentle." I was desperate right now. They were great separately, fulfilling what I wanted. Right now, I wanted what they had to offer together. I wasn't afraid to be overwhelmed anymore. I knew that feeling was something I could harness and then tell them what to do so that it could be eased and morphed into something that pleased all of us.

Grayson ripped his mouth away from my throat, stretching his hand out and palming my breast. He grasped the hem of my shirt and tugged it over my head, putting my lacey black bra on display for both of them. River was between my legs, kissing up my thighs, licking at my skin. He was dangerously close to where I wanted his mouth and I was squirming.

"I liked watching you, *aking sinta,*" Grayson said, his voice a little huskier than usual. "You take direction so well. Did you put on a little show for me that night when he took you from behind, when you were fucking his cock?" He dipped his hand into my bra and pinched my nipple, rolling it between his fingers.

River pushed my legs up, so that my heels were on the edge of the couch. My panties had gone back to cover my pussy, so he moved them over, blowing against my clit. "I think he asked you a question, gorgeous."

River blew air again, making me curl my toes and nearly lose my mind. Grayson pinched my other nipple causing me to cry out. It felt good, but far more stimulation than I had ever experienced. "Did you hope I was stroking my dick when you brought your fucking ass back against his cock? Every time that piercing hit just the right spot and made that pussy feel good. I know what that piercing feels like, Riley, no wonder you came so hard."

"Yes, fuck, yes, yes." My breath caught in my throat when River licked my clit, flicking his tongue over the sensitive bundle. His eyes were watching us while Grayson played with my nipples and sucked at my neck. I tried to undo his pants, hoping to get the right angle so that I could dip my hand inside and stroke his cock.

"Fuck, don't stop," I moaned; River's tongue pressed inside of me, coming back out to stroke my clit again.

River chuckled against me, pulling back and sliding one of his fingers through my wet slit. "I think she wants your cock, Grayson."

Grayson looked down at my hand, gaining a sigh of relief from me when he unzipped his pants and pulled them down. He kicked them off, his cock hard and laying against his stomach. It made my mouth water just looking at it. I grabbed it, running my thumb along the head and then stroked back down to the base. His hips moved, fucking into my grip.

Two fingers pushed inside of me, curling upward with each thrust. River's tongue focused back on my clit again. Grayson unclipped my bra, throwing the material onto the floor. He grabbed my throat, tilted my head back, and kissed me. Every moan that River pulled out of me went straight into Grayson's mouth, which he took with no hesitation.

River didn't let up and continued fucking me with his fingers until I had to shut my eyes when my orgasm barreled on.

"That's it, fuck that was beautiful," Grayson said at my cheek, looking down at River who was sitting back on his heels. They stared at each other as if they were having some kind of silent communication.

River nodded, getting up from the floor to start unbuttoning his pants. "I think that's an excellent idea."

I was panting and sweaty, clearly having missed whatever they were alluding to. "What are you talking about?"

My boyfriend threw his pants on the armchair, his pierced cock on full display. He leaned down to pick me up from the couch, holding me with one arm tucked under my ass as if I weighed nothing. Grayson removed his shirt, taking my place on the couch, gripping his cock while he spread his legs.

River slid me down his body, letting me feel the metal of his piercing against my skin and set me on my feet. "Turn around, get on your knees, then bend over." My vision was just settling back into place after my orgasm, but I did what he said. Grayson's cock was in my line of sight and I locked my eyes with his.

"You look so fucking sexy like this," Grayson complimented, moving his hand over his shaft slowly. "You'll look even better when your mouth is on my cock."

River tugged my panties down my legs, sliding the head of his cock over my entrance, teasing. "Show him how well you use that mouth, gorgeous. I want to hear those pretty gagging sounds." He removed his shirt, shifting me forward, while Grayson tilted his cock towards me. I reached up to grab it, but my hand was snatched up by one of his shadows.

"No hands, just your mouth," he explained, as his shadow brought my hand behind my back. Another black rope extended from him and snatched up my other arm, placing it parallel to the other. He held them in place, leaving me with only the use of my mouth.

River pushed inside of me and a moan escaped my throat, but that was quickly snuffed out when Grayson took my head and guided it down to his cock. I bobbed up and down, trying to use my tongue to get as much of his taste in my mouth as I could. River's hands held onto my waist as he fucked me, pushing me so that each time he thrusted in, the more of Grayson's cock I took.

"Does being with us make you so wet? You're fucking dripping right now." River collected my braids in his hand, pounding into me harder. Grayson gripped my face and thrusted his hips up, fucking my mouth. He was gentle enough to where he wasn't making me choke, but he was going hard enough for me to be so close to coming again after only a few minutes.

I felt River's dark chuckle vibrate through my entire body. "Tell me how much you like it, baby."

I coughed when Grayson let up and he leaned in, running his thumb over my bottom lip. "I like it."

River's thrusts were slower now, that achingly slow movement that had me feeling everything. It always prolonged my climax, but it continuously had me shaking and nearly begging him to make me come. He hovered over me, bringing his hand around to cup my throat. His mouth was at my ear when he said, "do you want him to fuck you?"

Grayson looked over my head at his best friend, nodding at something he'd likely been told in his mind and replaced River's grip on my throat, while my boyfriend placed his fingers at my clit. He kept a hold on my hair, while I moaned at the feeling of his fingers strumming against me.

I waited to catch my breath before replying, "I really want *you* to fuck him."

They both laughed.

"I will...next time. This time is all about you, gorgeous."

Grayson rubbed his nose against mine. "We want to use that pussy until you're sated and screaming."

I didn't know if it was the words or the way River was working my clit, but I started to come and it felt like it was never ending. Grayson released me from his shadowy hold, so I could stretch out my arms. My legs shook when it was over and River pulled out, wrapping his arms around me and bringing me up with him. Grayson held his erection as he got up, helping River move me onto the couch. He kept me facing forward, letting my hands and head hang off the back, while my knees were firmly planted on the cushions.

"Keep your ass out just like that. Let him see that pretty pussy." River went over to the back of the couch and Grayson stayed on the other side. My boyfriend crooked his finger, beckoning for his best friend to come closer. Grayson placed his knee on the couch and River gripped his chin. "Be a good boy and please her. Make her come." I saw Grayson lick his lips and nod. River leaned in and kissed him, their mouths moved in this harmonious way that had me whimpering.

It was like I was invading a private moment. The energy in the room was so charged, but this was a different kind of electric spark and I could have watched it for hours. I wanted to be shocked by it and feel its effects for the rest of my life. River bit Grayson's bottom lip, letting go and lightly slapping his face.

"I have fucked girls before, I know how to treat a pussy," Grayson got behind me, kneading his palms into my ass.

River used his cock to trace my lips. I stuck my tongue out and licked over the silver balls on the underside of his shaft. "Yeah, but this pussy is special." He looked down at me in adoration.

That twinkle in his eye was back, and this was probably the only time I would have wanted him to read my mind, but he'd conditioned himself for over a year not to do it to me, so I wasn't about to ruin that. My mouth flew open when Grayson inched inside, feeding his cock into me, while maintaining a hold on my hip.

"Your pussy takes my cock like it was made for it." He rolled his hips, making my moans grow deeper and more needy. River lifted my chin, using his thumb to pull at my bottom lip and open my mouth. I flattened my tongue and tasted the metal, making sounds against his shaft as he held the back of my head.

Grayson started moving faster, using his shadows to claim my wrists and hold them against the back of the couch. River gathered my hair up and helped me move back and forth on his cock. "Is she going to make you come already?"

"Fuck, she's so tight." Grayson's pelvis slapped against my skin and my cries were muffled by River's cock. I wanted to scream from how good it felt.

River pulled out of my mouth, bending down so we were face to face. "Do you want him to come inside of you? Fill up that greedy little cunt?"

My body vibrated with Grayson's thrusts so I had to work to get my words out. "Yes, please. I want that so fucking much."

"Then tell him that."

I looked over my shoulder, pleading with my eyes. "*Please*, come inside of me."

"Whatever you want, *aking sinta*." He went harder and River shoved his cock back in my mouth. It only took a few more thrusts before my whole body felt like it was shaking. River held my head in place while he fucked my mouth and Grayson slammed into me a few more times before he came.

River followed shortly after, making sure I swallowed before stroking my cheek. "You did so well. Good *fucking* girl."

Grayson kissed down my back, pulling out slowly. He bent down and licked at my overly sensitive pussy. My legs tensed at the sensation, and I shivered. River ran a hand through his hair, leaning down to kiss me. I turned my head, waiting for Grayson to kiss me as well and when he did just that I'd never been happier. Grayson released my wrists from his shadows, massaging them.

"You know what it's time for?" River said, reaching for me.

"What?" I asked, confused. My body was tired, and I was a sweaty mess.

"A bath," River answered, picking me up and carrying me bridal style. Grayson clapped his hands together adding, "and then we'll feed you."

Chocolate .PSD
Bar Mock-UP
Food   Packaging   Collection
157
156

23
ASHER

I sat at the bar, instantly regretting telling myself that one more drink wasn't necessary. I wasn't a lightweight, but I also didn't need Tommy, the bartender, to make the next drink stronger than the last and I would be fucked.

"You are allowed to have fun, you know that right?" Graham, a friend I'd gone to UC Berkeley with said, downing the last of his drink.

"I am well aware."

"You've ignored the last three women that have looked in your direction."

I rolled my eyes. "I told you that's not why I came out. I have no papers to grade and all my plans for the next two weeks of classes are set. It's more of a celebratory drink."

He tipped his empty glass towards me. "Okay, I suppose you're right. From one professor to another, that is something to drink towards."

I hummed, looking up at the TV where something referencing the NFL was on. Tommy came over and I shooed him away before he could offer me another drink. Graham leaned back in his chair. "How's that brother of yours?"

"He's good. Still graduating on time and still annoying the fuck out of me."

"And his girlfriend? Boyfriend? I don't want to get it wrong."

"Riley's his girlfriend. Still together and I guess they're fine. I rarely ask the details of his relationships, besides if they're legal and not a completely horrible influence." As much as I wanted to just let it be and treat her like an everyday student, her face wouldn't leave my fucking mind.

I heard my empty glass whine from me holding it too tight, so I let it clang against the wood of the bar.

"Is she pretty?"

"How would I know that?"

"I'm sure you've looked at her once or twice, Asher."

"She's just fine. It doesn't matter if she's pretty. I don't have to date her."

Graham snorted. "You should try to date someone. I love my time with you, but you know interaction with a female could do wonders. Even if it's not for mutual sexual pleasure, but then again, you could also use that too."

I groaned, jumping off my stool and heading for the bathroom.

I was alone with the porcelain sinks and wood interior. The low music could be heard from outside the door, but I could at least think straight. I pressed my hands to the sink bowl, looking at myself in the mirror.

I had no interest in talking about my brother tonight and especially not his girlfriend. Her work in my class had been superior, which had me second guessing that school wasn't a priority for her. She had to be an excellent multitasker because she was up to something, but I was on the fence about giving a flying fuck about what it was...unless it involved my brother.

I hated insufferable students who argued and talked back. She didn't really raise her voice, but she did have a sass to her that I found myself wanting to entertain. We'd hardly spoken since she happened to find her way to my office, but that didn't mean she didn't find ways to antagonize me, even when she didn't know it.

The genuine laugh she let out on occasion when her and her friend left my class. The way she threw her braids over her shoulder to expose the column of her neck. The way she bit her fucking lip.

I ran a hand over my face, walking backwards and into one of the stalls. I pressed my back against the wall. I thought about that mouth of hers and all the things I could do to it. I was professional in class, so calling me Asher just wasn't right, but when she called me *sir*...when she said it in that way that told me she was trying to get under my skin, *fuck* it made my dick hard.

I imagined what it would sound like when she was whimpering and doing as she was told. I wondered how she would look saying it on her knees. My hand was starting to reach for my zipper, but I stopped. She was River's girlfriend and this was a line I wouldn't cross. My brother and I had shared girls before, but none of them were ones he or I dated long term, if we ever really dated them at all.

Something like this would be a delicate matter and would need to be spoken about, but...I didn't want that. I had to stop picturing her bent over my desk and just keep her upright and several feet away from me across the room.

My cock was screaming at me to let it out, think about all the filthy things I wanted to do to her so I could wrap it in my fist and relieve the ache, but that couldn't happen. I wanted another drink tonight, but I said no to that. I'll say no to this too.

My phone buzzed and I dug into my back pocket pulling it out. My dad was calling, but I hit ignore. He was going to ask me if I'd talked to River about the meeting. *'You're his big brother, Asher, let him know it's the best thing for him.'* I wasn't in the mood for his shit tonight.

Speaking of fathers.... I let my mind wander back to Riley, but for a more honorable reason. Her dad died a few months before she transferred and now, she was at the university. She looked like she was searching for something outside of the academic building and I still highly doubted she was coming to see me when we ran into her.

They may be small things, it could be small pieces to a bigger puzzle. I may have been correct about her being a good multitasker because as much of a good student as she may be, I think she might be masquerading as an amateur detective.

Chocolate .PSD
Bar Mock-Up
Food Packaging Collection
157
156

24
RILEY

I snuggled with River in the backseat as Grayson drove me home to San Jose. After what happened last night, I honestly didn't want to be away from either of them, but Grayson had told his parents he would visit, and he was dragging River along with him. My mom had been overly excited when I informed her that I was still coming and I could hear Beau in the background panting as if he'd just run a marathon.

We'd spent the rest of the night cuddled on the couch, watching my favorite movies while they each fed me tiny pretzels. It was like all the big sexual energy had dissipated and we were back to how we used to be. We discussed one thing in particular though.

"So how does this work exactly?" I asked, pulling my knees in while the guys settled on either side of me on the couch.

"How does what work, gorgeous?" River dumped the pretzels in a large bowl.

"So, are we not allowed to just have sex...you and me?" I looked over at him, chewing on my lip.

River pushed his bottom lip out in thought. "Interesting. What do you think?" He gestured towards Grayson, who scratched his chin.

"What do you want, Riley?" Grayson tilted his head towards me.

"No, this is about all of us. I can't make all the decisions."

River scrunched up one side of his mouth. "Well, no, but we are fine if you'd like to. We are both here for you. I would love to fuck you with him around, but I would also really like to fuck you with no one else but us."

Grayson nodded. "My thoughts exactly."

I shook my head, giggling. "You guys are something else." I grabbed a few pretzels. "So, we're all fine to have sex in pairs and also very eager to have sex all together."

"Now you're getting it." River playfully knocked his knuckles against my jaw.

"That goes for you two as well. Although, I'd really like to be a part of it the first time you do it again, if that's okay." I smiled at both of them through a mouth full of salty snacks.

River raised his eyebrows. "Alright, alright. I think you just really want to see me make Grayson come so hard he'll be afraid I've emptied him out."

Grayson choked on his beer he'd just taken a drink from. "Let's not exaggerate."

River winked at him. "We'll see."

MY MOM THREW OPEN THE FRONT DOOR WHEN WE PULLED UP. I GOT OUT, followed by River and Grayson, who each gave my mom a hug that could have cracked her back.

"Are you guys staying for a little while?" my mom asked, nodding towards the house.

The door was wide open and I could see Beau sitting right at the threshold, mouth open and tongue out, waiting for me to come inside.

"Unfortunately, we have a slight drive to Grayson's parents," River said, patting his best friend on the back.

"We'll be back to pick her up though," Grayson offered.

I raised my eyes to the sky. "I can take the train…"

"No." Both boys were unanimous on that front.

My mom gave each of them another hug. "Alright, well be safe and make sure to let her know when you get there, so I know you made it."

River handed me my bag, kissing my forehead. Grayson swiftly kissed my cheek and a comfortable sigh left my lips.

My mom hustled me inside when they drove off and Beau nearly knocked me over the minute I stepped inside. I bent down to his level and scratched him all over, rolling on the floor with him and gaining all the Beau kisses I was overdue for.

"Are you hungry?"

"I'm not super hungry. I could snack though."

My mom laughed walking into the kitchen. I followed behind her and snagged one of the four bags of my favorite strawberry gummies off the counter. I ripped open the bag, tossing two in my mouth.

"I have some more for you to take back," My mom opened up one of the cabinets, revealing two six count boxes of them.

"Aw, you do love me."

My mom smirked, waiting for Beau to trot by her legs before she came over to me. She placed her hands on my cheeks. "I'm so happy you're home."

"Me too." I gave her a smile that hopefully conveyed all of my feelings.

"How are classes? Maintaining your grades? New friends?"

I hopped up on the counter. "Mom, I answer all these questions when we talk generally. School is good. My grades are perfect as usual and my roommate is great. I lucked out." I left out how one of my classes in particular had the most frustrating professor.

"Okay, well how are you, then?"

I sighed, popping another piece of candy in my mouth. "Mom…"

"I'm serious, Riley. I know you don't want to talk about it, believe me I understand, but you are at that school, and you've actively avoided talking about your dad. I would think that I'm the one person that you *could* talk about it with." Her voice was steady and concerned. She sounded worried but not enough to ask me to transfer to a different school.

I put my candy down, placing my hands on my knees. "You are, Mom. I just don't want to bring anything up while I'm not here and what happens if you break down and all I can do is be on the phone and do nothing."

She sighed, her shoulders dropping. "Honey, you are my number one priority. I love that you worry about me, but your job is to get through school and have fun. My job is to worry twenty-four seven about you. You want to talk to me about your dad and I start to cry? Okay, then let me cry and feel things. Stay on the phone with me until I stop."

I hadn't even been in this house for five minutes and I already wanted to fucking cry. I had only let myself miss my dad in small moments since I'd been at Mystic Riegan. "I get it, I get it." I twisted my fingers together, avoiding her eyes. "I miss him."

She rubbed my leg, squeezing in a way that only she could, making me feel like I could give so much weight to her and she wouldn't falter. "I miss him too. He would be proud of you for doing so well though. You've always done so well, so I'm not surprised."

A tear escaped from the corner of her eye and she wiped it away, shaking her head and then her entire body. She blew out a breath. "Enough of that for now. I want to make your first night stress free, so I'm making dinner tonight and you can tell me about how you are not spending all your time with River." She side-eyed me playfully. My dad had tried to be very parental when it came to River, but it was an ill-fated plan because River had a way to get what he wanted in the sincerest way possible. There was one conversation that always made me laugh, but it stuck with me.

"So, you're going to be a senior at Mystic Riegan?" My dad asked my boyfriend.

River nodded, stabbing at the food my mom made especially for tonight. This was the first dinner we'd all had since River and I had started dating and I wasn't the least bit hungry. "Yup, nearly perfect grade point average if that helps with your assessment of me."

I kicked him under the table. I knew he didn't mean it in a rude way but my anxiety was already through the roof.

My dad chuckled. "It does, especially since my daughter has a literal perfect grade point average. Always has."

My food was looking more and more unappetizing. "Dad, stop. Yes, I am very smart, but so is River. Can we talk about something else?"

"Eh, I'm smart, but not quite like you," River complimented.

My mom smiled down at her food, keeping her thoughts to herself.

"My daughter already likes you, kid. You don't need to kiss up to her."

I choked on air, gaping at my dad.

He put a forkful of food in his mouth, not paying my expression any mind. "He should be saying lots of nice things to me and making me feel like the most special person in the room." He pointed his fork at River, a little smile on his face.

River twisted his mouth to the side, considering his next words. "Mr. Monroe, I really like your shirt, I think it suits you well. Have you been working out? Because you look great. Mrs. Monroe is a very lucky lady."

I placed my elbows on the table, putting my head in my hands. My mom barked out a laugh. "No, he has not been working out."

My dad picked up a dinner roll and threw it at her. "That's because I get my workout from you, baby."

I watched my parents flirt right in front of me and I made a gagging sound. River just watched as if this was the best thing he'd ever seen and a gleam of joy was in his eyes. My parents stopped laughing and my dad picked his fork back up. "Well, my door at the university is always open if you need it."

River gave him a smile and nodded in thanks.

"So, how did you guys meet?" River asked my parents, moving his fork between them.

My parents looked at each other for a long time and they both sighed. My mom cleared her throat, wiping her mouth with her napkin. "That is a very wild love story."

"I'm sure I could handle it," River assured her, taking his last bite and throwing his napkin on his plate. "I can be a softie when it comes to your daughter, but I promise I'm a tough guy."

I giggled. "A softie indeed." I poked his stomach, only to be met with his abs.

My dad shook his head. "Alright, dishes in the sink and then we'll move to the living room to tell you this very boring but wild love story that River promises not to fall asleep to."

River laughed. "I'm wide awake and ready to learn about the art of wooing a woman." He saluted my dad, picking up his plate and going to the kitchen.

My dad grabbed my plate from my hand, pulling me into his side. "He's good to you?"

I nodded, butterflies fluttering in my stomach anytime River crossed my mind.

My dad kissed the side of my head. "Good. That's good."

I SHOOK MY HEAD, COMING BACK INTO THE PRESENT AND TRYING TO remember what my mom was saying. Ah, right, she thought I was spending all my time with my boyfriend.

"I am not," I answered, knowing my response was less than believable.

I tried not to at least. Now that his new dynamic with Grayson was on the table, I had a feeling it would be much harder not to, especially with how they worked so well as a *team*. Fuck, I had to get my mind back to mom appropriate topics. Getting railed by my boyfriend and his best friend less than twenty-four hours ago was not something I wanted to subconsciously bring up.

I COULD SMELL THE FOOD FROM UPSTAIRS WHILE I LOUNGED ON MY BED. Beau had his head resting on my pillow, his eyes closed as he snoozed. His body was as close to me as possible, radiating heat I didn't think was possible, but I didn't mind.

I stared up at the ceiling, putting everything I knew into perspective. My dad didn't just fall out his window, he was pushed. He was pushed by someone with the powers to do so...and then some. There had to be something in his office that was left behind, like the glass piece I'd found outside. I started to think about the missing witches Corrin had mentioned and how that all fit in. From the outside, I would assume they were two completely different issues, but I'd read way too many books to think anything was simply just a coincidence. The real question was how the hell were they connected.

My phone vibrated causing Beau to jerk up, stunned out of his sleep. I laughed, turning my phone over.

CORRIN

My determination is my best attribute because I was able to extract some other powers from the glass piece. Yes, I might have burned myself again, but never fear, I am fine.

That doesn't make me feel better.

CORRIN

Do you want to know what I found or not?

Of course I do.

CORRIN

So, there's a ton of elemental magic in there, some green witch skills, slight healing. It's like little bits of everything. Magic has a shape and form when you break it down on a molecular level and some of these are misshapen. Whoever's magic this is, they've been harboring all these skills for a while, farming them.

Can anyone actually have multiple powers?

CORRIN

Yes and no. You can gain both your parent's skills if you are born from two magic wielders. Or some witches can learn another skill if they are really that determined, but it doesn't happen often. It's usually easier when it's a skill that molds well with the one you've already been born with. I couldn't just decide to try out Ike's metal magic on a whim.

I considered River's powers and knew that most people heard him say telepathy and put him in the only mind reading category. He had developed his magic into so much more than that, but he didn't like to use it all the time.

Another text came through.

CORRIN

Multiple powers of this magnitude isn't normal unless you're siphoning it.

Like stealing it?

CORRIN

Exactly.

Let me add that the only time that is
possible is during one of the witches' moon
gatherings. You would have to know exactly
what you're doing to take powers and not
have anyone really notice. Telekinesis and
one of the elements was an original power
from them, something they were born with,
but that's all. They are clearly a powerful
enough witch to siphon for however long
they've been doing it.

> Witches' moon gatherings? Like what your
> coven does?

She sent me a thumbs up.

CORRIN

I'm not saying it's my coven specifically, but
the witches that are missing are ours, so it
just makes sense to assume.

> How would my dad fit into any of this?

CORRIN

Ike thinks that he found out what they were
doing, accused them of harming students
and how he would report it. People do a lot
of things when they get backed into a
corner.

> Ah, well that's something new. Now you're
> leaning towards it being a witch.

CORRIN

I don't love saying it, but yes. I'm rotting at
home this weekend, so I'll see what else I
can dig up, maybe get some coven
members to talk. The moon gatherings are
only twice a year so I don't even know if they
will remember if they felt anything off during
those times. I could ask the interim coven
leader, but that bitch is literally no help for a
regular problem.

Interim coven leader? Is that a thing?

CORRIN

It's a whole thing. Yes, I know this very odd fact is not lost on me. We got an interim coven leader a short time after your dad died…now that I think about it…

Okay, let me get Ike and go into a deep dive! Report back soon.

I blinked, trying to find a place to add this new information in my mind. I leaned over my bed and grabbed my backpack. I rifled through and found the police report again, my eyes going straight to River's dad.

He wasn't a witch, but something in my gut told me he had a part in this, even if it wasn't actually hurting my dad. If nothing else, he failed to tell the police *everything* and was covering up for someone, maybe this person Corrin was talking about. What was he even doing there that time of night?

He may have said all those nice things about my dad at that assembly, but I could guarantee he didn't mean any of it. I tried to imagine him offering me condolences if things were different and River actually enjoying his company and wanting me to meet him. His name started to blur as I looked at it too hard.

I felt a wet tongue slide across my cheek and the smell of dog breath entering my nostrils. Beau maneuvered himself into my lap, making me move my hands and allowing him to cuddle into me. He let out a heavy sigh but remained still.

I massaged his neck, digging my fingers into his scruff. I leaned down and kissed the side of his face, feeling my anxiety decreasing. "Thanks, buddy."

Chocolate PSD
Bar Mock-Up
Food Packaging Collection
157
156

25
RIVER

I sat on Grayson's bed, leaning back on my hands. I'd left him downstairs to talk to his parents, walking out awkwardly when they gave me a look that said they wanted to talk to their son alone. He was aware that this was going to happen, but as someone who grew up with less than wonderful parents, seeing his mom and dad actually act accordingly was a little mind blowing. Grayson's parents treated me like I was their son the moment I walked into their home and devoured every piece of food they put in front of me.

I'd been sitting up here for nearly an hour with the door closed, but I was nosey and wanted to know what was going on. Grayson had told me vaguely about his scholarship issues, but it was all fixed now, so one would assume: case closed. He worked hard to get into Mystic Riegan and have as little debt as he could when he graduated. Besides Asher, I think I learned a lot of my discipline from Grayson and his family. Well... most of it. I wasn't a saint.

I hadn't heard *that* much of the conversation, but I'd let my powers wander and filtered through enough thoughts to get the gist. Their talk went back and forth between Tagalog and English so keeping up was a feat, but I'd learned various words and paid attention during conversations to be able to understand some things.

Most of what they'd said revolved around wanting him to be okay and that if anything was wrong to come to them. That this was his senior year and this kind of thing made them nervous. Before I heard him come up the stairs, he had assured them that he had handled it. Grayson had the best voice for reassurance, the inflection would have you thinking there was never a problem at all.

That and his charisma was probably why I was attracted to him so fucking much.

He gave me a tight-lipped smile, closing his door.

"How was that?" I asked, moving over to make room for him on his bed.

He scoffed. "Oh, like you weren't trying to read our minds."

I held my hands up. "For the record, I have not mastered simultaneous mind reading and translating so well, so I only heard a few things when I could."

He bumped my shoulder, laughing. "It's fine. You know how they are."

"They care. Can't blame them."

He raised an eyebrow at me. "Mhmm, well, mom is getting ready to start making food. I asked her what it was and she said it doesn't matter because River will eat it anyway."

I barked out a laugh. "She's not wrong and I adore her for that. Also the fact that she packs up leftovers for me in that Tupperware that has the little sections. Very accommodating."

Grayson shoved me and then he sighed, rubbing the back of his neck. "So, about last night?"

I furrowed my brow. "What about it?"

We'd already had some version of an aftermath conversation, so what more was there?

Grayson gave me an incredulous look. "Oh, I don't know, it's just kind of wild that it happened in the first place. I mean we'd never really talked about that kind of thing, just you and me."

"I don't think anyone really knows how to bring up a topic like hey, *I would really love to fuck you and your girlfriend, is that cool?*" I said, chuckling.

"It was just a little strange how natural it all felt, at least for me."

I mulled this over. "I can understand that. There probably should have been some fumbling around or like awkward moments, but nope, just a very sated Riley and two extremely satisfied cocks."

Grayson grabbed my chin and shook me playfully. "Are you really okay with whatever this is?"

"If I wasn't, last night wouldn't have happened. Despite wanting to do what made Riley happy, I have my own dealbreakers. Involving you in our sex life isn't one of them." I took his wrist in my hand and moved my fingers so that I traced lines on his palm. "Riley is a big turn on for me by herself, but watching you fuck her was.... something else."

He stared at where our hands touched. "And she wants us to fuck each other. She's almost eager about it."

I laughed. "It's been a minute since we've done that." I brought my hand up and traced the tip of my finger down the side of his jaw. He gave me a look of wariness, but it was slowly descending into desire. "I heard what you said to her, how you remember what my piercing felt like? Do you still think about it?"

I watched his Adam's apple bob as he swallowed. "That thing is hard to forget."

My lips twitched, morphing into a smile. "Your mouth on my cock is also very hard to forget."

He sent me a smile back, running his hand over the front of my pants. "The feeling is mutual." He rubbed his hand along me harder, but then stopped, starting to pull back. "Maybe we should wait for Riley."

I leaned towards him, my hand finding the button on his shorts.

"She said she wanted to be a part of the first time we have sex again, not the first time I stroke your dick again."

"I—*fuck*," he moaned when I had my hand inside his shorts, feeling how hard he was.

"No sex, just touching. Can you handle that?" I teased, using my free hand to unzip my own pants and pull out my cock.

He gripped me tightly, moving his hand up and down, letting my piercing move over his fingers. "I think I can handle it just fine."

I moved my thumb over the underside of his shaft, while I kept up my movements. My hand stroked the smooth texture of his cock, a small bead of moisture dripping from the tip. I swiped my thumb over it, bringing it to my mouth and tasting. My eyes closed when he dipped his hand in deeper and found my balls. He massaged and caressed, then moved his hand back up, stroking me again.

I stuck my tongue out and licked my palm, his eyes widening as I grabbed his cock and swirled my hand around the head then back down. I wanted to lean down and take him in my mouth. I wondered if he tasted just like he did before, but I would refrain and just feel him.

"Fuck, that feels good," I said through my teeth, when his hand started to move faster.

Grayson was panting, his dick harder than I'd ever seen it. "Please, fuck, go faster. I'm close." I did what he said, moving my hand at a more frantic pace.

Our breathing was harsh and desperate. It felt so intimate in this small space with his parents downstairs. I felt my balls tighten and my legs tense, then a wave of relief washed over me, like I was on a high.

A warm liquid hit my hand, running down my knuckles. I looked down and noticed that it had also gotten on his shirt and some had gotten on mine. I removed my hand from him, keeping my eyes locked on his as I brought my hand to my mouth, licking away all the evidence.

Grayson smirked at me, but he did the same, licking me off his hand. He tucked his cock back in his pants, leaning over and kissing me. It wasn't a long kiss, but it meant something. He kissed my cheek then let out a loud huff when he looked at his shirt. "Fuck, now I have to change."

26
RILEY

The guys had dropped me off at my dorm and I tapped my keycard, seeing Corrin lying on her bed with her arm thrown over her face. She could have been sleeping, so I made sure to be quiet when I closed the door.

"Ugh!" I heard her groan.

I walked over to her bed and sat down. "What is it?"

She moved her hand away, giving the most dramatic sigh. "Not the greatest weekend I'll say."

"Did you and Mateo have a fight?"

"Oh, I wish it was that simple. Mateo and I do not fight, we have discussions, by the way."

I kicked my shoes off, tucking my feet under my legs. "Then what?"

"One of the witches came back."

My eyes widened. She sat up, finding her glasses and placing them on her nose.

"Are they alright?"

Corrin shrugged. "She's in one piece. She doesn't really remember being taken, It's super fuzzy. It happened so fast and then next thing she knew she was back on campus. She was in one of the herb gardens last night. The interim coven leader called us and when I was about to leave my mom questioned me like I was on trial, so I spilled the beans."

I flinched, wondering how that conversation went. I didn't have to wait long.

"If you are wondering how that went. It went terrible. My mom has wanted me out of this coven for a while, no real reason, but ideally not every witch needs one. I like belonging okay, sue me." She waved her hands. "Back to the story, sorry, her parents are kind of livid...rightfully so. The school isn't letting much out to the public. They like to handle things in a certain way, especially when it comes to witches. They might call for the fucking chancellor, who knows. She isn't blaming anyone, she wasn't physically hurt that she can remember, and I checked her over and well, all her organs are in the right place."

"That's a good thing, right? She's okay."

Corrin tugged on one of her tight curls. "Yes, that's fantastic, but what the hell? Why take her and then let her come back like nothing happened? She said that the only thing that seemed off was that her mind felt like it had been probed and prodded at. She had a massive headache and said it felt like someone had searched around in there and then threw her back out. *Then*, she passed out."

"Like someone was searching for something." I said this more to myself, but Corrin was already nodding.

"Pretty much. It's probably happening to the other one as we speak."

"I'm sorry, Corrin."

She blew out a breath and then gasped, "That was the other thing!" She jumped off her bed, rocking back on her heels as she stood in front of me.

"Now I'm nervous."

"Ike was looking into each of the witches that were taken. Yes, they came from my coven, which could mean that someone in or close to the coven is shady. We know that already, but he also found out that all the witches that were taken all had the same powers inherently."

I nodded, letting her know it was fine to continue.

"Telekinesis."

I got off her bed, pacing. "The power that was used to throw my dad out his window. That person is taking people with the same magic skill, rummaging around in their mind.... for what? And they've been siphoning powers from witches in general...to what, gain more power for when people, even simple humans like my dad, try to confront them?" I placed my hand on either side of my head, my ears thrumming. Everything was stacking up on each other and I didn't like nor did I know what to do with all the things I felt.

Corrin came up and placed her hands over my own. "Riley, it's a lot, but I'm pretty sure we have a lot of pieces but no idea where they go. It's like we are missing the corners of the jigsaw puzzle. We have a lot of middles, but no place to really start from."

I laughed a little at her analogy. "I know, I know. Sorry."

"Don't be. This has to do with you as much as it has to do with me. If helping my fellow witches means also helping you then I call it a win all around." She took my hands from my head, keeping her finger interlocked with mine. "The coven is taking extra precautions, so far Ike says that the witches that are missing are the *only* ones who had that power in the coven, so maybe it's done for now."

I clucked my tongue. "Or maybe they'll start searching else-where." I looked over at my bag that I'd sat on the floor. I could have taken out the police report and showed her that River's dad was the one who found mine, that he likely was involved in some way.

I wasn't totally sure of that though and I also had no idea how he fit in with all the things Corrin was telling me. Maybe he had nothing to do with the witches, or maybe he knew who did. I needed a little more time before I attempted to expose my boyfriend's dad, but how much time did I really have?

Chocolate PSD
Bar Mock-Up
Food Packaging Collection
156
157

27
RILEY

I snatched my phone from the desk, before it could vibrate any louder. Asher didn't move to look in my direction but simply kept teaching. I sighed in relief and then refrained from the loud gasp I wanted to let out when I saw the text.

RIVER

> I may or may not have jerked off to the memory of you gagging on Grayson's cock.

I quickly looked to check my immediate surroundings, seeing that Corrin was looking straight ahead and the guy next to me was typing away on his laptop.

> I'm in class. You can't tell me things like that.

RIVER

> Ah, yes. I'm sorry that you should know how hard you make me.

> I'm well aware of what I do to you.

RIVER

Oh yeah? Tell me more.

> Not now.

RIVER

Now is the best time, gorgeous. My class is boring and I miss you.

> Aren't you sweet.

RIVER

I miss you. I miss the cute way you cuddle up in the fetal position when you sleep and the way your cunt squeezes my dick when you're about to come.

> Jesus, River.

RIVER

Grayson feels the same way. You may be an addiction, tsk tsk.

I started to tune out Asher and the rest of the class, thinking back to that night. The vivid image of feeling so full and satisfied filled my mind. I remembered their hands on me and the way they looked at each other at times had my heart racing. I thought about the way they were so in sync with one another when it came to how to treat my body. I could still feel the way River felt inside of me while he pushed me closer to Grayson, making me take his cock deeper into my mouth. It was like the taste and the overwhelming sensation of it all was still present and heady.

I suddenly felt the urge to create friction between my legs. I wanted to recreate that feeling I was remembering. The thought of River and everything else was gone and all that was available in my mind was the feeling of pressure between my legs, rubbing where I wanted it. I didn't understand what was going on, but I didn't want it to stop. It was like I wasn't thinking of anything or anyone in particular anymore, but I was still getting pushed closer to the edge. The sensation between my legs grew and I wanted to beg for it to give me more.

Whatever this dream was, it was providing me with the greatest distraction.

I could feel the back of my neck start to sweat and I wanted to spread my legs more and increase the pressure. Whatever this was had a mind of its own and I could feel my breathing increase. I had kept my mouth closed up until this point but the moment I opened it; a short moan came from my lips.

I felt a kick at my leg and I blinked, bringing myself back into the present. I looked over to see Corrin giving me a questioning look. A hushed silence fell over the room or had it always been this quiet? I flicked my eyes up to see multiple students looking at me, including one very annoyed professor. Asher put the cap on his dry erase marker and cleared his throat.

"Would you care to answer, Miss Monroe?"

I opened my mouth, but nothing witty wanted to come out because I didn't know what the hell he was talking about. All I was aware of was that I was pretty sure I just moaned out loud. It was small but it happened...and the universe should swallow me whole right fucking now. A different kind of heat was blooming inside me and that was one of sheer embarrassment. The ticking of the clock overhead was almost grating as I attempted to regain my composure.

I didn't understand what the fuck—*wait....*

I had been daydreaming. I had been daydreaming in a class with a teacher who uses dream magic.

"I'm sorry, what did you say?" A few giggles echoed in the room and all I could think was, of course, River had to be the reason I got called out. The man isn't even here and he gets me into trouble. I had been thinking about River and then my mind went to an unsafe territory and his brother was right there to pick up the pieces and.... make me think I was going to come?

Asher gave me a less than enthusiastic smile, his eyes still keeping that cold calculating glare about them. "You want me to repeat my question?" He showed no indication that he was involved in what just happened nor did he look like he had any remorse about it.

I wanted to sink down into my seat. "I—I...well, you don't have to if you don't want to."

He pointed the marker at me. "Funny. I am well aware of what I can and cannot do. Are you aware of the rules of my classroom?"

I ground my teeth together. "I'm vaguely familiar."

"Let me remind you. No cell phones unless it's an emergency. Was your conversation an emergency?"

Corrin had her eyes closed as if she was trying to wish us both out of this fucking room. "No, it wasn't."

Asher hummed, crossing his arms over his chest. His biceps made the arms of his shirt tighter. "Hmm, are you sure? Because clearly whatever it was had you so engrossed you missed my question entirely. I would hate to know I interrupted something so important that you couldn't think to pay attention to the class you signed up to take and hopefully pass."

I wanted to scoff and honestly, tell him to fuck off. He was the one who made me moan out loud, in front of his class. "It won't happen again. I'm sorry." I would do everything in my power to never daydream in his class again. I wanted this to be done and over with. I needed him to start talking about different disorders and the new version of the DSM.

"I'm sorry, what?" His tone was a little demanding, but there was a different kind of inflection at the end. It was almost like he wanted to hear me say it because he liked it and not because he wanted some kind of respect as a professor. It could have been both knowing Asher.

I sat up a little straighter, licking my lips. "I'm sorry, *sir*." His eyes flashed with this spark of...something. The hand on the clock ticked and Asher finally looked away from me, leaning towards his desk and tapping his phone.

"Alright, put your homework on my desk and get out of here."

The guy sitting next to me leaned over towards me. "Don't worry, he fucks with everyone who looks unfocused." He let out a quick laugh. "Some daydream you were having." He laughed again, getting up from his seat.

I gaped at him, watching his back as he walked down the stairs. Corrin blew out the longest breath, letting out a shaky laugh. "That was brutally hot."

"Excuse me?"

She gave me a small shrug. "As much as I hate watching you in a tension filled situation. That was the most intense eye fucking I've ever seen. It's like when I opened my eyes you guys were still going at it."

"Please stop. Also, I'm dating his brother, so nope."

Corrin shuffled around me to get into the aisle so we could leave. "And your point is? You have two boyfriends, what's wrong with a third?"

I walked behind her as we descended the stairs. "I don't have two—."

"Miss Monroe, can I speak to you for a moment?"

His voice caught me off guard seeing as it still sounded stern but a watered-down version. Corrin looked over her shoulder, her eyes floating between the two of us. She wiggled her fingers at me as she walked out, giving me a knowing look. I shook my head at her, watching as the rest of the class filtered out until it was just Asher and I.

"What do you want?" I asked, not in the mood for his snarky attitude that was severely unwarranted. I also really had no interest in talking to him after the stunt he pulled.

He placed some papers in his messenger bag, not looking at me. "You may think I'm being harsh, but I'm owed a little respect as your professor."

"Respect?! After what you did?!"

He furrowed his brow, the look of faux confusion on his face. "What did I do, hmm?"

I looked over to where I had been sitting and back at him. "You... I...ugh. You know what you did."

Asher placed his bag around his neck, letting the strap land against his chest. "Perhaps. Hopefully that will teach you to pay attention to my lessons and not mentally gallivant off into less than appropriate territory. I understand my brother has a way with words, especially ones of the provocative variety, but I would think someone that continues to do so well in my class would know how to prioritize her responsibilities."

"What goes on in my head is my business." I walked up to him, pressing my finger into his chest. He towered over me, but I didn't deter my confidence.

"My classroom, my rules."

"Fine, then I'll tell someone above your head about what you did."

He barked out a laugh, looking at me as if I just told the funniest joke he'd ever heard. "Please do and when they ask you about what exactly I did in great detail so they can file the paperwork correctly, make sure to let them know that you were thinking about getting fucked and that I was just helping you along so that you could go back to being a good student who follows my class rules and pays fucking attention."

My chest was heaving, but I realized that my heart was also racing. His green eyes glanced down at my mouth and then he blinked, clearing his throat. "I won't stop you, so by all means be my guest."

"I'm sure your dad would bail you out anyway. Nepotism is in your favor."

He scoffed. "There is that. I'm not a fan of it, just so you are aware."

"I don't care."

He wrapped his hand around his bag strap. "Speaking of fathers... is that why you came here?"

My stomach dropped. "What?"

"My question was simple enough. Is your dad the reason you enrolled here?"

"Again, something else that is none of your business."

He lifted one of his shoulders. "I'm not asking for a shit ton of details. I just want to make sure you aren't getting involved in something that could involve my brother."

I gave him a tight smile. "River has nothing to do with anything. I wouldn't do that."

"So, you are doing *something,* little liar?"

I found myself stuttering. "I—I...no. Y—you...fuck... that's not what I said."

"Accidents happen, Miss Monroe. Maybe you should just focus on school and not get sidetracked playing Nancy Drew, hmm."

Accidents happen, yes, but I wanted to throat punch everyone who kept saying that's what happened. I also wanted to bust into tears, thinking about how fucking complicated and confusing this had gotten. The way he said it though, it was like he didn't quite believe it himself. I crossed my arms over my chest, severely pissed off. I had to focus on not letting my voice sound shaky. "Sounds like you have something to hide yourself, especially since that's something someone like that would say."

He tilted his head to the side, raising his eyebrows for a brief second before walking around me. Suddenly, I felt him behind me. His voice surrounded me, almost like I could feel him all over my body. "You seem a little tense. Maybe you should go find my brother to release some of that stress since I didn't let you finish. If you'd like me to apologize, you'll be waiting a while. Although, from what I've gathered about you, you like a little cliffhanger...to be left right. At. The. *Edge*..." Each word came out concise and right at my ear. I heard him walking away and I didn't realize I was squeezing my thighs together until I finally relaxed.

I swiftly turned around, catching him right as he got to the door. "Is that my homework? Getting myself off, *sir?*" I saw his hand flex as it wrapped around the doorknob.

Fuck his dream magic. And fuck this newfound feeling I had towards him, which was something I couldn't quite put my finger on.

28
RILEY

I wasn't hungry at all, so I made my way to the library. Something Corrin had said still hadn't left my mind.

They like to handle things in a certain way, especially when it comes to witches.

I knew things about Mystic Riegan, but maybe I didn't know enough. Now that Corrin and I were a collective unit on this adventure I'd started, anything I found out could help both of us. I felt like her and Ike had done their part tremendously, so it was only fair I discovered some information of my own.

The library had six floors, one of which had a section dedicated to the school's history. If something was going to lead me in the right direction, it would be in that area. At least I was crossing my fingers that I wasn't wasting my time.

I got off the elevator, looking up and checking the signs to figure out where to go. I walked past a few aisles, realizing how quiet it was up here. Usually, I would hear little whispers from other students, but this floor was just dead silence.

"Riley?" A familiar voice said, causing me to stop and back up, looking down one of the aisles. Grayson was on the floor, up against a wall, a book in his lap.

I smiled at him, looking around. "You do know there are tables and chairs, right?"

He let his book close, keeping his thumb inside to hold his place. "I like a little seclusion."

I placed one of my hands in my shorts pocket. "That's fair." I nodded towards his book. "Anything good?"

"Just started but it's good. Vampires and fae. Marriage of convenience, you know, all the good things."

I laughed. "You are really in your vampire era, aren't you?" I walked into the aisle, searching the shelves.

"What are you doing here? Like here as in this part of the library?"

I fiddled with the strap of my backpack. "Um, I'm looking for something on the school's history."

"That's very broad. You're going to need to be a little more specific."

"Well, something that has to do with the school and witches."

His eyes narrowed. "Also, really broad."

"How so?"

He searched around him, plucking his bookmark off the ground and placing it between the pages of his novel. "The school was founded by witches, so that part of its history would be in nearly every book you look into. The oldest ones are over there." His lips pushed out a bit as if he was using them to point, pushing his chin up towards the bookshelves behind me.

That wasn't anywhere on the school's website, so it was news to me. Maybe I didn't need a book to tell me the things I needed to know. I walked the rest of the way over to him, taking my backpack off and sitting down beside him. "So witches take up the majority of the student body, I assume."

He reached over, pulling me closer to him. "When the school first opened, yeah, it was pretty much primarily witches and then they let in other magic wielders. Eventually they opened it to humans and the school has been known for its extensive integration ever since."

"Hence prestigious university on the west coast."

Grayson ran his fingertips over my arm. "Exactly. It houses one of the largest covens in the state. They're the ones that decided to form the school."

"Any chance you know the name?"

"Of the coven, um, let me think..." He scrunched his mouth up, then he snapped his fingers. "Celica. This is like Mystic Riegan 101, shouldn't you know this?"

"I wasn't aware that understanding everything about the school was a requirement for admission." I shoved my body against his, causing him to reach down and tickle my side. I pulled my phone out, finding my text thread with Corrin.

> Does your coven happen to be named Celica?"

CORRIN

Yes...why?

> I assume you are aware that your coven created this school, so the influence they have has to be massive.

CORRIN

Oh fuck, how did I not think of that before?

> Of course, they would want to keep things involving witches close to their chest.

CORRIN

Whatever is going on though is being done
with someone's selfish interest at play, not
the coven. No wonder my mom is so wary
about them. I'll update Ike.

I should have put two and two together. I'm
a little all over the place with everything
going on.

I sighed, hesitating before I started typing.

You're all good. Just please stay safe.

I went back to my past theory. My dad found out what was going
on and threatened the culprit, which cost him his life. He threatened
a member of one of the biggest covens. What if it was their old coven
leader? Corrin did say they got a new one shortly after my dad died,
so maybe they removed themselves from the situation.... but stayed
around to continue to siphon powers and steal witches?

Stealing witches, just to give them back with their minds
rummaged through...

Nothing made any sense. My dad believed in fairness and not
because his job description forced him to. That was just his personality, and he would have done anything to fight for students he tried to
help every day. I bet he was happy to have stood up to whoever this
was, he probably didn't hesitate and stood his ground, unafraid of
the consequences.

That alone had me more determined than ever to keep going,
keep digging.

"Riley, are you okay?" Grayson shook my shoulder.

I inhaled, turning my head to look at him. "Yeah, I'm fine. Sorry."

"Where did you go just now?"

I shook my head. "Nowhere you need to be concerned about."

"You don't know me very well if you think I'm not always
worried about you."

I tried to hide my smile, but it was coming through. "Is that right?"

"Mhmm." He brought his face closer to mine, brushing his lips over my own. His hand slid up my leg, creating circles along my bare thigh.

"I should let you get back to your book," I whispered against his mouth.

He reached up to touch my cheek, his thumb grazing my skin and leaving heat in its wake. "Is that what *you* want, trouble?"

I wrinkled my nose, remembering what he called me when he shared me with River. "What did you say the other night?"

"What do you mean?"

"You called me a different name that night. *Aking sinta.* I'm wondering what it means."

Grayson ran his thumb over my lips, smiling at me. "What if I don't tell you? Are you going to pout about it?"

I opened my mouth, wrapping my lips around his thumb and sucking. His focus never left me, his mouth dropping open a little, I released his thumb, letting my tongue linger on it. "No. As long as it's not something mean."

"Believe me, it's not. It's something nice." He dipped his head down, moving my braids out of his way and kissing my neck. "Unlike all the things I'd like to do to you."

I bit my lip, moaning softly. He slid his hand down my stomach and rubbed between my legs. My words came out breathy. "We can't have sex in the school library, Grayson." I tried to say it with conviction, but it sure didn't sound that way.

He chuckled, continuing his tortuous rubbing. "Who said anything about sex?" He unbuttoned my shorts, reaching inside and plunging his fingers inside my panties. "I just want to hear you come."

I spread my legs out a little wider, feeling a little empowered as he watched me. He made no move to kiss me, but his eyes would scan my body, then return to my face gauging each of my reactions.

His fingers slid over my clit, circling it and taking it between his fingers, pinching.

I gripped his shoulder, pressing my lips together even though I wanted to be so loud. "Put your fingers inside of me."

"Say please, *aking sinta*."

I groaned as he teased me, skating his fingers over my pussy but not putting them inside. "Be a good boy and put your fingers inside me, *please*."

He shuddered and pushed in one of his fingers, slowly, watching my expression change into one of pure pleasure. Grayson pressed in another, letting his face fall into the crook of my neck. I squirmed against his touch, wanting him to move faster, but he was just rocking his hand back and forth. It was sensually antagonizing, but I wasn't going to tell him to stop.

It made the orgasm that was building that much more thrilling and the build up was making me feel light-headed. He thumbed my clit, pressing against it, while letting his fingers stroke inside of me. I was getting that same feeling I had when Asher was using his powers on me. The right friction, the right rhythm, and I couldn't fucking believe I was doing what he'd said and chasing that climax that he'd left me without.

Grayson curled his fingers just right and I started to pant, needing to release all the sounds I wanted to make. He stuck his hand behind my head, curling his arm around so that he could press his hand to my mouth as I came. I let all my noises out against his palm, causing them to sound muffled.

When it was over, he released my mouth, planting a kiss on my lips. He took his hands out of my shorts, putting his fingers into his mouth and sucking off my taste. I rebuttoned my shorts, watching him with hooded eyes. "Let me guess, you aren't going to wash my scent off your hands?"

He winked at me. "Maybe. Maybe not."

I pressed my hand to my face, peeking out between my fingers. My phone vibrated and I took a look, seeing a text from River.

RIVER

Coming in libraries, are we?

I looked around, assuming he was lurking somewhere.

How do you know that?

RIVER

How do you think?

I looked at Grayson, a little confused.

"How does River know what just happened? He can't use his power on campus."

Grayson gave me a playful smile. "He isn't on campus. He went home after his morning class. Me letting him in on what happened isn't a campus violation, so I was graciously letting him have a little play by play. He did tell me that you can get a little loud, so I should cover your mouth." He waved his hand around at our surroundings. "Library and all."

I rolled my eyes, looking back at my phone.

Are you jealous?

RIVER

Haha, no. As long as you're happy and so is that pussy, then I'm a happy man.

I am happy.

I would be even happier when I could just focus on this and not everything else that had nothing to do with them.

RIVER

Perfect. Keep it up and you'll have a very eventful weekend, gorgeous.

I'm going to tell Corrin she can bring her partner. Is that okay?

RIVER

Asher won't be home, so you could literally
bring whoever you want.

I smiled at my phone, clicking it off and pushing off of the ground. Grayson kept his eyes on me. "Leaving so soon. I thought you had school history research to do?"

"I actually figured that out. And I should probably grab something to eat and caffeine. I could take a nap after..." I motioned towards the area we were in, alluding to what had just transpired.

"You're welcome, trouble."

He handed me my backpack. "We're back to that?"

Grayson picked his book back up. "I like keeping you on your toes. Don't pretend like you don't like it."

Chocolate PSD
Bar Mock-UP
Food Packaging Collection

In the afternoon of that day my pocket diary shows me that at least six or seven drums were throbbing from various points. Sometimes they beat quickly, sometimes slowly, sometimes in obvious question and answer, one far to the east breaking out in a high staccato rattle, and being followed after a pause by a deep roll from the north. There was something indescribably nerve-shaking and menacing in that constant mutter, which seemed to shape itself into the very syllables of the half-breed, endlessly repeated, "We will kill you if we can. We will kill you if we can." No one ever moved in the silent woods. All the peace and soothing of quiet Nature lay in that dark curtain of vegetation, but away from behind there came ever the one message from our fellow-man. "We will kill you if we can," said the men in the east. "We will kill you if we can," said the men in the north.

All day the drums rumbled and whispered, while their menace reflected itself in the faces of our coloured companions. Even the hardy, swaggering half-breed seemed cowed. I learned, however, that day once for all that both Summerlee and Challenger possessed that highest type of bravery, the bravery of the scientific mind. There was the spirit which upheld Darwin among the gauchos of the Argentine or Wallace among the head-hunters of Malaya. It is decreed by a merciful Nature that the human brain cannot think of two things simultaneously, so that if it be steeped in curiosity as to science it has no room for merely personal considerations. All day amid that incessant and mysterious menace our two Professors watched every bird upon the wing, and every shrub upon the bank, with many a sharp wordy contention, when the snarl of Summerlee came quick upon the deep growl of Challenger, but with no more sense of danger and no more reference to drum-beating Indians than if they were seated together in the smoking room of the Royal Society's Club in St. James's Street. Once only did they condescend to discuss them.

29
RIVER

I'd gone back and forth on whether to show up to his stupid meeting, but I decided it would be more of a hassle *not* to go. At least he had picked a Thursday when I have a class in an hour, so I didn't have to stay here forever. I walked through the door, stepping up to my dad's front desk receptionist, Dorthea. She was an older woman, with kind eyes and tiny crows feet at the corners. She was far too good to work for my dad.

"River, oh my gosh, how are you?" she asked, smiling at me.

I granted her a genuine smile. "Good, Dorthea and you?"

"You know, same old. Picked up another hobby."

I rapt my knuckles against the wood of the counter. "Crocheting didn't pique your interest?"

She wagged her finger from left to right. "Hated it. It's for some people, but I am not one of them. Felt like I was giving myself early onset arthritis."

I laughed. Footsteps and a throat clearing had my laughter ceasing.

"River, come on in." My dad motioned for me to follow him. I sighed, cracking my neck and giving Dorthea a nod before stepping around her desk.

My dad's office was clean and put together. It reminded me of Asher's, but at least my brother tried to decorate his desk just a little. Even if it was just a fake plant. There were two chairs on the opposite side of his desk, so I chose the one closest to the window. I could look outside every so often if I got bored during this little encounter.

My dad unbuttoned his suit jacket and sat down in his chair. "How are you?"

"Same as last time."

"It's been a while since we've spoken."

"Not long enough," I mumbled, leaning back in my seat.

He rubbed his eyebrow, clearly already frustrated. "The fact that I have to force meetings on you doesn't make me happy. You know that, right?"

I let out a choked laugh. "Then why do you do it?"

"I want to spend time with my son."

I sighed loudly, looking over his shoulder at a picture of all of us on a shelf behind him. I couldn't remember how old I was during it, nor did I remember if I had been happy. Just because I was smiling didn't mean much.

"Are you seeing anyone special?"

My eyes widened. "Spying on me?"

He scoffed, sliding his hand down the front of his jacket. "No, River. I work at this school; I happen to see you every now and then. I'm just assuming."

I shrugged. "You assume right. She's not up for discussion, so I suggest you move to the next topic. She's a human, I love her, and she already knows she won't be engaging with you anytime soon."

He leaned over his desk, resting his forearms on it. "I'm sure your mother would like to meet her."

"Maybe she will, but not when you're around."

He let out a sharp laugh. "You act like you had this horrible childhood, that you weren't given everything you wanted. I have done nothing but want the best for you. You are the one who chooses to see it differently than the rest of us."

I reached out and wrapped my hands around the end of the arm rests. "The rest of us? Are you talking about Asher? You really think just because he teaches here and lets you oddly dote on him that he doesn't resent you?"

"Despite what you think, everything I've ever done has been in your best interest. You and your brother."

I squeezed the ends of the arm rest, looking down at my knuckles. They were turning white with the amount of pressure I was using. "You had me stand in front of a bunch of strangers and wanted me to fuck with their minds, Dad. You wanted to show me off to your fucking friends, you wanted me to enhance my powers when I was still going through puberty." I pointed an accusatory finger at him. "*You* resented me when you couldn't get what you wanted and somehow you think that because you keep me monetarily satisfied, I'm going to *like* you?!"

He ran his long fingers over his mouth, staring at me. "None of those people would have gotten hurt. It simply would have been practice for you. They were willing participants, River. You were just too young to understand. Your brother can attest that no harm came to those strangers you mentioned."

"You of all people should know that mental magic used for too much malicious intent can do harm more deeply than anything physical. I may do some reckless shit, Dad, but I at least know how to maintain my own powers."

"River, lets just leave the past where it's at and focus on the here and now." He always did this. Glazed over the past and kept trying to focus on the future. It was irritating. I didn't let my past linger so much that it ruined how I saw my life and my relationships, but that didn't mean I'd forgotten. I didn't care much about an apology. I just wanted the man to leave me alone.

I shook my head, pushing the chair back and standing up. "I think I'll go. You know if it wasn't for mom's continuous pleading for me to go to Mystic Riegan, I wouldn't be here. I don't know what you said to make Asher come here, but knowing you, it's probably not good."

I moved to start walking towards the door.

"River, sit down."

"Yeah, right."

I felt my body stop moving, feeling myself wanting to walk back over to my chair. I tried to push back against my mind, but I couldn't. Something much stronger was taking over.

"Sit. Down. River." My dad's voice was forceful and lacked any gentleness he tried to have before. I quickly did as he said, grinding my teeth together at my lack of control. My dad had telepathy just like me, but he'd focused much more on controlling the mind and thoughts, rather than just reading minds. It was very on brand for him, so whenever this kind of manipulation came out to play, it wasn't shocking.

"This is how you spend time with your children. You force them," I said through my teeth, continuously trying to push past his abilities to find the strength to leave. I was at a major disadvantage with my dampener ring on and he knew it.

"I don't like doing this. You want to be stubborn, well I can as well." My dad smiled at me as if we had been having the most pleasant conversation this entire time. "I could have forced you to do what I wanted when you were younger, but I didn't. That counts for something."

He walked around his desk and stood in front of me, his eyes assessing every single thing about me. "Now you are going to sit here and have a nice conversation with your father before your class, like the good son I know you can be."

Chocolate PSD
Bar Mock-Up
Food Packaging Collection

30

RILEY

I'd woken up Friday morning, realizing River hadn't texted me back after I sent him a casual checking in message. He was quieter than usual about his plans, but I never really pushed when it came to him. He didn't try to ever force me to tell him things when I didn't want to, so I took the hint and decided not to push my luck.

He could handle himself and whatever it was that he was doing. I decided to pull out the book I had been reading—a retelling of one of my favorite stories from when I was a kid—when Corrin came through our door, letting it slam on the other side of the wall.

"Well hello to you too," I said, slightly used to her antics, letting out a small laugh and focusing back on my book.

She hustled over to me, taking my book from my hands. I lifted my hands, confused. "Uncalled for, but I'm listening." The fact that I'd lost my place had my blood boiling.

"Do you have plans tonight?" Corrin asked, tapping her nails on my novel.

"Yes, getting lost in a world that isn't this one."

"It will have to wait, if you want to get closer to figuring shit out," she huffed, dragging me off my bed.

I slapped her hands away. "What are you talking about?"

Corrin turned around and strolled over to our closet. "I found a witch who can see into the past."

I nearly flew over to her, tugging her shoulders so she would look at me. "And we didn't think of this before, because...?"

"It's very fucking weird to go around and ask strangers at your university if they have seer magic. I might have asked Mateo to keep an eye and ear out if one just happened to come into the bar." Corrin tugged a few options off the rack and threw them at me. "Don't worry, I didn't tell them any details. Mateo is a great listener though, their temper could use some work, but maybe that's just a possessive thing they need to work on."

"I thought only wolf shifters went to a wolf shifter bar?"

My roommate pulled a jacket out, putting it on. "It's owned by shifters, but it's open to everyone. It's all about respect. If you don't show it to them, then well they might just go full wolf and eat you." Her tone was casual, while I thought that entire sentence over in my head.

I took a top and skinny jeans from the pile of clothes I was holding and went to the bathroom. "What makes you think she is going to want to help us?"

"She graduated from a university that houses the coven mine can't stand, apparently. If she has any chance of making an ass of mine then she will."

I poked my head out of the bathroom giving her a skeptical look. She was on her bed now, kicking her legs back and forth. "What? Mateo is a great bartender. Solid listener, like I said."

"You mean eavesdropper."

She mumbled *whatever*, while I pulled a claw clip out of my bag of hair accessories. I took a few of my braids from each side and pulled them to the back. I held the clip and secured them, then made sure there were no fly away hairs out of place that I would have to use gel to secure.

When I looked at myself in the mirror, a light bulb went off and I flinched. "I can't go."

"And why not?"

"My best friend since forever is coming down tonight and I promised I would see her." I would also see her this weekend at River's party, but this was our chance to be alone and spend time just us. I started to make my way back over to my bed, prepared to sit this one out and hope that Corrin came back with good news.

"Okay, then bring her."

I stopped, slowly looking over at her. "To the bar? She doesn't know what we're trying to do about any of this. It's going to be really hard to try to have a conversation with a memory witch and not mention some key details."

Corrin tapped her chin. "Hmm, you know how you fix that?"

I tapped my foot on the ground, waiting.

"You tell her. Shocking, I know."

At this moment, my hair clip felt tight and a raging headache was barreling its way through. "She'll think I'm insane for doing this in the first place."

Corrin chuckled. "I mean, it is just a little bit wild to transfer schools just to find the truth. It's also really fucking cool. And the fact that you still maintain good grades is like superhero level impressive."

"Not everyone is as overwhelmingly accepting as you."

She sighed dramatically. "True. I am one of a kind, but if she's one of your best friends, I think she'll understand more than you think. I understand keeping it from all your boyfriends, but not from your girls."

She plucked my phone off my dresser and handed it to me. "Hustle, babe."

I sighed, scrolling till I found my text thread with Marianne.

Can you get a ride to Marth Moon?

MARIANNE

I could, but why would I do that?

Meet me there, please.

MARIANNE

Isn't that the wolf shifter bar in Mill Valley?

Yup. I promise I'll explain everything when you get there.

MARIANNE

Here I thought we were just getting sushi tonight. You've gone and went all mysterious on me. Sure, I'll head that way when I get home and grab the car from my mom.

I swung my phone between my fingers. "It's done."

RIVER HAD FINALLY TEXTED ME BACK, PROFESSING HOW SORRY HE WAS THAT he hadn't responded and he would make it up to me tomorrow night. I sat in the passenger seat of Corrin's car and watched the trees go by as we turned down another street. The woods were getting a little thicker the deeper we went, but surprisingly there were still signs of civilization.

Neon lights and signs that matched came into view. Corrin parked on the gravel lot, turning off her car. I looked around noticing that Marianne's car wasn't here yet, so I got out, taking in my surroundings. The Marth Moon sign glowed brightly in a yellowish hue with a half-moon over the N. The parking lot wasn't packed, but it wasn't exactly empty. Laughter could be heard from inside and a few patrons were hanging out along the perimeter. The smell of cigarette smoke and something else filled my nostrils.

I sniffed the air, trying to figure out what it was.

"That's the marth."

"The what?"

Corrin motioned for me to follow her towards the building. "While also being a decently well-known shifter bar, they are also pretty sought after for brewing their own beer. Instead of yeast, they use marth. It has more of a scent, but it makes the most delicious drinks."

"And they just magically get this marth...how?"

Corrin gave me a devious smile. "Witches. There are a few ingredients you need to make it, but you also need magic to finalize the product. They had someone for years and then after I'd been with Mateo for a while, I offered up my services. Potions chemistry saves the day."

We walked up the steps and Corrin opened up the door for me. It was warm inside, which was a drastic change from the slightly chilly night air. There were a few pool tables, a life size game of checkers and an area that catered to the game of darts.

Tables and chairs were littered throughout the middle and the bar sat to the left, a few overhead lights along the top. A couple of TVs were placed in specific spots and that marth smell grew more and more potent. There was a well-worn couch in the front corner, now being preoccupied by a couple who were very into each other at the moment.

Corrin smiled at the girl at the bar, waving and walking over. "Where are they?"

The girl wiped her hands on a wet cloth and bit her full bottom lip. She had long silky, brown ringlets and light brown skin. "No idea. Stepped out I think. They get a little frustrated when the brew doesn't turn out perfect the first time."

Corrin looked as if she understood the meaning behind this girl's words. She turned to me, taking off her jacket and placing it on the stool next to her. "So, sometimes Mateo likes to go outside and..."

She was cut off when a loud cry was heard from outside.

The girl jumped over the bar, while we stayed close behind her, running out the door. The people from outside were now in clusters, looking fairly confused but also very interested to know what the fuck was going on.

"What happened?" The bartender asked one of the guys trying to look out in the distance.

He shook his head. "No idea. Just heard the scream. Like something out of a horror movie."

The sound of footsteps running along the gravel caught my attention. I pushed past Corrin and saw a wave of blonde hair. I squinted making sure I was seeing things right. "Marianne?"

My best friend came running towards me, her eyes wide and alert. She was breathing heavily, practically plowing me over when she reached me. "Oh my gosh! Riley! We have to go!"

"Wait! Marianne, go where? What happened?!"

She looked behind her, her body shaking.

She took in a breath, placing her hands on my arms. "I got a little turned around and then my car stalled a little bit down the street. I got out to check it out and then I heard something. It sounded like growling...I got a better look at it and its eyes flashed this yellow color that freaked me the fuck out, so..." Her shoulders tensed when a crackle came from the wooded area near the parking lot.

She shuffled behind me as if I was going to protect her from whatever it was.

"Growling and yellow eyes?" the bartender asked her.

Marianne nodded swiftly, pulling pieces of her hair from her face.

I noticed Corrin and the bartender give each other a look before rolling both their eyes. I really wanted to be in on whatever they had silently communicated. A large shadow extended against the ground, projected by the light from the bar and the moon. It wasn't monstrous, but it wasn't just a simple woodland creature. My breath caught when I saw paws, connected to a large, furry body, and the face of a wolf. Its canines were pronounced and just like Marianne had said its eyes were yellow. Its coat was deep brown, thick with a few broken leaves stuck to it.

Its eyes narrowed on Marianne, but it didn't make a move to attack. It looked like no one in the vicinity was necessarily backing away but just waiting.

Corrin let out a heavy sigh, turning around to look at me and Marianne. She smiled, stepping away from us and towards the wolf. "Mateo, you really need to learn that no one understands you when you're a wolf." She looked up at the animal and extended her hand.

Mateo?

The wolf dropped its head, pressing its snout into her palm. It shook its body, the leaves falling away, along with some dirt and dust.

"Like I said, Mateo gets a little tense when their beer doesn't go well. They're working on it." She smiled, apologetically.

A small wind gust formed, circling around the wolf and after a few sparks and what sounded like bones cracking, Corrin's partner was in front of us. And they were...naked.

A resounding *oh* and *fuck* echoed around us.

"For the love of fuck, Mateo!" the bartender screamed. She placed her hands in front of her eyes, turning her back to them. "As you can see, this is my younger sibling and they are nothing to be afraid of." She placed her hand over her chest. "I'm Jade and I actually don't love random people seeing me nude."

She gave us a tight smile and raced back into the bar.

Corrin tried her best to stand in front of her partner, but to no avail. "Just because you enjoy being naked doesn't mean everyone else enjoys seeing it, honey."

Mateo let out a loud laugh, giving their attention to Marianne over Corrin's shoulder. "My apologies."

Marianne stood with her mouth open. "The first time I encounter a fully shifted shifter and I also end up seeing them naked. This was not on my bingo card, but I'll take it." She wrapped her hair over one of her shoulders, catching her breath.

Jade came stomping back outside, throwing a robe in Mateo's direction. "Put some clothes on. *Deja de traumatizar a la gente, pinche idiota!*" She charged up to them, smacking the side of their head. She turned around addressing all the people around us. "Nothing to see here, please go back inside for free drinks on me."

Mateo started laughing again but stopped the minute Jade threw a look over her shoulder. Corrin helped them put the robe on, kissing their cheek.

"I assume this is just the beginning of the night and I'm about to be told more things that will shock me." Marianne followed behind Jade, who was muttering a multitude of Spanish obscenities, stepping inside the bar.

I gave her the most reassuring smile I could muster.

Chocolate PSD
Bar Mock-Up
Good Packaging Collection
157
156

31
RILEY

Mateo had changed clothes and now wore a fitted t-shirt and black suspenders. Apparently, there was a shower in the back room of the bar and they had cleaned up, coming to sit with us. Their hair was still damp, looking much darker than when I saw them on video chats with Corrin.

Jade sat a beer in front of her sibling, giving them a less than friendly smile.

"You can't be too upset with me. I tried to explain. *No todo el mundo habla lobo.*" Mateo pouted, wrapping their hand around the glass. Their accent wasn't overly thick, but they put a little more stress at the end of their words. Jade's was the exact same way.

"I don't think *anyone* actually speaks wolf," I answered, translating.

Mateo's mouth quirked up into a smile. "I like this one." Corrin was snuggled up to their side, tracing her finger through their trimmed beard.

"There are actually people who do speak wolf, but why anyone would want to hear what this one has to say, I'll never understand." Jade plopped down in her chair with her own beer.

"I'm sure River could have read their mind and not ran away like I did." Marianne took a sip of her drink. "I ran track in high school and I'm regretting not keeping up at least my stretching like I used to. My legs are killing me from all that running."

"You ran for like five minutes," I joked.

She balled up the paper from her straw covering and threw it at me. Mateo cleared their throat. "We're getting someone to fix your car. You'll be able to leave tonight, no problem."

Marianne nodded, looking over at me as if I was meant to spill everything I was supposed to say right at this very moment.

The door opened and Mateo looked over their shoulder. They patted Corrin's leg quickly. "*Mi amor*, there's your girl."

A tall girl with red hair down to her shoulders stepped inside. She wore leggings and an oversized t-shirt tucked into the front. A few other girls followed behind her. She scanned the room, catching sight of Corrin.

Her mouth opened and it seemed as if she wanted to laugh but no noise came out. She turned towards one of her friends, saying something and then turning back to head our way. "Corrin, how's that cute little coven of yours?"

Corrin heaved out a breath. "Just fine, thanks for asking, Pen."

"Funny, I heard one of your own just up and vanished and then got plopped right back into society, like nothing ever happened."

Corrin's face faltered for a moment. "How do you know that?"

Pen shrugged, "Just because I graduated doesn't mean I'm completely above university gossip. I also know your pretentious little school isn't doing fuck all about it."

"Woah, what..." Mateo started, casting a look over at Corrin.

"We're trying to fix that," I cut in, knowing this little back and forth spat between them could have gone on for a while if I let it.

Pen swiveled on her heels to give me her full attention. "And who are you?"

I swallowed, throwing a glance at Marianne, who was desperately trying to keep up with the conversation. I pushed my chair back, stepping up to Pen who raised her eyebrows. "I'm the girl whose dad likely died due to someone associated with that coven, and I would like you to help me figure it the fuck out. You'll know that Celica Coven isn't all it's cracked up to be and you'll be doing me a large favor."

Pen smirked, sizing me up. "I don't care much about doing you a large favor, but you had me at proving Celica Coven is a shit show. What exactly do you need from me...." She sighed expectantly, waiting for me to give her my name.

"Riley."

She nodded as if my name would stay in her mind until our dealing was over and she could forget about me. Pen tucked her hair behind her ear, tapping Mateo on the shoulder. "Do you mind letting us talk and getting me a drink?"

Mateo grumbled but got up. "We are still going to talk about this." They gave Corrin a knowing look, walking over to the bar.

"Riley, what the fuck. This is about your dad?" Marianne scooted her chair closer to me.

"Yeah, I need to explain—"

Pen cleared her throat. "Whatever you're about to say can wait, I'm sure. You want me to put all the pieces together for you?" She blinked, waiting for my response.

"Maybe not those words exactly, but yes," I said, leaning into the table.

Pen looked around at us and then started laughing. "Listen, the way my magic works is I need to be in the room where it happened. I need to touch things, stand in the same place as your dad and then the whole imagery comes to mind. It's not as simple as you telling me some shit and I can just solve the crime."

Jade huffed. "*¡Que increíble!* Why are you even fucking sitting here then." She downed her beer, leaning back in her chair. Mateo's sister didn't know anything about, well, anything, and she was just as frustrated as me.

Pen let out another laugh. "I don't want to step foot on your campus, that's all. That doesn't mean I can't help you. You'll just have to do a bit more work." She swung her head to face Corrin.

My roommate pressed her lips together. "What do I have to do?"

Pen sighed, giving Corrin a patronizing look. "What you do best, potions witch."

"How is a potion going to help?" Marianne questioned, one of her blonde eyebrows raising.

"Ugh." Pen pulled at her hair, plucking out a strand and reaching for a napkin. She placed the hair on top, sliding it over to Corrin. "Witches' magic flows through our entire bodies, from the top of our head to the tips of our toes. Therefore, if you are as good at creation and extraction as you say you are, then you won't have a problem pulling some memory magic from this and using it."

Corrin stared at the hair. "You want me to create a brew that mimics your powers for what? Riley to drink?"

"Or you could grind it up and create a powder to throw in her face. I don't fucking care what you do, but you'll need to do the same thing as me to even make it work." Pen looked up when Mateo came back around with her drink. She gave them her fakest smile, while Mateo just rolled their eyes.

"I'll have to get into my dads office." I tapped my fingers against the table.

"Can't you just ask to be let in?" Marianne asked, placing her hands in her lap.

"I'm trying not to draw so much attention to myself. It already seems like only a handful of people even knew he was my dad and just a lot of people suspect. I want to be absolutely sure before I go causing a scene about it."

"There's also no way you could take something like that and no one ask questions, especially when you actually learn the truth,"

Corrin said, taking the napkin and folding it over so she wouldn't lose the one thing we needed to make this work.

"The truth being that your coven isn't taking care of their own and they're probably murderers?" Pen clucked her tongue, picking a piece of lint off her shirt.

"I think we're done here." Jade placed her elbows on the table, her loose curls falling over her shoulders.

The redhead picked up her drink. "Good luck with your witch hunt." She cackled as she walked back over to her friends. Mateo immediately took their spot back, forcing Corrin to give them her attention. "Explain, right the fuck now."

Corrin rubbed her temples, and I gave her a sympathetic look. I felt a tug on my jacket and looked over at Marianne. "I love you and all, but you are going to have to open your fucking mouth right now and spill."

"Let me get this straight. You transferred out of community college to go to Mystic Riegan, so that you could set the record straight that your dad didn't fall or jump out his office window like everyone said? No one knows besides your roommate and her partner...and their sibling now, I suppose?" Marianne said each word slowly.

"Yup."

"Okay ...and now you know that witches are going missing from the central coven of the university, all of which had the power that pushed your dad out a window." She snapped her fingers. "Also, the witches are now slowly reappearing but like someone fingered their minds? And your big bad is stealing powers somehow...sort of, because you saw a bunch of powers on a piece of glass you found in the grass." Her words trailed off, but then she caught my eye again. "And you need this Pen girl's magic to see who did it or how it happened, but you will need to sneak into his office to do said...

magic." She closed one of her eyes as if she was a bit iffy on that last part.

I snorted. "Fingering their minds?"

"I don't know how else to put it, Riley. It all sounds a little convoluted."

I pressed my tongue to the inside of my cheek, leaning my body against the wall. We'd moved away from everyone and had a little corner to ourselves. "So you don't believe me or any of this?"

Marianne reared her head back, looking insulted. "I never said that. I'm all the way in a different fucking state. I come here to see you and I'm hit with all of this. Give me a break, pretty please."

I nodded, placing my head against the wall.

"Are you planning on telling your mom?"

I let out a choked cough. "Not yet. She was already mildly against me going to Mystic Riegan in the first place. I'm not going to bring up anything that could cause her to backslide when she's made so much progress since he died."

"And what about you, hmm? This is a fucking lot for someone. You lost your dad and now you plan to go find his killer. I'm a little nervous that you'll just combust one day, and at the wrong moment at that."

I scoffed. "I can handle myself and my feelings. My dad would want me to figure it out. The fact that I let people in on anything at all is a good sign, right?"

Marianne took my hands in hers. "Fine, I suppose you're right. If you think it wasn't an accident, then neither do I. I just hope you're being careful in all this. You're going after someone who might have killed your dad, Riley, so what makes you think they won't hurt you also?

"It's a risk I have to take."

"Rebelliousness is kind of hot on you." She squeezed my hands. "You'll find your truth, whatever that ends up being and I'll be here to gush about how my best friend maintained a straight A average while being only a sophomore and attempting to take on a coven and a university in the name of justice."

I held my stomach as I laughed. "I'm not Batman, stop it."

She tapped her chin. "Well, have we ever actually seen you and Batman in the same room?"

I was practically wheezing from laughing so hard.

Marianne tugged me over to the bar. "I thought your lack of text messages meant that you had replaced me, not that you were starring in your own thriller. I did always think you were a fan of spicy romance and that's it."

I hummed, wanting to hide my smile. Marianne gasped. "Wait, is there spicy romance?" She held her finger out in front of my face. "Hold on, you're already in a spicy romance with your boyfriend, so that's old news."

"Yeah, you might want a drink for this."

Marianne's mouth dropped into an O before she squealed. "Riley Marie Monroe, what have you done, or should I ask *who*?"

32
RILEY

I made sure my hair was set and that my dress looked good enough to pass Corrin's party test when she saw me. She told me when she decided to stay with Mateo last night that if I came to my own boyfriend's party looking far too casual for her liking, she would be driving me back to the dorm to change.

The dress was short, but not so short that I would flash anyone the minute I bent over. My ruby gem necklace sat comfortably at my chest. The weather had been warm today, breezy, but the nights were getting chiller than I liked so I unhooked my jean jacket from the hanger. I pulled my braids out once I had it on, letting them fall down my back. I slipped my Converse on and put on the most minimal amount of makeup, looking down at my phone at Marianne's text.

MARIANNE

> I have arrived so hurry up. Take your time but do it quickly.

We had to park on the street a few houses down since plenty of cars I didn't recognize had gotten closer spots. I had told River we were coming far later than I would have liked since Marianne took forever picking me up. Despite telling me to hurry up, she always ended up being the one not on time.

The music had a deep bass and my body was vibrating with it the minute we stepped inside. There was loud laughter and the thick smell of alcohol in the air. Marianne moved out of the way as other people pushed open the door to get inside. I took her hand and guided her into the living room, finding that the couch and the armchair were already taken.

"So, where's your boyfriend, or is it *boyfriends*?" She wiggled her eyebrows at me.

I slapped my hand against my face. "I shouldn't have told you that."

She shook her head, her blonde hair moving from side to side. "Oh, no. I loved learning that my best friend got plowed by two guys who are obsessed with her. Honestly, we all deserve to be worshipped like that."

"Please, any louder so everyone can hear you," I said sarcastically, placing a finger over my lips.

"Mhmm..." She nodded over my shoulder, but before I could turn around, large arms wrapped around my middle.

"There she is." River pressed his lips to my ear, squeezing me. He gave Marianne a simple wave, kissing my cheek.

"Where's the other part of your triangle?" Marianne asked, looking around.

"He's around. How about we get you two something to drink?" He took my hand, leading us to the kitchen. He asked Marianne what she wanted, since he already was well aware of what I enjoyed. He opened the fridge handing her a beer and pulled out various bottles and two different fruit juices.

"What's that?" I asked, watching as he placed everything on the messy counter.

"Everything I need to make your favorite." He bent down, opening a cabinet and straightening back up with a shaker in his hand.

"River, you are not about to do that." I pressed my hands to my cheeks, taking into account all the things on the counter that made a Sex on the Beach.

Marianne took a swig of her beer. "That is so disgustingly sweet I think I'm going to puke."

He started to add the different ingredients to the shaker, heading to the freezer for some ice. I couldn't help the smile that spread on my face at how this very filthy mouthed man could be so cute.

"Don't fuck it up." Grayson appeared in the doorway, creating a V with his fingers and pointing from his eyes to River's. He moved around my boyfriend and over to me, kissing me on the cheek and giving me a hug where his hands landed right above my ass. I could hear Marianne choke on her drink, but she didn't say anything.

"Hand me a glass, will ya?" River looked over at Grayson who nodded at him, opening one of the cabinets up top, setting a crystallized glass down on the counter. My boyfriend opened the shaker, poured the drink into the glass and slid it over to me.

"No fancy umbrella?" Grayson joked, nudging River who shoved him back.

I picked up the drink, bringing it to my nose. It smelled just fine, but that didn't mean much. I brought it to my lips, tipping it back so I could take a sip. Both boys and Marianne were all looking at me with bated breath.

I smacked my lips, purposely prolonging my reaction. "It's actually really good. You could always put bartending skills on your resume."

"You can come work under me." I heard Mateo's voice and turned around. Corrin hurried around the counter and hugged me, pulling back and assessing my outfit. She gave me one small nod that spoke volumes.

Introductions were made and the conversation flowed seamlessly. Mateo had mentioned that their sister was tending the bar, so she was sorry she had to miss us tonight. The music entrapped us and soon the beat was one that I could move to and River knew exactly how to find a rhythm with me. Marianne was chatting up a girl in the kitchen, while Corrin and Mateo danced enthusiastically with each other. I held my drink in one hand, careful to keep it in the glass. River spun me around and pressed me against his chest, bringing his forehead down on mine. He grabbed my hips, sliding his hands back and gripping my ass, which bunched up my dress.

"Any higher and the whole worlds going to see what we share." Grayson came up behind me, his body heat surrounding me. His fingers played along with River's, teasing at the hem of my dress.

"We have a lot of plans for you tonight, gorgeous." River leaned in to kiss me. Grayson slipped my drink from my hand and I pulled away from River's kiss.

"Hey, I wasn't done with that." My tone was playful.

"We need you to be coherent and willing tonight, *aking sinta*." That phrase again. Something about it made my insides flutter.

"Well then, water it is for the rest of the night." I placed my hands on River's chest, reaching up to try to kiss him and then I heard a crash.

"What the fuck was that?" River's mouth formed into a hard line and he groaned. "I'll be right back, don't go anywhere." He kissed my forehead and then went in search of the reason for breaking up our good time. Grayson followed him and I pressed my hand to the back of my neck.

Water actually sounded amazing right now since I felt like I was burning up. I started to head towards the kitchen when a hand gripped my forearm. I turned to come face to face with a burly guy who I'm pretty sure I'd seen around campus.

"Can I help you?" I asked, trying to pull my arm out of his hold.

"You can dance with me." His voice was a little slurred.

"I'm okay, thanks." I tried to remove myself from him, but he just held on tighter. "You can let me go now."

He laughed a little, teetering on his feet. "It's just one dance. You had no problems with the two guys before."

I gave him a forced smile. "Well, I know those guys and I don't know you, so let me go."

He pulled me into him, causing me to smell the alcohol on his breath up close and personal. "You can get to know me then, come on." He started trying to drag me to where a throng of people were dancing, but I planted my feet and pulled back.

"Just let me..."

My entire body was yanked backwards into a hard chest. Fingers held my arms, moving me to the side. I looked up, coming face to face with the person who had pulled me away.

Asher. He had on a grey henley that shaped his body nicely; it was hard not to look at him.

The burly guy blinked, looking more annoyed. "Go find your own girl." He shoved his hands against Asher's chest.

River's brother let out a deep laugh. "I wasn't aware she belonged to you."

The guy looked past Asher at me, scanning my body in a way that made me think I was completely naked. "She might if you'd stop being a massive cockblock and let me show her a good time." He tried to move past Asher, who didn't hesitate to pull his arm back and connect his fist with the guy's face.

I watched him stagger back, shaking his head, becoming even more unstable on his feet. He lunged toward Asher who moved out of the way, grabbing a beer bottle from the coffee table and smashing it over the guy's head. He stumbled and fell on the ground with a loud thud.

"What the fuck are you doing here?" River placed his hands on either side of his head, looking at the mess around us.

Asher placed the other half of the broken bottle on the coffee table. "I fucking live here."

Grayson pointed to the unconscious body on the ground. "You didn't kill him, did you?"

Corrin and Marianne fought through the crowd, crouching down next to the body. Corrin pressed her fingers to his neck. "No, he's fine. His pride will probably hurt like a bitch though." She fluttered her fingers, moving her hand over his body. A shimmer of magic laid over his body and then disappeared. "Just for good measure, but he'll be fine."

She looked up at Asher, her eyes widening. Both she and Marianne looked at me, mouthing 'are you okay'. I nodded, more concerned about the people now giving me way too much attention.

River came over to me. "Baby, are you okay?"

"You really shouldn't leave your girlfriend alone for drunk idiots to try to prey on," Asher chastised.

River pointed at me, facing his brother. "I wasn't aware I needed to hire the fucking Secret Service to watch her like she's a fucking child."

Grayson cleared his throat. "Guys, this is really not the time for this."

"Better yet, maybe you shouldn't have parties without my say so, like you're fucking sixteen sneaking out of the house," Asher ordered.

River barked out a laugh. "Oh, don't blame the party. The guy was an asshole and you saved the day, good for fucking you. I'm sure Riley is very grateful that you knocked him unconscious. Would you like a medal for doing something nice for someone?"

"You can't have fucking parties and underage drinking going on under my roof. You can't have me coming in and pulling your girlfriend from less than friendly idiots. I'm her teacher, River, fuck!"

"Now you consider that, huh?"

Asher narrowed his eyes and my heart stopped. "Excuse me?"

River stepped up to his brother, getting in his face. "You think I don't listen to your thoughts sometimes. Sometimes the things you let run wild..."

"All of you just shut up!" I screamed, shoving past them and running up the stairs.

"Riley!" Grayson shouted, but I paid him no mind. I didn't pay attention to where I was headed but I found myself in a bathroom. I pressed my back against the door, taking deep breaths in and out.

A knock sounded at the door, but I didn't move.

"Riley, come out, please," River pleaded, knocking again.

I sighed, but I didn't budge. Maybe if I just stood here, making no noise, they would just go away.

"Move, fucking move." Asher's deep voice commanded. I heard the knob turn and then I quickly moved away from the door when he shoved it open, causing it to swing wildly. I was breathing heavily, my eyes finding all three of them standing there. I noticed behind them was a large bedroom that I'd never really seen before which told me in my lack of thinking I had run into Asher's room—well, his master bathroom.

"Can you please just get out?" I said in a small voice.

Asher sighed, stepping into the bathroom. "No, it's my bathroom."

I scowled at him. "Fine, then I'll leave."

He stepped in front of me. "No, that's not happening either."

"Would you like me to say thank you for helping me out and knocking some guy out? Okay, thank you, I truly appreciate it. Now may I fucking go?"

Grayson squeezed between Asher and his best friend. "Are you okay, though?"

I rubbed the side of my head. "Yes, I'm just fine. This one moment will not haunt me for the rest of my life. This—" I motioned towards the four of us, "is actually really annoying."

River put his hand out for me to take, "Then I'll take you home."

I was about to take it when I stopped, finding Asher's green eyes hiding behind his glasses. "What was he talking about?"

Asher rubbed his hands together. "What?"

I rolled my eyes, officially done with being coy. "Downstairs, when you guys were yelling at each other. River mentioned that your thoughts ran wild. Wild how?"

Asher blew out a breath and turned to leave, gripping the bathroom door. River reached for my hand but I moved it away. "What kind of thoughts do you have, Asher? The kind that violates the code of conduct?" I said each word sharply. Asher stepped back a little, closing the door and hearing it click, trapping all of us in the bathroom together.

He turned around slowly, stalking towards me while Grayson and River stood along the wall. They were watching as if this was something they couldn't miss. They had no idea what the outcome would be, what the stakes were. "You need to be careful about the assumptions you are trying to make..."

"Miss Monroe? Is that what you want to say?"

He got a little closer to me. It was a large bathroom, but the space felt like it was shrinking the more in my face he got. "I'm happy you are fine and I'm happy I could be there to help when I did. That's all. My brother has no fucking idea what he's talking about so leave it alone."

I tilted my head to the side. "And if I don't?"

"This conversation is over." He looked at my mouth, his chest rising and falling with calculated breaths. His hands flexed at his sides as if he was trying to regain his composure. Composure that was slipping little by little by the looks of it.

River let a soft laugh leave his lips. "Fuck, Asher, your thoughts are loud as hell."

Asher put his hand out, letting his palm face his brother. "Shut. Up."

River leaned over, whispering something in Grayson's ear. Grayson's eyes widened but he just licked his lips, remaining against the wall.

"You are allowed to invade my daydreams at your leisure, but you won't share your thoughts with the class? You don't play fair." I let out an exhaustive laugh.

"Maybe I don't want to play with you," Asher shot back.

"Of course you do," River said, staring at the ceiling. "Let's stop pretending like we've never shared a bed with the same girl. While we're at it, how about..."

"River, please stop fucking talking!" Asher balled his hands into fists.

I furrowed my brows. "You two have had sex with the same girl before?" There were things I knew River had in common with his brother, like their dislike for their father, but I wouldn't have considered this to be something to add to that list.

"It doesn't happen frequently, but yeah, we have. And he's usually way less pretentious while we have that dynamic. You like when you have someone to boss around that isn't me," River pushed, eyeing his brother and then me.

Asher ran a hand through his hair, looking as if steam would start to blow out of his ears. His jaw worked like he was grinding his teeth together. He moved to try to leave the bathroom again and I found myself wanting to stop him...again.

I reached out to grab his arm. "Are your incredibly wild thoughts about me? Is that why sometimes in class, you can't look at me, because you're thinking about me a certain way?" He turned around, removing my hand as if my touch burned him. Asher was looking at the ground, refusing to give attention to anything else.

I peeked over at Grayson who flicked his eyes to Asher, nodding his head towards his best friend's older brother. I licked my lips, wiping my hands down my dress. "Do you really dislike me or is that how you hide how much you actually.... want me?"

"You keep my brother and his friend. That's perfect for you to handle." He looked at me, that resolve of his shrinking.

"I don't think what I'm able to handle is really for you to decide, now is it?"

"Don't test me, Riley." His words came out through gritted teeth.

I was so close to figuring out the answers to my dad's death and even finding out that this school had a much deeper fucked up foundation than I thought. Things were going in a good direction for me and I wasn't about to back down because my teacher has chosen to keep me at arm's length in hopes that he wouldn't think inappropriate thoughts about me. To his higher ups sure, those looming thoughts were against school policy, but to me...I wanted to know every detail of what his mind consisted of. I wanted to know if every time he snarked and disciplined me, he was just trying to push down his need to bring me closer.

"Do you sit in your office and try to remember all the reasons you shouldn't like me just to be reminded that—" I stepped a little closer, mustering all the courage I had, "all you really want to do is fuck me."

The look he gave me could have sucked all the oxygen out of the room. Our mutual breathing surrounded us.

Asher licked his lips slowly. "You should *really* quit while you're ahead."

My lips twitched into a tiny smirk. "Oh, but good students always go the extra mile. Isn't that right, *sir*?"

He didn't move, but his eyes flicked over to the wall at the men next to us.

"Tell me I'm wrong. Tell me you aren't attracted to me. Tell me your brother hasn't caught you thinking about me. Tell me that you didn't enjoy making me almost come during your class. I will go home and we can go back to our everyday back and forth dynamic if that's the case." I raised one of my eyebrows. "Or..."

"Or. What?"

My voice was soft. "Or you see what I can handle."

I was starting to think this entire situation was a waste of time. If Asher was this stubborn, I truly wondered how their experiences with women together had gone. I was happy with Grayson and River; I was excited to keep exploring what that was, but as much as I wanted to be settled with just the two of them, there was something that was telling me I wanted this broody fucking man to be involved.

I huffed, turning slightly to tell River to take me home, when

Asher released a sharp breath. He reached out and grabbed my waist, yanking me to his chest.

"Fuck it," he groaned, his lips crashing down on mine.

33
RILEY

Our mouths moved and his tongue licked at my lips. I wrapped my arm around his neck as he held me tighter, kissing me deeper, groaning into my mouth. Asher pulled away, taking my bottom lip between his teeth and pulling until I whimpered. He rubbed his nose against mine, a smirk shining along his face.

He tightened his hold on me, pushing me back until I was pressed against the sink. He reached down, claiming hold of my thighs and picked me up. The cold porcelain hit my skin and I could have shrieked at the sensation, then Asher's hands found my face again. He pulled me closer, kissing me and leaning his body in so he could find a place between my legs.

My dress rode up higher, the metal faucet digging into my back, but the pain didn't matter when he trailed his mouth down to my jaw. His facial hair tickled my skin and caused me to shiver.

I heard a small laugh, finding River and Grayson staring at us so intently. There were no looks of jealousy or anger. Their eyes were hooded as they followed every movement and took in each and every sound I made like it was the most ethereal music they'd ever heard.

I felt cooler the moment Asher tugged my jacket off my arms and threw it to the ground. He grasped the back of my neck, forcing my face to his. "Is this what you like? Getting watched and touched. I didn't know you wanted all that..." His other hand slid up my thigh, getting dangerously close to where my panties were soaked. "From me. I didn't even think you liked me." His fingers pressed between my legs and I hissed. He moved my panties to the side, sliding over how wet I was, a smile creeping onto his face.

"I don't." I said through gritted teeth, trying not to moan when he circled over my clit. I didn't actually know if I liked him. I didn't have to *necessarily* like him to want this.

"You're already so wet. I think you do like me, no need to pretend, little liar." His fingers rubbed against me and my eyes started to flutter close. Asher tugged at my neck, my eyes coming open immediately. "You don't get to close your eyes. You like being watched like a pretty little slut, then it seems fair that you watch them while they see you come apart all over my hand."

I let out an unbridled whimper at his words, at the rough way he said them. His hold on my neck was tight, my mouth dropping open when two of his fingers pushed inside of me. "Oh, *fuck.*"

"Do you think you can keep your eyes open for me?"

I let out a breath, trying to gather my words, but every movement of his fingers, every thrust inside of me had me gasping. "Yes."

He pulled my head back, leaning in and licked up the side of my throat. His teeth nipped at my ear. "Yes, *what?*"

His fingers moved fast and my thighs felt exhausted from all the tension I held in them, keeping my legs open. I forced my eyes to stay open even when all I wanted to do was let them roll back and relax. "Yes, *sir.*"

Asher pulled back from my neck and smirked at me. His mouth found mine, plunging his tongue inside and fucking me with his fingers harder. I couldn't keep up with his kiss, my panting becoming harsh and unsteady. My orgasm washed over me as he kept pumping his fingers, pulling out every sound I could muster.

He ripped his fingers out, hooking them into the sides of my panties and pulling them down my legs. He looked over his shoulder at River and Grayson. River's green eyes found Grayson's brown ones, silently communicating. Grayson nodded, his shadows pulsing around his body as if they were eager to come out and play. River looked back at his brother, rolling his lips together before giving me a look of sincerity,

"I'm not the one you need to ask, Ash. I haven't stopped you, so you know where I stand. You want to fuck her, then ask if she *wants* you to fuck her." He winked at me, running a hand through his hair and letting the other slide over the front of his pants. "Besides, we all know how much I love verbal confirmation...right, gorgeous?"

Asher placed his hands on my thighs, moving his fingers lazily along my oversensitive skin.

"We'll both be right here, watching," Grayson added, moving his hand so his fingers could thread through River's hair.

Asher moved his hands further up my thighs. I looked down and saw his erection pushing against his pants. My pussy pulsed at the idea of it inside of me. I tried to remember that this man—being with this man—violated so many rules and he was the most aggravating person I'd come to know in a short amount of time.

He took off his glasses, folding them and placing them on the sink. I could see his eyes better and they were so full of conflicted desire that I couldn't help it when more heat bloomed at my core. He tucked his finger under my chin, lifting. "You want me to fuck that wet little cunt in front of your boyfriends? Let them hear all those slutty little sounds you make."

I reached out, brushing my fingers over where his cock was straining to be released. "Yes," I answered, fiddling with his belt. "It doesn't mean I like you."

He slapped my hands away, making quick work of his belt, before unzipping his pants and pushing them down. "Whatever gets you to come on my cock, little liar. Your pussy seems to like me just fine." He took my thighs and pulled me closer, taking his cock in his hand and rubbing it against my slit. I started to tilt my head back and let my eyes close, basking in how good it felt.

Asher's hand slipped over the front of my throat, jerking me to him. "What did I fucking say? They watch you and you keep your eyes open. You don't listen and I'll edge you until you can't take it anymore and we both know how much you fucking hate being right on the edge, don't we?"

He moved my dress up higher, exposing to River and Grayson how coated in my arousal his cock was. He was simply teasing me and he'd made me a fucking puddle. I nodded, biting my lip. "Yes..."

He raised an eyebrow, testing me.

"Sir. Yes, *sir*," I said quickly, finding that I didn't want to be the cause for this moment being cut short.

"She's a good girl, isn't she?" Grayson said, his voice full of pride towards me.

Asher held his cock, moving the head over my clit. "We'll see how good she is." He fed his cock into where I wanted him and I brought my hand out to grab onto his arm.

He let me feel him before he started moving. "Fuck, that little pussy takes my cock so well." He started to move slowly, sliding in and out. I clenched around him each time, finding his eyes watching me and it made every feeling coursing through my body that much more intense. "If this is how you show your disdain, I couldn't possibly imagine what it looks like when you actually like someone."

River chuckled, readjusting his cock through his pants. "Oh, she acts the same way. She loves me and that pussy takes my cock just perfectly."

Asher lifted my leg a little higher, pulling his cock out to the tip and then plunging it back in deeper. I sucked in a breath, feeling the heat rise in my cheeks and the sweat percolate along my chest and between my breasts.

"Let me tell you something else, Ash." River tilted his head to the side, but not looking at his brother. He was staring right at me, but I knew he was using his powers to communicate.

Asher licked his lips, grabbing my hips and moving a little faster. There was a steady slapping of skin and the feel of him inside of me which sent my heart into rapid speed.

River looked pleased with himself. "Don't worry, gorgeous. I just told him he doesn't need to be so gentle."

I wanted him to touch me, I wanted River's hands on my body and I wanted Grayson to caress me with his shadows and make me shiver. The way they looked at me told me they felt the same way, but they were just as content to sit and watch me scream and writhe at the hands of someone else. Asher moved faster, pounding into me.

I moaned, wanting to beg him to go harder.

"You stretch so pretty around me. Must mean you and that slutty," *thrust*. "Little," *thrust*. "Pussy must like me." He pulled me in to kiss him, our lips aggressive and needy. He fucked me hard and fast, pushing my thighs back, so I had to grip the edges of the sink counter to keep my balance.

He released my lips right as a scream barreled out of me. His name came out of my mouth and as much as I wanted to take it back, I couldn't. This moment would be one I replayed in my dreams at night and with my luck, he would slither his way in just to watch me come apart again.

My thighs tensed at the thought, causing my pussy to grip his cock. He groaned, his eyebrows furrowing and I knew he was close to coming. "Are you on the pill, an elixir, anything?"

I nodded, biting my lip. "Yes, yes, fuck."

"Do you want me to come inside of you? I could come all over that perfect stomach of yours or pull that dress down and see it paint your chest." Asher sounded serious while having a deep desirable voice filled with need. I could have come again with all his questions.

"Come inside of me, please *sir*." I pleaded, trying to rock against him and get friction even though I was still trying to come down from my own high.

He muttered a *fuck* through his teeth, thrusting one last time and giving into his orgasm. The heat in this bathroom was overwhelming and it was starting to feel like an inferno. I leaned back in for another kiss, but Asher reared his head back, narrowing his eyes at me. He slid out of me, reaching down for his pants, pulling them up.

His green eyes slipped down to my open legs, his lips twitching ever so slightly in a small smile. "You stay here and wait." He picked up his glasses, placing them back on his face when he looked over at River and Grayson who were also both sweating, their eyes dilated and their breathing harsh. "You two get everyone the fuck out of my house."

Chocolate.PSD
Bar Mock-Up
Read Packaging Collection
157
156

34

RILEY

River and Grayson went downstairs to clear out the party while Asher got a washcloth, added water to it and handed it to me. He helped me off the sink which was a mistake because the minute I landed on the ground, I could feel his release slowly dripping down my thigh. I grabbed the cloth from him, muttering a thank you.

Asher ran a hand over his mouth and sighed, leaving the bathroom. I groaned, realizing that the repercussions of this entire situation would rear its ugly head soon. I didn't know what I was doing. I was so close to getting a clear truth when it came to my dad, but now the more intimate side of my life had become a little...complicated.

Others may say it's simple. Three men have some form of affection for you, they all are very good at sex and at least two out of the three dote on you like it's their day job. Nothing to complain about, right? I rinsed the cloth when I was done, running a hand over the back of my neck. Grayson was one thing. He and River had a relationship outside of me that I don't think I'll ever truly understand, but I was just happy to be one of the things they shared and adored. Asher, on the other hand, was a beast I didn't know I needed to be worried about when it came to...any of this.

He sure did fuck like he'd been wanting this for a while. Then again, I accepted his cock like I did too. I swung the door open, finding an empty bedroom. I spun slowly in a circle, taking in the space. The walls had a few unique art pieces, but otherwise they were bare. Bookshelves that housed what I would only assume as textbooks and non-fiction novels were up against the wall. Asher didn't seem like the type who wanted to be whisked away to a fantasy land in hopes of finding his destined soulmate; he liked things to go his way and to frame his narrative perfectly.

He was suspicious of me and I didn't know if it was because I took his neatly aligned narrative and fucked with it, or if he legitimately knew something. I clearly wasn't going to ask, but it seemed like none of it was important right now if what happened in the bathroom was any indication.

The door opened as I made myself comfortable on the bed. They all walked in, River swinging my phone back and forth. He handed it to me, the soft feel of his fingers grazing my own. "Your mom texted."

"What?" I woke up my screen, seeing that I had less battery life than I would have liked and found her message.

> MOM
>
> Haven't heard from you in a while. Proof of life, please.

I laughed a little, starting to type.

> I'm alive. Busy with school and everything else. I promise everything is fine

My mom's reply came immediately, as if she had been waiting with her phone in her hand.

MOM

Thank god. Beau has been pacing around
your room and I was a little alarmed but then
he stopped. I always feel like he knows
when something is up.

> I'm sure it's a dog thing. Don't they have like
> a sense about those things?

MOM

That does not make me feel better, Riley.

> I promise I am in one piece and okay. Being
> social does require me to be a little MIA, but
> I'm trying.

MOM

I know, sweetheart. How is Marianne? Her
mother told me you guys were headed to a
party tonight.

I sighed knowing that if I indulged in this conversation, I would be texting her for a good minute. I peeked up at the three guys who were casually pretending to be engrossed in other things, but in reality, they were watching me. Actually, one of them was, without an ounce of shame, staring at me. Asher sat in his desk chair; his elbow propped up on one of the arms.

> Yeah we are actually still here so can I talk to
> you tomorrow?

MOM

Right, right. My bad, I forgot it's not cool to
be texting your mom at a party. I'll talk to
you tomorrow. Love you, always and always.

"Everything okay?" River asked,

I nodded. "Yeah, she's just checking in on me. I do need to charge this though." I raised my phone for them to see.

River plucked it from my hands, walking over to Asher's desk. His brother followed his movements, watching as he searched until he found the right charger. Grayson jumped onto the bed, getting comfortable.

Asher scoffed. "By all means, please make yourself at home."

"You're going to have to loosen up, Asher. We all just got very close in the last hour, so deal with it." Grayson stuck out his tongue, shooting his shadows out and smacking Asher on the cheek.

Asher groaned. "And you will single-handedly make me regret it."

"So, you don't currently regret it?" I asked, toying with the end of one of my braids.

Asher readjusted his glasses on his nose. "At the moment, no."

I chuckled, realizing that that was the best answer I would get for now. I scooted back so that I was next to Grayson at the headboard. He put his arm around me, his shadows coming out and smoothing themselves over my legs.

"Corrin also told us she would see you Monday to figure things out," River said, cocking his head to the side. "Figure out what?"

"Nothing, just roommate stuff."

"She made it seem like it wasn't so simple."

I shrugged. "You can't assume something sinister by only a few words, River. If it was something dire, I would tell you."

He crossed his arms over his chest, his more colorful tattoos popping out next to his black shirt. "Okay, fine. This really makes me hate promising not to read your mind."

"You promised what?" Asher asked, his eyes narrowing.

River walked over, sitting at the foot of the bed. "That's old news. Well, clearly not for you. Her mind is a purposeful mystery to me."

"Quite the mental workout for you, since you love reading minds," Asher pointed out.

River looked over at me, a mischievous smile on his face. "It's what she wanted, so I did as she asked. Also, I mean it's a little fun not being able to know things. She gets to *tell* me what she wants..." He turned around and moved up the bed, trailing his fingers up my leg, mingling with Grayson's shadows.

"Did you happen to put your panties back on, *aking sinta?*" Grayson asked.

"I—" I started but River cut me off. "She did not." River got onto his knees, walking his fingers up my legs and spreading them open. "I can see that sweet little cunt perfectly."

Asher spread his legs in his chair, his eyes fixated on us. "Sweet isn't the word I'd use."

Grayson was already pulling on the straps of my dress, exposing my strapless bra. River grabbed my dress from where it sat on my waist and dragged it the rest of the way down. "Well, it won't be when we're done with it." He kissed up my leg, planting a kiss to the inside of my knees. "We're gonna make a pretty little mess out of you, aren't we?"

Grayson unclasped my bra, cupping my breasts and playing with my nipples. He bent down, taking one in his mouth and flicking his tongue over it. I let out a moan, looking down as I watched River kiss up my body, moving his hands up to my stomach, splaying fingers out to keep me steady.

I ran my hand through Grayson's hair as he dragged his mouth to my other nipple. I looked over and noticed Asher's piercing stare. He had a finger over his lip as if he was really looking at every move I made, every kiss his brother and Grayson graced me with. River kissed my clit and my eyes closed from the sensation, but then I opened them again quickly to look at his brother.

Asher balled his other hand into a fist. "You want to be shared, Riley? You want all our hands on you?"

"Fuck, yes, I do." I managed to get out before River pressed his fingers inside of me, causing my words to come out rushed. Grayson brought his hand down my body and used his fingers to pinch and circle my clit.

"You look so *occupied* over there, so I'll let you finish that. One thing about me is that I'm not selfish." Asher raised his eyebrows at me.

"Yes, just like that," I begged, feeling River's fingers move back and forth while Grayson played with me alongside him.

River pulled back, removing his shirt and unbuttoning his pants. Grayson followed suit, putting a pillow behind my head to prop me up. Grayson moved so that he was on his knees, next to my head. He slid his cock against my lips and I reached for it, stroking him. I stuck my tongue out and licked the underside of his shaft and then back up to the head.

River slapped his cock against my clit, making me squirm. He rubbed the metal of his piercing against it, the silver balls now wet from me. He held himself and pushed inside, grabbing my thighs and holding them as he pumped his hips.

"Oh, fuck, fuck..." I said, the bed shaking with his movements.

Grayson turned my head, his bicep flexing as he angled his cock near my face. "Open your mouth."

I did as he said, tasting him on my tongue when he put it in my mouth. His shadows came out grabbing my hands and moved them over my head, connecting them to the headboard. I was naked and on display, being pleasured by two men while the other one sat in a chair and looked on like this was the most natural thing in the world.

"Your cunt looks so pretty filled up, gorgeous," River praised, lifting me a little higher so his thrust could go deeper and faster.

I sucked Grayson into my mouth, moaning around him. He moved his hips, pushing further back and then he pulled out. He slid his cock over my mouth again, wetting my lips and then pressing against them to be back inside. I was clawing at the headboard and my toes curled, my orgasm brewing.

"Eyes on me, I want you to look at me when you come." Asher's deep voice had me moving my eyes so I could see him. He had gotten out of his chair and was leaning over the bed. I came hard, my eyes never leaving his. River slowed his movements, sliding out of me and walking backwards on his knees off the bed.

I was about to ask him where he was going, but Asher grabbed my ankles and pulled me to the side of the bed until just the top half of my body was against the mattress. He flipped me over, making sure I arched my back and raised my ass towards him.

"I should see if your pussy is as sweet as my brother says it is." Asher bent down and licked me from behind. I buried my face into his sheets, stifling my cries. He moaned against my backside, sticking his tongue inside of me.

"You keep that up and you might make her come again," Grayson said, lifting my head up.

Asher left me wanting more, the moment he stood up, spanking me. "Is that right?" He moved around me, removing his pants before getting on the bed and taking over Grayson's hold on me. "You want to come again, like a needy little slut." He pressed his forehead to mine, giving me a deep kiss. It was sensual in a way I didn't think was possible for him.

Grayson jumped off the bed and Asher took his place, removing his shirt. I knew Grayson and River had nice bodies; I'd seen them without shirts plenty of times. Asher was no different, but seeing him with nothing on, looking down at me…it was something else I couldn't put my finger on.

I hadn't realized River had left the room, until he appeared in the doorway. "Perfect, you all know how to follow directions." He must have mentally communicated with them before he snuck out. He held a small bottle in his hand, rounding the bed towards Grayson.

The shadow wielder moved his hand between my legs and massaged my pussy. I whimpered, pushing back against his hand. I looked over my shoulder seeing River take Grayson's face, bringing him over to kiss him. Grayson continued to play with me while he and my boyfriend shared a kiss.

"He's going to fuck you, gorgeous, and I'm going to fuck him," River said, giving Grayson room to stand behind me, positioning my body how he wanted.

Asher turned my head so he could angle his cock towards my mouth. "Don't worry, I'll give that antagonizing mouth something to do." I wrapped my lips around him as he pushed inside. I swirled my tongue around his shaft as best I could, bopping my head back and forth.

I felt Grayson's cock inside of me as he held onto my hips. Each thrust pushed me forward causing me to take more of Asher's cock. I heard the sound of a cap opening, then the sound of something being squirted out.

Grayson's movements faltered, but he rallied and his rhythm returned. He was moaning, but due to Asher's sudden hold on my hair, I couldn't turn my head and see.

"Fuck, I remember your ass being tight, but this is just my finger. Are you sure you want my cock?" River asked, speaking to Grayson.

I felt Grayson's body shudder. "Yes, just go slow."

Chocolate.PSD
Bar Mock-UP
Food Photography Collection
157
156

35
RIVER

I took more of the lube and squirted it into my hand, adding some more to Grayson's ass. I stroked my cock, covering it with the liquid, watching my hand slide up and down my shaft, glistening. All the hairs on my arms stood up hearing Riley gag on my brother's cock and being able to fuck Grayson again, while he fucked her was something that had been secretly on my bucket list. I was never going to be the one to ask for it though.

I said some very out of pocket things, but this was something I wanted Riley to want.

I spread Grayson's ass cheeks apart, pressing two fingers inside his tight hole. I spread my fingers apart, massaging. I felt some resistance but nothing I wasn't used to. He started to relax even more, while I rubbed his back. I eased a third finger in, feeling push back but then it eased. I would stop if he couldn't handle it and I would find another way to please him. I pulled my fingers out, spreading more lube onto his ass and placed the head of my cock at his hole.

I pushed forward, feeling him tense, so I stopped. He stopped thrusting into Riley and even Asher slowed his hips.

"You okay?" I asked, brushing his hair back from his face.

He took a deep breath, starting to move inside my girlfriend again. "I'm okay. Keep going."

Getting the piercings in was going to be the hardest thing, but he wanted to do this and so did I. Riley wanted it just as much. I watched her back muscles move and marveled over the perfection that was her brown skin. I inched in some more and then a little bit more. I watched the head of my cock slide in and I stopped, rubbing my hands down his sides. "Is that good? Feel good?"

Grayson moaned, moving back against me as he pumped into Riley. I was delicate about the metal of my piercing. It was agonizing the amount of restraint I had, but I watched each section go in, stopped and then started again. I had gotten past all of them when Grayson started pounding into her and begged, "just fuck me, for fucks sake!"

I pulled back a little and then pushed in, grabbing his hips and moving. I didn't want to go too fast, but I made sure he would feel everything. I let go of one of his hips and grabbed his shoulder, pulling him back against me. "Did you miss my cock?"

Grayson's hold on Riley's hips tightened and the way she moaned around Asher's cock told me everything I needed to know. I slapped his ass. "Did you miss me filling this tight little hole?" I moved quicker, making sure to look for any signs that he was uncomfortable while still enjoying myself.

Gagging sounds came from Riley causing my body to shudder. "Oh fuck, that mouth is going to make me come," Asher warned, causing her to choke. He let up a little, his chest heaving when he came.

Grayson and I moved in unison and there was a tingle in my spine. "River, god, I'm close."

He was so tight and Riley's now unmuffled noises were like ecstasy. I groaned, moving faster. "Make her come again and then we can come together." I reached around, circling my fingers around his throat. I squeezed his neck, feeling his pulse point rhythmically beat against my thumb.

Grayson nodded, moving his hand between Riley's legs and played with her clit. She looked over her shoulder, her face stained with small tears from when Asher was face fucking her. The look of desire and intrigue was not lost while she watched us together.

Her mouth dropped open and her body shivered. She came loudly, Grayson not letting up on his thrusts.

"Come on, come for me." I demanded. He moved against her, his body jolting when he finally came. That feeling of him releasing had me seeing stars and coming with a groan, holding him in place.

Riley let out heavy breaths from her place bent over the bed. Asher looked relaxed as he stretched out on his bed, watching us. I eased my cock out of my best friend, licking my lips when he pulled out of Riley. I rubbed his shoulders, kissing the side of his face. "Next time you can fuck me, I promise."

36
RILEY

I asked to shower by myself which had gotten me disgruntled looks, but I was able to get clean with no distractions. My mind had wandered to the vision of River and Grayson together. It was erotically intimate in a way I'd never seen. The amount of care River had for him pulled at my heartstrings. Watching him fuck from a different perspective had that same heart racing.

River had given me some of his clothes to wear as he usually did and I stepped out of Asher's bathroom, feeling clean and refreshed.

"You could have just gone to sleep smelling like all of us." River smiled at me, pulling at the hem of the shirt I wore.

"Maybe next time." I lifted up on my toes and rubbed my nose against his.

Asher leaned against his desk. "I think it's time we went to bed. So, get out of my room."

"Can you pretend you like all of us for maybe a fraction of a second?" Grayson said, chuckling.

Asher rolled his eyes. "I do like you. I would like you more if you left and let me get some sleep. Let her get some sleep as well. No midnight fucking."

River walked over and grabbed my phone from his brother's desk. He looked at the screen. "Well, it's way past midnight, so I think a mid-morning fuck is not off the table."

"Your brother is right. Lack of sleep will not be pretty for you." I poked him in the chest.

He pouted but held his hand out for me to take. Grayson followed behind us as we left Asher's room and walked down the hall to River's.

"I think I'm gonna sleep on the couch." Grayson threw his thumb over his shoulder before we stepped into the room.

"No one is kicking you out," I said, tugging at his shirt playfully.

He caressed my face, his thumb hanging onto my bottom lip. "Oh, I know. I also know that River did not spring for a queen-sized bed when he and Asher went mattress hunting."

"A full can fit us just fine," River argued, attempting to throw his best friend in the room.

Grayson slapped his hands away. "I also think it's better for Riley if we both aren't there to cause her to overheat, in the good way and the bad way."

River rolled his eyes but conceded. "Fine, you know where the blankets and shit are."

Grayson blew him a kiss, then grabbed my face and kissed my lips. I leaned into it, wanting more of his mouth. "Good night, *aking sinta.*"

I'D SPEND THE ENTIRE REST OF THE WEEKEND WITH RIVER. GRAYSON HAD left early in the morning, leaving us with a simple text that he couldn't stay till Monday and that he'd find a way to make it up to us. River had put me on the back of his bike and taken us to Lucina, which was a small town near where the school was located in San Francisco. It had pretty architecture and I could listen to River talk about art for hours.

I hadn't realized he'd invited Marianne out as well. She'd pulled up in her mom's car and was happy to see me, but she'd waited until River had gone to get me a snack before diving into her questions. My answers were honest, but the most exciting part was that in a short period of time I'd gained two additional sexual partners. I had no idea what that meant for me in the long run. The excited expression on her face told me she was happy I was satisfied in the present and that she should have bet money on Asher and I colliding in a way I'd never considered until last night.

I was sad that she was leaving Monday morning, but we had already marked on our calendars each time she would be back.

We'd all sat outside of a small grab and go food place while I video chatted my mom. Beau was more than happy to be in the screen the entire time. The only thing I could think of that would have made it even better was if we were all there together. Yes, even Asher, who we'd invited, but he claimed he was too busy to go to a town he'd been to loads of times.

Corrin kept trying to ask me questions during Asher's Monday morning class, but now that the sex haze had lifted, I wanted to focus on what I'd originally come here for. I shushed her for the fourth time, and she practically hissed at me. I would tell her things, just not right now, not while the man who I'd seen naked and panting taught in front of us. He was so good at pretending like he hadn't made me come on a bathroom sink or that he hadn't shoved his cock in my mouth, causing tears to run down my face.

I grabbed my things when class was dismissed and Corrin pulled me to her when we were off the aisle steps and proceeded to throw a million questions my way, but Asher had other plans. "Miss Monroe, a minute?"

Corrin let out the most obnoxious groan and stomped out. Asher walked around his desk when we were alone, closing the space between us. "You can't go around telling your friends about what happened."

I raised an eyebrow. "I'm not doing that. *You* are the one who knocked a drunk guy out at your house. *You* are the one who ran after me and into your bathroom."

He sucked his teeth, nodding. "A dire mistake on my part then."

I scoffed. "Is that why you wanted me to stay back? So, you could scold me?"

"I'm not scolding you."

I pulled my braids to one of my shoulders. "Tell yourself whatever you want. You can forget about that night and we can go back to this fun little repartee, where you constantly think I'm up to something and I don't give a fuck what you think."

He stepped toward me, taking up any space that had existed between us. "I do still think you're up to something, little liar, but that doesn't mean I'll forget about that night. To be honest, if you just opened up your pretty mouth and told me I was right, that your glowing education isn't the whole reason why you transferred, then I might be inclined to repeat all the things I did to you."

"I don't owe you any explanation. I'll be completely fine writing it off as a lapse of judgement and have a story to tell when I'm much older. It will be fascinating and not—what is it you said about how my story telling goes—oh, right, mundane."

His laugh echoed in the empty room. "Lapse of judgement? I don't really think you even considered thinking about it. You just knew what your needy little pussy wanted and I gave it to you."

I shoved him back. "And you are just the king of thought-provoking decisions. It didn't take you long to join in on the fun with your brother."

He put both his hands on the side of my head, bringing his face close to mine. Our breathing mingled and his glasses started to fog up. "You don't know how badly I want to bend you over this desk and pound your pussy until you're screaming. You and that fucking attitude."

"You don't know how badly I want you to stop treating me like I've got something to hide."

His lips brushed mine. "Oh, little liar, but you do. You were very conflicted in your dreams the other night."

My eyes widened. "You went into my head? Again?!"

He dropped his hands. "My brother made you a promise. Not me."

"Did you see anything?" My voice was hesitant, and I was nervous that I had dreamed of a prior conversation or dreamed of a future plan.

"Was there something you didn't want me to see?" Asher put his hands in his pockets, searching my face for some indication that I was about to be forthcoming with him.

"I..." I was cut off when my phone vibrated in my back pocket. I was grateful for the distraction.

CORRIN

Northside courtyard, now!"

I started to back away from Asher who looked more than frustrated with me.

"Riley, where are you going?"

I shook my head. "It's important. Your interrogation can wait." I spat back, opening the door and running out.

I ran as fast as I could to the northside courtyard, noticing that a bunch of people were crowding the otherwise open space. I shoved students out of my way, getting disgruntled looks, but I had to find Corrin. When I got to what I hoped was the front of the crowd, she grabbed me and pulled me into her.

"Look!" Corrin pointed to what had everyone so enthralled. There was a girl with dark hair and olive skin on the ground. The school nurse and other medical professionals were around her, but I could see her face clearly. She looked confused and lost. Her clothes were a little dirty and she was flinching each time one of the medics tried to touch her, but there were no signs of blood or external injuries.

"Who is that?" I asked, noticing that school officials were starting to disband the crowd and the sound of cop cars were in the distance.

"It's another girl from my coven, Riley."

A Dalmatian barked erratically while being held back by two school officials. The dog ripped out of their hold and was at the girl's side in a matter of seconds, starting to growl at anyone who came near her.

She held her hand out and softly touched its body, rubbing her hand down its side and the dog ceased its growling, nuzzling its face into her neck. It must be her familiar.

I looked over at the girl, shuffling back when we were finally shoved out of the perimeter. "We need to do this then. You need to do what Pen said tonight, and I'll find a way to get to my dad's office."

A few people lingered, but the rest of them moved on with the rest of their day. The girl from Corrin's coven was carried off somewhere, her dog following closely, and I had an inkling to follow her as well, but I wouldn't have known what to do when I caught up with them. She wouldn't remember anything. I would leave any conversation I had with her the same as when I started.

"You won't have to look that hard. It's the department meeting night. It happens one Tuesday every month. It's around eight in the auditorium." Ike stepped up behind us, causing Corrin to shriek.

"And how do you know this, brother dearest?" she asked, putting her hands on her hips.

"It's on the school calendar. Public knowledge." Ike rolled his eyes.

"That gets the staff out of the building, but what about getting in in the first place? It's not like I'll be able to just grab a key off of security." I looked at Corrin. "Could you make one through magic?"

She tilted her hand from left to right. "Um, maybe. It's not something I've ever done and I don't even know how long that would take me to figure out. Your faith in my magic is appreciated, but I'm still just a sophomore witch."

Ike scrubbed a hand down his face. "Fine, twist my arm."

"Huh?" I said, scratching my head.

"Listen, I may not want to use my powers in my career, but I still know *how* to use them. Locks are made of..." He waited a moment. "Right, metal. And what do I do?" He paused again, giving us a patronizing expression. "Metal magic. Does it all make sense?"

Corrin punched him in his arm. "You don't have to be so annoying, you are aware of that right?"

37
RILEY

I paced back and forth in River's room waiting on any word from Corrin about the extraction. She had texted me that she was working on it, but after a few hours I'd grown nervous.

"What's with all the back and forth?" River asked, lounging on his bed, scrolling through his phone.

"Just nervous about some school stuff, that's all."

He chuckled. "You are probably the smartest person I know, next to Professor St. James, so I think whatever it is will be fine." River put his phone down. "Do you want to talk about it?"

I smiled over at him. "No, but, um, thanks. If you want to be helpful, I do have a question for you." I rocked back and forth on my heels.

He patted the spot next to him on his bed. "I'm an open book, gorgeous."

"You aren't allowed to look too deep into it?" I demanded.

He lifted his hands. "Of course not. Shoot."

"Did your dad ever talk to you about mine?" I actually wanted to close my eyes when I asked this, not knowing how to anticipate his reaction.

River pursed his lips, rubbing the back of his neck. "I already asked my dad questions about what happened and he told me what he could. I don't like talking to the guy that much, so I must love you a lot if I tolerated speaking with him enough to question him on things."

"I don't mean about what happened, I mean like did your dad ever mention mine at all. Even before we started dating?"

"Uh, no. The relationship I have with him now is exactly the same as it was then, so I don't have any new information for you. Why are you asking?"

I narrowed my eyes at him and he waved his hand, as if he was trying to erase his question. "Right, not looking too deep into it. Got it."

"What exactly did your dad tell you about what happened anyway?"

He gave me a skeptical look. "I told you all this. He reiterated pretty much everything the police said. He said there were no suspects, and I think he was found by one of the school's probably underpaid security guards."

My spine straightened as my ears perked up. "Security guard?"

River nodded, placing a hand on my knee. "Yeah. He moved on to another topic after that and as per usual I stopped listening."

Oliver St. James lied to his own son, which meant that him finding my dad had more to it than I thought. My phone buzzed loudly in my hand. I looked down at the screen seeing Corrin's name flash.

I lifted my finger up, telling River to give me a minute. I stepped out of his room and into the hallway. I answered the call, putting the phone to my ear.

"Hey, anything?"

Corrin's voice sounded like it had a smile in it. "We are a go for tomorrow night. I don't know how this shit will taste, but it should work. You'll be able to mimic Pen's gifts long enough to solve this bitch."

"Perfect. So, I'll see you tomorrow night at the northside courtyard."

"See you there."

She hung up and I jumped when I heard Asher's door close.

"What's in the courtyard?"

I shrugged. "If I said none of your business, would you leave it alone?"

He smirked, his beard looked as if he had trimmed it recently. "Is that a real question?"

"Grayson wants to know if you want to go to a movie tonight..." River started, staring down at his phone while he came out of his room. He noticed both of us, looking back and forth between us. "What's happening here?"

"Absolutely nothing." Asher walked past me down the stairs, his arm brushing mine. Our fingers touched and I had the overwhelming feeling that I wanted to wrap my fucking pinky tightly around his and never let go. No idea where that idea came from. If I hadn't been the center of all their attention the other night, I wouldn't have believed it ever happened.

"Hmmm, I would have thought that all the bonding we did would have brought you guys closer," River said, sounding a little disappointed.

"We are a millimeter closer than we were before." I threaded my fingers through his. "So, a movie?"

He snapped his fingers. "Yes, a movie. Let me text him that we are on the way." River walked ahead of me down the stairs, grabbing his motorcycle keys.

Asher eyed me from the kitchen, but I said nothing else. I was far too close to let new people into the plan now. I had what I needed and who I needed. I had to make sure it went off without a hitch.

38
RILEY

I silenced my phone, not wanting any mishaps before I went to meet Corrin. I had gotten a text from both Marianne and my mom, but I could answer them later. I passed by a few teachers heading towards the auditorium and attempted to look as uninteresting as possible. An email had gone out this morning about what transpired in the courtyard.

The entire thing sounded as if they knew things were off but tried to act as if they had it all under control. It was downright infuriating. I leaned against an adjacent building to the one my dad's office was housed in. It was humid out even though the sun wasn't around, the air a little muggy. I heard footsteps, making my breaths a little softer not knowing who it was. My roommate patted my shoulder, standing in front of me. Ike was right behind her, looking around as paranoid as ever.

"Calm down. You didn't have to help us, you know," Corrin scolded.

Ike shook his head, heading towards the building. "If anything happened to you, mom and dad would never let me live it down. And I know you would come back and haunt me."

The meeting had started five or ten minutes ago, so unless a teacher or faculty member was running really late, they would all be there by now. The school security was really meant for certain buildings that housed more priceless things that the university cared about or the potions building, since Corrin had told me that something in there was likely explosive.

The door had two basic bolt locks and a chain lock on the top. Ike held his hand out, tiny wisps of gold and silver whipped around. The wisps connected themselves to each piece of the various locks and I heard them being bent and molded, the chain lock at the top melted into a golden pin that slipped right through. The bolt locks pulled back and Ike yanked the door open.

We didn't want to spend time waiting on the elevator, so we took the stairs, to Corrin's dismay. I took them two at a time, my determination overpowering the fact that my legs were burning. I opened the door to my dad's floor, realizing how eerie it all felt this time of night. None of the overhead lights were on and I had the odd feeling that someone was watching.

I stopped in front of my dad's office, the nerves I'd placed in the back of my mind shoving their way to the front. Ike stepped up to the door, lifting his hand, then slightly lowered it. "Are you sure you want to do this? We can turn back and just, like, go to Leif's for food."

"Open the fucking door, Ike," Corrin said, exasperated.

He let out a sigh, using his powers on the door. It swung open slowly and I pressed my hand against it to keep it ajar. Ike looked at his sister. "Please check your phone just in case. I'll be back downstairs and text you if I see someone." He gave us one long look and then went back down the hall.

I stepped into the room, the feeling of dread washing over me. I wanted to turn on the light, but that would cause suspicion, so I worked with the tiny piece of moonlight we had. It looked like an office my dad would have. There was a tiny basketball hoop on the back of the door for when he got bored, there were so many open books on his desk, and when my eyes roamed over the ground, I found a picture of me, him and my mom when I was just a kid. We looked so happy, and it would never be like that again.

It was like besides the window being fixed, nothing in this office had been touched.

"Riley, are you ready?" Corrin reached into her bag, pulling out a small bottle with liquid that looked like apple juice.

"Is this safe?" I asked, trying to sound smart even though I didn't actually care at this point.

"If I did everything right, yes. If not, it will still work, but you might end up with a shit stomachache tomorrow." She removed the cork from the bottle and handed it to me.

I nodded, inhaling deeply, then exhaling. The bottle shook a little in my hands when I brought it to my lips. I tipped it back, drinking the contents. It had a tangy aftertaste, but it wasn't horrible. I walked over to my dad's window, trying to find some way to turn this power on. I looked out the window, placing my hand on the glass.

"Do you feel anything?" Corrin asked and I was about to answer her when things got fuzzy. I fell against the window, grabbing onto the sill to keep me elevated. Corrin started to come over, but I held my hand out to stop her.

The room started ripping apart and moving. Different colors filtered my vision and I felt a wave of vertigo. The sky outside changed over and over as if it was trying to find the right timeline to put me in. Corrin disappeared from my sight and I saw someone moving around the desk, but they weren't fully put together. I blinked hoping that the more I tried to focus the clearer the past would be. I stepped away from the window, trying to find my balance. I landed against the desk, my hand shaking when I picked up the picture of my family—the one that had just been on the ground—but now it was on the desk like it was always meant to be.

My head was throbbing, but there was a lamp on in the room, creating a dim light around me. I saw my dad's handsome face, working hard at his desk. A knock came at the door and a person came in. Suddenly the vision changed and my dad was being jolted out the window. I turned my head too quickly, the swift movement causing me to press my palms to my temples.

My dad was back on his feet when I blinked, but he was right in front of the window and I backed up giving the past some room, so I could pay attention.

I don't understand, my dad said. *That can't be true.*

The lamp got thrown in one direction, cutting off any solid light supply I had. The room was surrounded in darkness, no moonlight to guide me.

You don't get to take things that don't belong to you, the other person said. It sounded like a man. The lack of light made it hard to make out his face, but he was tall. His voice sounded angry and like he was at his wits end.

I will tell them. You won't come near my family, my dad said, prepared to charge at this man. The jolt of magic that shot past me hit my dad and he collided with the window. I hadn't thought about the consequences of doing this, seeing this. I held my quivering lips together because I needed to know who did this. I wanted to reach my hand out and save him from falling. I wanted to tell him to just back down and say whatever he needed to, so he could get out of this situation.

If I knew anything about my dad, he was thinking about me and my mom the entire time, and I didn't know what hurt more. The fact that it seemed like we were the reason for his death or that we were the last things on his mind.

I tried to get closer, needing to see who I was going to expose. I needed to see who was snatching girls from Corrin's coven. I took one step and then another, but then a loud scream came from near the door. It sounded like my name.

It sounded like Corrin was screaming my name.

Chocolate PSD
Bar Mock-Up
Food Packaging Collection

39
RILEY

I felt my body shake as if someone was pulling me back and forth. The world I'd seen felt distorted now and everything was out of order. Time moved forward and I tried to find purchase on anything I could get my hands on to stop it. Then my mind stalled like it had found its place to stop and I was back in my father's office, in the present.

I slammed my hand against my head, feeling like my entire brain had been heaved right off my spinal cord. Corrin was at my side, taking my face in her hands and forcing me to look at her. We weren't alone though. I ripped her hands from my face and saw one security officer and Oliver St. James in the doorway.

River's dad had Ike by the arm, giving each one of us a skeptical expression.

"You were supposed to keep watch, Ike," Corrin hissed, pressing her lips together when the security officer gave her a menacing look.

"I was! They came out of—" He was cut off when River's dad started speaking.

"What the hell are you doing in here?" He reached back and cut the light on; the room now shrouded in a bright overhead light.

"We were just leaving..." Corrin started, trying to sound nonchalant.

"What happened in here?" I asked, looking back at the window.

Oliver quirked a brow. "Whatever do you mean?"

"You know exactly what I mean!"

He stared at me, his gaze one of uninterested coldness. "I have no idea and you really shouldn't concern yourself with things that don't involve you." He huffed out a breath when I started to argue, looking over at the security officer before throwing Ike towards Corrin. "Do it and we'll deal with it in the morning."

The security officer reached into his pocket, pulling out a tiny tube of silver dust. I watched River's dad walk out as the officer removed the cap, flinging his arm out and let the dust wash over us. I had no idea what it was meant to do, but I started to lose all feeling in my limbs and my head felt foggy again.

This time was different. My vision wasn't turning into anything; it was simply going black.

I'D WOKEN UP IN A LESS THAN COMFORTABLE BED AT THE CITY HOSPITAL. I didn't remember getting there, but the image of my mom's face would always be ingrained in my brain. It was one of the worst things to wake up to. The look of fear and confused anger, because your mom has no idea if you were hurt or if you brought this upon yourself, is something you can't easily remove from your memory.

My mom had spoken to the doctors and River was at my side, trying not to question me during the two hours I was there until they released me. All my scans came back clean, there were no signs of drugs or alcohol, which I knew there wouldn't be. Any traces of what

Corrin had me drink were gone as if once it had done what was required of it, it just vanished from my system. Grayson had run through the doors with Asher strolling in behind him. Asher looked like he could snap the neck of the next person that pissed him off and I wondered if that rage was because of me.

River had assured me Corrin and Ike were fine. I wondered what that word even meant...*fine*. I couldn't tell my boyfriend that his father had put me to sleep after I snuck into my dad's office and became a dupe of a memory witch. My head pounded just thinking about the massive amounts of questions I would get after that.

I still held my secrets, and all Oliver St. James suspected was that I was just a nosey student. Nothing more.

I hadn't wanted to go home, but my mom demanded that I get in the car in that voice that she hadn't used on me since I was twelve. She'd driven in silence, her hands gripping the steering wheel with a deathly hold. I had planned to bolt to my room when I got inside, let Beau follow me and snuggle with him until I was whisked back to school, but I wasn't so lucky.

"Living room. Now." My mom didn't look in my direction, she just walked past me to the couch.

I heard Beau sigh as he sat down at my feet. His tail wasn't doing its happy wag and his ears were back. It was almost as if he was in trouble as well. I reached down and slid my hand over his head, trying to reassure him that everything would be okay. I made my way into the living room, sitting on the opposite end of the couch.

My mom rubbed the place between her eyebrows, her eyes closed as she took deep breaths. "You can start explaining at any time now?"

Beau walked in front of the couch, laying down in front of my feet. I smacked my lips together, hoping that at any moment the words would just come to me. "I'm sorry, Mom."

"Riley, I'm sorry is no good at the moment. I have no idea what you are even sorry for, that's my point."

My mouth opened and closed but nothing seemed good enough.

"River's dad said that you were a bit erratic and so were your friends, which is why they decided to put you to sleep. Honey, what were you doing in your dad's office? I told you that if you needed to talk to me about something then you could...you promised me you would."

I reared my head back, waving my hands. "Wait, *erratic?*"

She nodded. "I'm not completely okay with their methods, but if you were in danger of hurting yourself I would rather them use something on you to keep you from harm."

"Mom, I wasn't.... *erratic* is not the word I'd use. I was..." I trailed off, groaning.

"You were what? What could you have possibly been doing in your dad's office so late at night, hmm?" She tapped one of the couch cushions, waiting for my response. She had this way about her that made you nervous to answer, but also afraid that if you took too long she might bite your head off. "Not to mention Beau was having a field day last night. He barked for hours on end and nearly broke down the front door."

Beau peeked up at me, huffing.

"I hadn't ever been in there and I knew I would get looked at and questioned if I asked to see it myself. Dad never got to take me in there as a kid, just the campus. I guess I wanted to feel close in some way..." It wasn't a lie. Not completely. My reasoning for going there behind people's backs was valid, so it could all make very logical sense. I didn't have the answer to who had jolted my dad out a window, so allowing my mom into the fold wasn't an option just yet.

"Riley..."

"I wasn't erratic though. That's a lie." I might not be so open when it came to certain truths, but I wasn't going to have someone say something so blatantly false.

"Why would he say that then?" My mom scooted closer to me, placing her hand on my leg. Her skin was smooth like velvet when I placed my hand over hers.

"I don't know, but if I'm honest about anything, Mom, it's that I was completely sane before I got dusted with magic."

She nodded, taking in my words and considering them. "And you being in your dad's office, did it help you at all? I'm still highly upset by your choices, but I guess I understand feeling the things you do. Did being there give you any clarity or maybe even some closure?"

I squeezed her hand. "No, but I'm working on it."

Her eyebrows furrowed with alarm. I stopped her before she could start yelling at me. "I'll find a less invasive way to do it that doesn't involve school property or trespassing."

She placed a hand over her heart, letting out a breath. "Good. You have a meeting with the Dean of Students anyway, so if you were even considering another stunt then I'm sure that would have you thinking twice."

"The Dean of Students?" I smacked my palm against my forehead. "But..."

My mom pointed her finger at me. "It's still misconduct. You violated school rules and a little thing called breaking and entering. They aren't pressing charges on that front thankfully, but you and your friends are having a meeting to discuss potential punishment, if there is any. Hopefully it will just go on your record and get removed in a year."

I sucked in a breath, exhaling when I leaned back against the couch. Beau jumped on me as if he was small enough to be a lap dog and snuggled into my lap. "Just perfect."

40
RILEY

I tapped my foot against the floor, way too antsy to sit in my chair. I wasn't nervous because I thought I was going to get reprimanded, but I didn't want to go through another moment of having to dodge questions about a topic I had no interest in discussing. Corrin, Ike, and I were all called in, finding ourselves in the spacious office of the Dean of Students.

An older woman with short brown hair motioned for us to sit down, while she sat in the chair behind her desk. She placed her hands in front of her, clasping them together. Her name plate read Mercedes Wales.

"In my position, it may seem hard to believe, but I don't like disciplining my students. I do believe that people make mistakes and should learn from them without being made out to feel like everything they do from then on needs to be perfect. I try to understand the reasoning behind incidents before I take action and then plan accordingly."

I snuck a glance over at Corrin, who was also looking at me, but quickly looked away. What she was saying was promising, but until I heard her whole speech, I wouldn't take my chances.

"Would anyone like to explain to me how you ended up in Mr. Monroe's office?"

We were all silent until Corrin cleared her throat. "Don't you already know all that?"

Ike's breath caught. "Corrin!"

My roommate gave her brother an incredulous look. "What?!"

Dean Wales cut in. "I really just wanted any explanation that might enhance the things I already know, but Mr. Hayes, you do know the consequences for using your magic on campus unsupervised or without written approval from a faculty member, correct?"

Ike nodded solemnly.

Dean Wales shook her head, leaning back in her chair. "Since you have been a model student thus far, and from the looks of your academic track, your magic is not your chosen career path, then I give you disciplinary probation for the rest of the year. You will also reform the original locks that you messed with."

Ike seemed to physically relax. He would be watched more closely, his choices put under a microscope to make sure he stayed on the straight and narrow. Dean Wales focused on Corrin and me. "I know both of you have had a hard semester so far with everything going on with your coven," she eyed Corrin, "and with..."

Knock, knock.

Dean Wales straightened in her seat, while each of us looked to see who it was.

"Come in."

River's dad peeked his head in, catching sight of us. He closed the door behind him, stepping further into the room. "I am very sorry to bother you Dean Wales, I was just bringing these for you to look over." He sat some papers down on her desk.

She smiled up at him, giving them a quick scan. He gave each of us a simple nod as if he hadn't barged in on us that night and put us to sleep. Oliver fiddled with the cufflinks at the end of his shirt. "I am truly sorry for what I had to do to you all. I was only working in your best interest. I would have hated for you to hurt yourselves or get into something you weren't supposed to."

His words were meant to sound sincere, and Dean Wales ate it up. For me, all it did was make me curl my hands around the chair's armrest. I wanted to scream that *I* wasn't the problem here.

"No one blames you, Oliver. I was simply telling them that I know it's been difficult with that mess with the covens that needs to be looked into and with Thomas's death."

My eyes widened when I heard my dad's name. Mr. St. James tilted his head to the side. "Thomas's death?"

Dean Wales gave him a quizzical look. "Yes. I don't think it's completely fair to cast aside the fact that his daughter was the one breaking into his office. It's concerning, but not of an academic nature. Things need to be cared for more delicately with this matter."

River's dad slowly looked at me. His eyes gave nothing away, but the tension in his shoulders sure did. "You're Thomas's daughter?"

I licked my lips, tearing my hands away from the armrest and placing them in my lap. "Yes."

"I spoke to your father a couple of times. He spoke about his daughter, but I'd only seen pictures from when you were smaller. I had no idea you'd joined us at the university." The way he spoke to me was like he wasn't talking to me at all. His voice sounded distant.

Dean Wales put the papers he gave her to the side. "Your father was a delight and he will be missed, but if there are any issues you are dealing with, you seek one of our counselors or ask for help in another way. Disregarding school rules is not the way. You have such a brilliant transcript from your last school and so far at Mystic Riegan and I would hate to see you tarnish that."

I gave her a polite smile. "Of course not, I apologize for not thinking clearer." I wanted to vomit saying anything that went against what I was trying to do.

Seek a counselor. I'm sure that was what she and anyone else told students and then sent them to my dad. No counselor here was going to be able to help me because my problem was hidden within this school, so trusting anyone that worked for someone higher was tricky territory.

Mr. St. James rubbed his chin, tapping his fingers against the desk. "I should let you get back to your meeting."

Dean Wales nodded. "Thank you. Make sure everyone is ready for the assembly tomorrow."

He stopped right next to my chair, turning to look at her. "Ah, yes. The assembly." He looked over at us, his eyes finding mine and giving me a tight smile. His gaze drifted and it could have looked as if he was being a creep and staring at my chest, but I knew that wasn't it. His eyes twitched a small fraction when they landed on something at my sternum.

My necklace.

He hummed. "I'll make sure the rest of the faculty is on it. I'm sure you are already sending an email."

Dean Wales laughed and River's dad made his way out, not giving me a second glance.

"Assembly?" Ike asked.

The Dean of Students got up from her chair. "As I told Corrin, this witch situation needs to be dealt with and we are wanting parents, students, and faculty to come and address it. The Chancellor thinks it's in our best interest to involve everyone as a school community, so he's coming to speak and hopefully find a solution." She raised her wrist to her face, looking at her watch. "Alright, well disciplinary probation for all of you. Please be on your best behavior and follow the rules. Your futures are far too promising for something like this to trip you up."

We said our thanks and made our way out the door.

I walked in step with Corrin who nudged my shoulder as we got outside. I looked over at her, watching as she reached into her bag. She pulled out a folded photo and handed it to me. I could feel my eyes start to brim with tears, but I held them back. I looked at the photo from my dad's office—with me, him, and my mom.

I blinked up at her and she was giving me a small smile. "I grabbed the entire frame right before I heard them come in. I thought if we were gonna go down during our little mission then at least you would have this."

I pulled her into the biggest hug, burying my face in her shoulder. Ike stood behind her, giving us some space.

"Thank you. I'm sorry I got you into this just for it to go to shit."

Corrin laughed. "It's not shit just yet. It just went off the rails for a moment, but we'll figure out another way." She lifted her phone from her back pocket. "Ah, Jade is here to pick me up. You want to come to the bar?"

I shook my head. "Nah, I think I'll head to the room."

"Okay well let me know if you want us to come pick you up at all." She gave me another quick hug, turning to walk away with her brother.

41
ASHER

"Did you even ask them why they were there?" I said through my teeth. I held onto my dad's desk so tight that I started to lose feeling in my fingers.

"I didn't have to, nor did I really want to." He had one of his legs bent out and crossed over the other, looking uncharacteristically relaxed.

"You could have hurt them? I understand what they were doing was wrong, but for fucks sake." I pushed away from the desk and walked away from him. I looked at the back wall, my chest heaving.

I heard him chuckle. "I didn't, though. Listen, son, I really don't quite understand why you are so damn upset with me. Aren't you the one who told me they would be at the courtyard?"

I may have fucked Riley and felt something for her that needed to be thoroughly investigated, but my brother came first. As much of an asshole as River thought I was, his best interest was my priority. I'd gone back to my office after I'd overheard her phone call and gotten bombarded by my dad.

He started asking so many questions about my brother and kept prattling on about the less than joyous meeting he'd forced River into. He was exhausting. I'd said that if he cared so much about his son then he should probably figure out what's going on at the court-yard that night. I slightly regretted that now, but not enough to go to Riley and tell her the truth.

He scratched under his chin. "Besides, your brother wasn't even there, so you can stop worrying about him."

"I just didn't want River connected with something that seemed off, that's all. I thought you would peep in, see what they were doing. Not this!" I took my glasses off, pinching the bridge of my nose.

My dad rolled his eyes. "It's a sleeping powder, Asher. Not a flesh-eating virus. I needed to get them out of there without issue. Who knows what kind of outbursts would happen if I had tried to remove them with tender care." He waved his hand in my direction. "None of that matters anyway. Now that you are here, I have to ask you a question."

"You really think I want to help you out with something?"

My dad paid my response no mind. "Did you know that girl was Thomas's daughter?"

I readjusted my rolled-up sleeves. "Riley?"

His eyes sparkled with my recognition. "So, you know her?"

I stepped up to his desk. "She's in my class. That's all."

My dad's laugh was boisterous as he settled back in his chair. "Asher, we may not see eye to eye on many things, but I am still your father and I like to think I know when you're lying."

I scoffed. "You can check the roster; she *is* in the class."

"That's not all though."

"What the fuck does that mean?"

He got up from his chair, some of his hair getting out of its perfectly done style. "Why would your brother be hanging around with her? Why would you act as if you are so confident that he would be there?"

"None of this is of any importance. I'm leaving." I stalked across the room, prepared to open the door and slam it closed.

"River's mysterious little girlfriend."

I swallowed, my stomach dropping.

"That does complicate things, doesn't it?"

I turned my head, noticing that my dad was talking more to himself than to me. I left the room, wondering what exactly he meant and whether or not I cared enough to dig more into it.

42
RILEY

The assembly was packed when I walked in, flanked by River and Grayson. I'd been overly evasive with them, but just like my mom, they only wanted to know how they could help. I was so fucking tired of explaining myself and trying to figure out how to keep everyone in their own lane. I decided that right before the assembly I would open myself up, just a tiny bit. Just enough to satisfy.

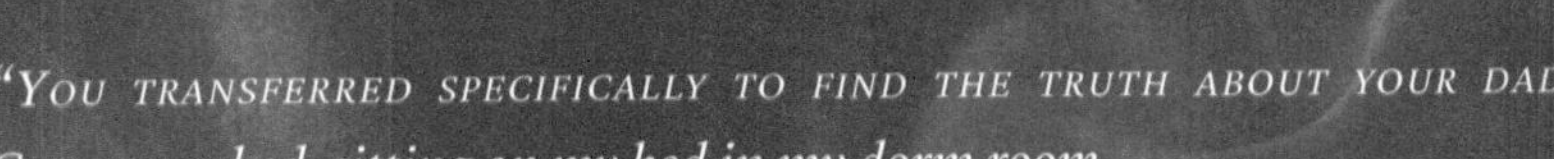

"You transferred specifically to find the truth about your dad?" *Grayson asked, sitting on my bed in my dorm room.*

"Mhmm."

"And I was right about things being weird after the party, about you and Corrin being fucking sneaky," River added, leaning against the wall next to the bathroom.

I nodded, standing in the middle of the room and moving from foot to foot.

"Are you sure this isn't just grief talking? Like you want to think there is more to it but..." Grayson started but I shot him an irritated look.

"No! I'm not an idiot. If things made sense, I would let it go, but it doesn't. A lot of people want to say that well, you never really know people, when shit like this happens, but this is not one of those cases. I knew my dad and this isn't something he would have done."

Grayson gave me an apologetic look. I felt bad for snapping at him, but I was so damn tired.

"How many people know about this?" River questioned.

"Umm, only three know about it to its full extent and maybe like two know about in a more minor way."

River's eyes widened and he placed his hands over his mouth. "Riley! You can tell everyone else, but you can't tell us. You can't tell me?" He sounded a little hurt.

One of my braids fell into my eye and I tossed it back, so I could focus on him. "I didn't want to tell anyone, okay? Corrin just kind of fell into it and everything else...I just...ugh. I want you to know enough so that you aren't in the complete dark, but not enough so that you think you need to help me."

"You want us to just sit back and watch?" Grayson asked, the irony of his question not lost on me.

I pointed at him. "You have a scholarship to worry about," I moved my finger to River, "and your dad, well he is a part of the faculty and there is the matter of your brother. Also, you're both seniors and graduation is really fucking important."

"And so are you." River rushed over to me, placing a hand on my cheek.

THE SEATING WAS SCARCE, SO WE STOOD ALONG THE BACK WALL. PARENTS, including Corrin's, sat with unappeased faces waiting for it to start.

Corrin pulled at the collar of her shirt, her face the epitome of anxious energy. I found Asher near the front of the stage. He was speaking with someone, but I could tell he was a little tense.

Someone tapped the mic and feedback littered throughout the room. Dean Whales cleared her throat, greeting everyone. "I know you all came here for answers and to speak your thoughts. We want to listen and find a way to keep our students safe."

"We want to know who's doing this!" someone in the crowd shouted.

"We want you to increase security!"

"Why weren't we notified about this sooner!?"

Corrin's mom's voice was clear throughout all the noise. "My daughter loves this school and her coven, but I will not tolerate her being put in danger."

Dean Whales put her hands up, trying to calm them down. "I understand your grievance with the university..."

She continued to speak, but my eyes focused on Oliver St. James. He was looking right at me, but almost like he was looking through me. I was uncomfortable and felt like this meeting was so much more than what I was seeing.

"I would like to bring out Chancellor Erik Fowler, who wanted to address you and your concerns and give you insight into what we have discovered thus far." She looked to her left and a man started walking up the stage. He was tall with a head of curls and bronzed skin. He smiled at Dean Whales, a smile that could have rivaled the brightest light bulb.

He stood behind the podium and his voice rang out around the crowd. "Hello parents, faculty and students. I am tremendously sorry that this is why you've all been gathered here tonight. We've made a grave error in thinking we could keep this as just a university matter and I take full responsibility for not reaching out sooner."

His voice was deep but compelling, nearly charismatic. If his personality was as appealing as his voice, then I didn't understand why he was almost nonexistent when I had searched the school online.

My thoughts barreled on when I felt a presence near me. Grayson and River were on my right side, so why did I feel so boxed in? The crowd was thick, but there was still space to breathe. I was about to ask Grayson to switch spots with me when whoever it was got even closer and I found myself finally looking at them.

I didn't recognize them. They looked like a normal student just here for a general assembly. Their eyes though held a far-off look, like their mind was somewhere else and they were moving on autopilot.

"Can I help you?" I asked, annoyed. A few people in the back row peeked over their shoulders to look at what was going on.

The dazed student blinked and then reached for my neck. It happened so fast that I didn't have time to push them away. I thought they were going to choke me, but they ripped my necklace from my body. I staggered back, landing into River and Grayson.

"Woah, what the fuck?" River yelled, shooting daggers at whoever had harmed me. The Chancellor had stopped talking and was looking in our direction. Corrin was tugging her brother through the crowd of people to get to us.

The student gazed at my necklace and then looked towards the stage. I charged towards them. "Give it back!"

Within the blink of an eye, they threw down the necklace, ripping their dampener ring off and pointed their palm at the gem. It rattled and shook as if it was being overtaken with so much energy. It was lifted from the ground and then exploded into a million tiny little pieces. I moved my hands in front of my face, shielding myself.

The explosive energy rattled the room, causing everyone to try to regain their balance.

The student started breathing heavily and then they dropped to the ground, slumped over near the multitude of tiny ruby shards. My mouth dropped open as I looked around, confused and stunned at what just happened.

"Riley, are you okay?" Grayson said, touching my shoulder.

I turned around, reaching my hands out to pull him into me for some sort of normalcy, when a burst of power shot out of my hands and shoved him backwards. It was invisible, but you could almost just see the energy it released. He collided with a crowd of people, stumbling back.

River's eyes expanded, looking between Grayson and myself. My hands shook as I looked down at them. My veins pulsed like something was growing, but it didn't hurt much. It stung a little and was cold as if something foreign was being directly injected into my body. River reached for me and I forced him back, shooting out another stream of magic, but he jumped to the side, dodging it.

The magic sailed through a crowd of people who shrieked and tried their best to move out of its way.

"What the fuck..." I was walking backwards, whispering to myself as everyone in the room started talking, pointing at me and attempting to find an exit.

"Riley..." River started.

"No! Stay over there!" I yelled, the magic bolting from my hands again. I saw Grayson looking over at the stage of overwhelmed faculty and staff, blinking rapidly as if he couldn't believe what he saw, then he looked at me, something like sympathy in his eyes.

The room turned into chaos, but I saw Asher circle around the stage and push past some of the people trying to find their way out or shouting at anyone who would listen. I didn't know what he was doing or if he was trying to get to me, but he needed to stay where he was.

People were quickly exiting the auditorium, while the staff were trying to contain an already hectic situation. I heard my name being yelled from the stairs below and then I heard it closer as if River was trying to get my attention, but the rampaging crowd was too much.

Grayson ran towards me, grabbing me around my waist and encircling us with his shadows. The room disappeared around us and there was silence.

43
RILEY

I stumbled forward when we got to our destination. Grayson's shadows dispersed and he stood back. I took in a few deep breaths, trying to take in my surroundings. We had landed in a massive room, a study. There were tinted windows, floor to ceiling bookcases, and multiple couches made of velvet. A bar cart was in the corner and a chaise sat by one of the windows, a quilted blanket draped over one end.

Chandeliers hung from the vaulted ceiling and a coffee table that looked like it was hand carved was placed in the middle of the room.

"Grayson, where are we?"

He ran a hand through his hair, looking towards one of the doors.

"Grayson. Where. Are. We?" I repeated, my tone sharper.

His eyes looked sad when he answered me. "Riley, I'm sorry."

I furrowed my brow, cocking my head to the side. "Sorry? I don't understand why…"

The double doors near the far end of the room flew open and

River's dad walked in, looking pleased. He strolled past us as if he didn't even see we were there.

He headed to the bar cart, beginning to prepare a drink. "I almost thought you were going to go against me, but you did as you're told like you've always done."

His back was turned to us, so I had no idea who he was talking to.

"I knew you would be conflicted, but I have to say the anticipation was a little thrilling. I was astonished myself when I came to figure it out," he prattled on, putting ice in his glass.

"What the hell are you talking about?" I pressed, feeling that surge of energy. It was hectic the way it moved through my veins.

Mr. St. James turned around, his eyes finally accepting our presence in the room. "Oh, sweetie, that's a very long story. You'll have to be more specific."

I started to point my finger at him and shout, but the glass was yanked out of his hand and thrown at the wall. His face grew red with anger, and he stomped towards me. I put my palm out and he was thrown backwards, knocking into the bar cart and hitting the wall.

He smoothed a hand over his hair. "You insolent fucking girl."

I didn't let his anger bother me. I was too busy trying to understand everything that was going on. "You told that student to tear my necklace off, didn't you? To destroy it?"

All he did was give me a sly smile, confirming my accusation.

"Now, now, let's play nice and this will all get resolved." A voice sounded from beyond the door. It was one I'd heard before. *Charismatic.*

I looked over my shoulder to see Chancellor Fowler, unbuttoning his suit jacket as he came into the room. He looked over at River's dad, noticing the glass that littered the floor. He stuck out two of his fingers, making a sweeping motion. I watched as all the pieces gathered together and set themselves on the bar cart.

He sighed, casting a glance at Grayson. "Your parents should be so proud of you. You know how to get things done and succeed. You can breathe easy, my boy, at least when it comes to me your senior year will be without hindrance."

I gave Grayson a look of confusion, swinging my head back to the Chancellor.

"Oh, don't be upset with him. Anyone in his position would have likely done the same thing. I don't like threatening my student's college careers, but when push comes to shove and all that." The Chancellor walked over to Grayson, patting his shoulder. My shadow wielder tensed, his brown eyes finding mine, pleading with me as if I understood any of this.

River's dad cleared his throat. "I can take the boy back. He served his purpose."

Chancellor Fowler thought this over, nodding. "Right. Have him release the new girls while he's at it."

New girls? What the fuck was going on?

"Girls? Wait...the witches..." I shook my head at Grayson. "The ones that went missing and then they came back. They said they got whisked away but don't remember anything..." I thought back to how we even got here. It was like being in a silent black tunnel. It was soothing but only because I knew it was Grayson. The feeling wouldn't be the same for someone who has no idea it's him. I looked down at his hands, seeing that his dampener ring was missing. "It was you."

Grayson closed his eyes. "I'm so sorry, I didn't have a choice."

"You always have a fucking choice! Why did you do it?"

Mr. St. James laughed darkly. "Because we told him to. Unless he wanted to explain to his parents why his scholarship money just went away and why his senior year would be an entire fucking waste."

"I never hurt them, Riley. I just took them to a location and I would bring them back when I was told. Please, you have to believe me," Grayson begged.

I ignored him, tuning him out and looked at Chancellor Fowler.

"Why am I here? All those girls you took were witches. I'm not a witch."

Chancellor Fowler held his stomach as he laughed, looking at me almost fondly. "Of course you are. Everything you did back at the school, the little mess I just cleaned up. Undisciplined telekinesis."

"I—I, but...." I stepped away from him, my eyes narrowed. "You have...you.... all the other witches..." My mouth moved but I couldn't seem to finish any sentence I started. I swallowed as he raised his eyebrows expectantly. "You killed my dad."

Grayson's brows turned down. "You did what?"

Chancellor Fowler raised his hand up, silencing Grayson and stalked towards me. "I killed a man that was getting in my way."

"He knew you were siphoning magic from the Celica coven witches, so you killed him," I accused.

His lips tipped up in a smile, as if what I said was funny. "While I did do those things, Thomas didn't know about it. There is nothing wrong with gaining a little more power from the witches that serve you."

"Witches that...you aren't making any sense!" I yelled, moving my hands and two vases flew off the mantle and crashed against the wall.

"Thomas wanted to claim something that wasn't his and I was going to get it back. With the help of your dear Grayson, I was able to weed through the wrong ones and finally find the right one." He reached out his hand, dragging his knuckles along my jaw. I flinched, stepping back.

He sighed, walking over to one of the velvet couches and sat down. He motioned towards the couch across from him. "Sit down, Riley, and let's talk this through. Like adults. Clearly your mother did not teach you how to speak to your superiors." He casually moved his hand toward the large fireplace and flames shot out of his fingertips. The flames jolted towards the wood and took hold, creating a luminous fire. Corrin had said the murderer had natural born elemental magic and telekinesis powers.

I stood my ground. "No."

"Riley."

"*No.*"

Chancellor Fowler nodded at River's dad, who looked over at Grayson. The Chancellor leaned back, putting one of his feet up on the coffee table. "Grayson, why don't you grab me my little surprise for our guest? It's where we kept the girls. You'll know what I'm talking about when you see it."

Grayson let air out through his nose but shadowed himself away. After a moment he was back with someone in tow. I pressed my hand to my mouth when I saw Marianne with him. She looked scared. Her voice shook. "Riley...what's going on?"

"I swear I didn't know I was going to get her. I didn't think she was even a part of this!" Grayson yelled, trying to get my attention, but I paid him no mind.

"Of course you didn't, dear boy. Do you really think you're the only shadow wielder that works for me?" Chancellor Fowler shook his head. "Now that you have support here, will you please sit down?"

I ran over to Marianne, who grabbed me as if her life depended on it. "No, you're a monster."

"You and your mother, both so difficult. That's what I loved about her. So damn stubborn." He slung his arm over the back of the couch, getting more comfortable. "Be reasonable and listen."

I groaned, stomping my foot in frustration and the coffee table flipped up, falling against the ground with a bang. "Stop talking about my mother like you know her!" Marianne held onto me tighter. She looked as if she had been ready for a night out, ill-prepared to get whisked away for an unknown reason.

"Oh, you are so confused, and it hurts my heart to think you have just been wandering this world in the dark." He placed a hand on his chest. "She is the reason for all of this, but I'm here to correct it. The thought of Thomas will hurt a little less every day..."

"You're crazy and a murderer," I spat out.

His eyes turned cold. "Oh, well, you should blame your mother." He casually moved his hand to the side and I was thrown backwards. Marianne reached for me, but Chancellor Fowler held her in place, so she wouldn't move. "So stubborn." He said before moving his hand up and the glass pieces from earlier lifted from the bar cart. He crooked one of his fingers and all of them came flying at Marianne piercing her body.

Blood immediately gushed from the deep wounds. Too many pieces were in her neck and face. Her knees hit the ground first and she looked at me, her mouth moving like she was trying to speak, but nothing came out. Her eyes that always had so much life, descended into pure nothingness. The cry I let out was piercing and hurt my throat.

"Unless you would like to see your sweet mother and father in the same way, I suggest you grab her." Chancellor Fowler told Grayson as I started to run to Marianne's body. I felt ropes around my body, holding me tight. Black shadows intertwined themselves together to hold me upright. "Oliver, see to it that the school is in one piece. I don't need that to go to shambles when we're just getting started."

Mr. St. James nodded, walking out of the room. I pulled and squirmed, trying to tear through Grayson's hold. "Grayson, stop!" I pleaded, watching the thick, red blood pool around my best friend's body. Tears streamed down my face as I sobbed, begging the person I thought cared about me to let me say goodbye to my best friend.

Chancellor Fowler stepped up to me, grabbing my hand and slipping a ring on my finger. Through my tears, I realized it was a dampener, and I felt all the magic that I had become dormant. He smirked at me, heading to his place on the couch again. He motioned towards the other couch and Grayson lifted me within his shadows and placed me in front of it. The black ropes unraveled themselves, their usual warm feeling, now distant and something I couldn't recognize.

The Chancellor stared at me from where he sat. "I hope we've come to an understanding. Now then, Riley.... sit down."

I slowly descended to the couch, casting a glance at Marianne's body. My vision was shaky since my entire body hadn't stopped vibrating. How would I explain this to her mom? How would I get over this? Maybe he would kill me too and none of that would be something I had to worry about. "What do you want?" I said in a low voice.

"I want to get to know you."

I scowled. "I don't want to know *you*. You killed my best friend." I clutched at the fabric of the couch. "You killed my dad." I flicked my eyes to Grayson who had his head down, almost like he was too ashamed to even give me his attention.

Chancellor Fowler balled his hands into fists and then unclenched them. His voice got louder with every word he spoke in my direction. "Your powers have been hiding in that ruby around your neck since the moment they manifested! I don't know how she did it, your mother, but it's also concealed you from me for years! The minute you stepped onto this campus I could feel you, but I just couldn't find you. She kept you simple and human for far too long! " He jolted from the couch and grabbed my arms tight, the feeling almost like he was burning me. My eyes widened at his closeness. "You were not born to two commonplace humans, Riley! Your mother may be a plain human woman, but Thomas is not your father!"

I blinked, the air in my lungs nonexistent.

Chancellor Fowler gave me a small, crazed smile. "I am."

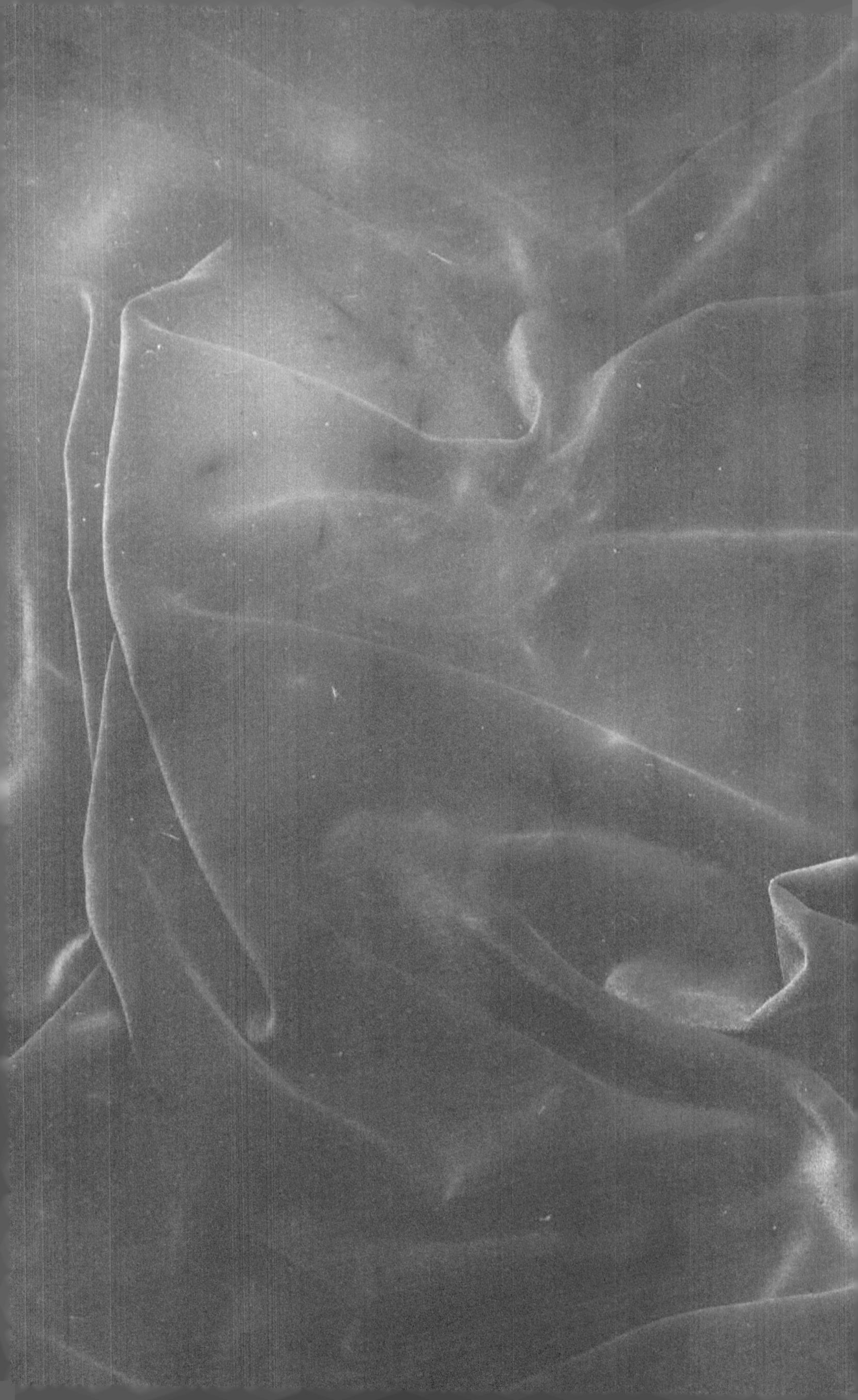

ACKNOWLEDGMENTS

Well, that ending was something…right?

This book has been in my head for a long while now and finally getting to write it was like letting out a sigh of relief. The amount encouragement I've received while watching this story become what it is, well…it's astonishing. My heart is in these characters like it always is and I really hope it shows.

To my husband who, no matter what, supports me. I could write the dirtiest, most filthy smut and he would give me a standing ovation for it. River's love for Riley and his unhinged flirty nature had to come from somewhere.

To my mom, I swear….do NOT read this book, please. I love you to the moon and back.

To my sensitivity readers, A.E. Cosby, Aurora, Julia, Marylife & Evie... thank you for helping me make this story even better. Thank you for helping enhance it in ways I could have never done on my own. Also, thanks for letting me know that google translate is actually the worst.

To Ashley, Jenny and Gabby, thank you for reading this story ahead of time and giving me all the unhinged thoughts. I adore you to pieces.

To Nikki St. Crowe, Sarah Blue and RD Baker for telling me to just go for it and write the book because why not? I had the most fun I've had in a while.

To my editor, Brittany, sorry I made you read all this smut. Actually, I'm not sorry.

To all my readers, ahhhh! A thank you will never be enough. Your support means the world to me. You are the reason I get to keep doing what I'm doing.

Chocolate PSD
Bar Mock-Up
Food Packaging Collection

ABOUT THE AUTHOR

Allie Shante was born and raised in Georgia and graduated from Georgia State University with a biology degree. While science was fun, books have always been a part of her heart and writing right up there with it. After writing and never finishing any of the books she started, she buckled down years later to finish a novel she never actually expected to write, let alone finish.

When she's not reading and writing confident females and stubborn men, she enjoys being an overprotective dog mom and crushing escape rooms with her husband.

Check out her out at: www.authorallieshante.com
Instagram: instagram.com/allieshantewrites
TikTok: tiktok.com/@allieshantewrites

www.ingramcontent.com/pod-product-compliance
Lightning Source LLC
Chambersburg PA
CBHW020352010826
48973CB00005B/1367